Night Sky, Morning Star

Native Writers' Circle of the Americas/Wordcraft Circle

FIRST BOOK AWARDS

Janet McAdams, *The Island of Lost Luggage*

Evelina Zuni Lucero, *Night Sky, Morning Star*

SERIES EDITOR, GEARY HOBSON

Night Sky, Morning Star

Evelina Zuni Lucero

THE UNIVERSITY OF ARIZONA PRESS   TUCSON

The University of Arizona Press
© 2000 Evelina Zuni Lucero

∞ This book is printed on acid-free, archival-quality paper.
Manufactured in the United States of America

05   04   03   02   01   6   5   4   3   2

Library of Congress Cataloging-in-Publication Data
Lucero, Evelina Zuni, 1953–
Night sky, morning star / Evelina Zuni Lucero.
p. cm.
(First book awards)
ISBN 0-8165-2055-0 (paper : alk. paper)
1. Indian activists—Fiction.   2. Isleta women—Fiction.
3. Ex-convicts—Fiction.   I. Title.   II. Series.
PS3562.U2544 N54 2000
813'.6—dc21
00-008119

Song lyrics, page 50, from "Indian Car," by Keith Secola © 1989. Used by permission.
Song lyrics, page 107, from "Help Me Make It Through the Night," words and music by
Kris Kristofferson, © 1970 (renewed 1998), TEMI COMBINE INC. All rights
controlled by COMBINE MUSIC CORP. and administered by EMI BLACKWOOD
MUSIC INC. All rights reserved. International copyright secured. Used by permission.

British Library Cataloguing-in-Publication Data
A catalogue record for this book is available from the British Library.

Publication of this book was made possible in part by a grant from the National
Endowment for the Arts.

To my best friend, Ed

For Fayla, Derek, Dwayne, and Tessa
For all my friends

In loving memory of Jose Abe Zuni,
Superintendent, Consolidated Ute Agency, 1961–1966
Superintendent, Nevada Indian Agency, 1966–1975

Contents

Prologue,
JULIAN, JUNE 1996
~ 3 ~

Voice Mail,
JULIAN, A YEAR EARLIER
~ 7 ~

Dreamcatcher,
CECELIA, JUNE 1996
~ 13 ~

Communications,
JULIAN, JUNE 1996
~ 33 ~

Sounds of Silence,
MARLI, JUNE 1996
~ 49 ~

Fancy Dancer,
MARLI, 1974–1976
~ 71 ~

Home of the Braves,
JULIAN, 1968–1972
~ 87 ~

Heaven's Blue Door,
JUNE 1996
~ 105 ~

That Guy,
REENA, JULY 1996
~ 111 ~

Seasons,
REENA, 1953–1996
~ 122 ~

Patty Hearst Did It,
JULIAN, 1972–1976
~ 144 ~

In Recovery,
JULIAN, JULY 1996
~ 158 ~

The Whole Truth,
CECELIA, JULY 1996
~ 164 ~

Practically My Whole Life,
JUDE, AUGUST 1996
~ 180 ~

The Real Thing,
CECELIA, AUGUST 1996
~ 197 ~

When Time and Chance Meet,
CECELIA, AUGUST–SEPTEMBER 1996
~ 211 ~

The Race Is Not to the Swift,
JUDE, SEPTEMBER 1996
~ 226 ~

Epilogue,
JANUARY 1997
~ 227 ~

Acknowledgments

I would like to thank the following people for their assistance and expertise in the writing of this book: Elizabeth Cumby, M.D., Isleta Indian Health Center; Christine Zuni Cruz and Margaret Montoya, University of New Mexico Law School; Lenny Foster, Navajo Nation Corrections Project. I am also indebted to Louis Owens for his invaluable advice, for faithful encouragement, and for showing the way; Aaron Carr for all the discussions of writing, publishing, and works-in-progress and shared laughter; Simon Ortiz and Geary Hobson for their excellent comments, generous encouragement, and unfailing kindness; Rudolfo Anaya for his critique and professorial challenges; Francis Geffard for his editorial advice; Rory, Austin, and Garrett for sharing their stories of the fathers they never knew; and my family for their patience, laughter, prayers, and loving support.

Excerpts from the following chapters were published previously in slightly different versions: "Sounds of Silence" as "Sacred Wraps" in *Native Roots & Rhythms*; "Heaven's Blue Door" as "Deer Dance" in *Returning the Gift, Women on Hunting,* and *Native American Literature;* and "That Guy" and "Seasons" as "Seasons" in *Northeast Indian Quarterly*.

Night Sky, Morning Star

Prologue

Head erect, eyes forward, I walked down the corridor that led to the yard. Each step took effort as if I walked in deep sand. I felt the weight of my thick braid down my back, its flayed end brushing the waistband of my fatigues.

"Pick it up, Morning Star," the guard growled behind me.

I gritted my teeth. My parole hearing—what a farce. But no, don't give the pig any satisfaction. *Think of nothing but getting where you're headed.*

I increased my stride. The gray concrete floor passed in a blur beneath my feet. Call it progress. Time had no meaning. Each day was already old when it started. Days passed gray and unnatural, marked not by sunrise and sunset but by clocks, buzzers, whistles, metal gates clanging open and shut.

I glanced up at the fish-eye perspective of a surveillance mirror mounted at the end of the long corridor. I was a small figure moving along a concrete plain, walking toward myself, the guard trailing close behind. I stopped before the thick steel door. The guard, big-bellied, sour-smelling in his sweat, took his time unlocking the door. As I passed, he sneered, "Better luck next time, chief. Chow time. Get to the count." The door clanged shut as I stepped into the open yard.

Long shadows fell along the concrete wall that enclosed the yard. Two basketball goals, backboards with metal hoops but no net, faced one another, kept each other company in the deserted area. I stood a moment and looked up at my only view of the natural world. Clouds, thin and feathery like brush strokes, stretched across the pale blue sky. I took a deep breath, let it out slowly, and found myself shaking.

What would I tell the others? They'd be waiting, reluctant to speak, waiting on me to go first. Willie, blue bandanna on his head, would be the one to break the silence, to ask, "So what's the word, Julian? What'd the Man say?" Last night, the Indian brothers held a drum and prayer ceremony for me. They had fasted for the day, and as we drummed, I thought I detected an undercurrent of urgency. Our drumming and singing surely were heard across the prison.

Sylvester led the prayer, imploring the creator to look with pity on me as I faced the parole board. "We're just men made frail by you, our creator, and we need your help." His voice trembled. He cleared his throat, dropped his head, and spoke to the floor. "Grandfather! Julian needs your help. Help him be strong. Give him a warrior's heart. We don't understand the white man's ways, his ways of justice. Help us all to be who you made us to be in this world. Help us to be free." The words had brought tears to my eyes, and the tears brought strength. I raised my head bowed in prayer and opened my eyes to see Willie watching me.

I took a step forward. I had no answer for them, or for myself.

Fly rounded Unit Three and headed down the walkway, moving with the nervous energy that had earned him his name. He met my eyes, then ducked his head, but not before I saw the familiar smirk on his face. Fly was Sluggo's first wife, a faggot, the lowest of the low. One of the Indian inmates, Benson, had once acted like that, a bitch in heat, putting the rest of us at risk. A couple of his homeboys from the rez took him aside and laid it out for him that he was affecting the honor of the whole group, that we'd be forced to defend it if he kept it up. Benson got the picture and had himself placed in protective custody. My mouth twisted at the memory. Keeping tight was how the Indian brothers got through the long days, the longer nights.

I was drawing a deep breath, raising my head, when Fly suddenly whirled and landed the toe of his shoe right in my throat. My head snapped back, a brushfire of pain erupting in my throat. I gasped for breath, experienced the terror of falling, and heard a hollow thud as my head hit cement.

Fly hissed, "A little reminder, chiefie, dear. Mind your own business." Spittle hit my face, traced down my cheek. His footsteps moved away quickly.

I tried to cry out, but no sound came. I struggled to breathe, grabbing my throat and pushing my heels against the ground. My throat was swelling, closing. My body instinctively fought for air, but another part of me, suddenly free, whirled through time and distance. I saw my mother, the way she looked when I was young, smiling her approval of me, her only son. Her hand touched my cheek. I smelled the delicious, sweet aroma of her kitchen, warm and cozy in winter, felt the damp heaviness of snow in the air, then felt it falling on my face, cold and wet. I tried to catch a snowflake on my tongue.

A wind shrieked. I cocked my head, listening hard. "Son," my father called weakly. My mother's face lifted, grew concerned. She looked at me, fear in her eyes. I turned toward my father's voice. He stood mute and helpless, began to age before me, eyes saddened, his large frame sinking into itself. *Wait, wait,* I wanted to say. The melting snow on my face felt like tears. Arms reached out for me. *Cecelia!* I struggled to speak her name. Her face floated above me, came closer till I felt the cool brush of her lips on my forehead. I rested completely.

I felt a downward pull that I didn't resist. Darkness was closing around me, warm and private, my first moment of absolute privacy in almost twenty years.

"Eeiii! The chief got it."

The voice startled me, drawing me back from the peaceful state I was entering.

"He was gonna get it sooner or later. Pat him down. See if he has any smokes on him."

Rage tore through me. The bastards with their monkey noises! I had been free! I twisted my body to get away, felt a shoe planted on my burning chest.

Cheers for the home team echoed in the Kit Carson High School gymnasium. *"Julian, Julian, he's our man!"* The words bounced against the gym walls and rose to the rafters along with the shrill whistle of the referee, the bounce of the basketball, the players' running feet, the squeak of rubber soles. Among the rafters, the sounds gathered and came bouncing back down in a surge of power that lifted me, sent the ball sailing from my hands, slicing through the air, swishing through the net. The fans thundered, *"Julian, Julian, he's our man! Let's give Julian a great big hand!"* They clapped and stomped their feet on the bleachers. The cheerleaders marked the tempo with upraised fists clenching pom-poms as they leaped and kicked, swirling their short skirts.

The gym's bright lighting grew dim.

The ball was in my hands again. I tried vainly to see the backboard.

"Eight, seven, six . . . ," the crowd counted down together, heightening my tension. A hand firmly patted my bottom. "Pass it. Pass it to me, Julian." Herman was behind me, working a wad of chewing gum. "I got a clear shot." I handed off the ball around my back and raised my arms to block the shot for him.

"Three, two. . . ."

I couldn't see anything, but I heard the crowd roar. The buzzer sounded loudly, signaling the end of the game.

I sensed a terrifying, dank presence like a shadow. Coldness penetrated my bones. My body shook uncontrollably; I felt a warm liquid between my legs, around my thighs, beneath me. My lungs burned and I longed for solitude, for sleep.

"Poor guy. It might help if I stuck him, huh?"

"Go for it. Ain't got nothing to lose."

I saw a glint of steel. A honed shank? I gave myself up to it, heard a strange gurgle, felt something wiped on my shirt, heard footsteps hurrying away.

My lungs filled with air. *Cissy,* I breathed, then lost consciousness.

Voice Mail

JULIAN — A YEAR EARLIER

I still remember the shock I felt when I was leafing through an artsy Southwest lifestyle magazine in the prison library. The articles, so highbrow and smug in their dumb simulations of Southwest living, didn't much interest me. But the ads did. I gazed at the shapely bare shoulders of a young Indian woman. My eyes dropped down the page. Her back to the camera, she was nude to the waist, posed provocatively with one arm bent back to her shoulder, the other behind her head, her hand atop a pile of silky, ebony hair. Her long fingers spread wide in a display of rings. I whistled softly between my teeth. *Raw beauty*, the ad proclaimed, an obscure reference to the handcrafted silverwork the woman modeled. I smiled. Raw beauty, yes. My eyes followed the course of gleaming silver around curves and contours of brown skin. Bracelets clamped strong wrists; earrings dangled from delicate earlobes. A necklace of inlaid coral spilled down her back. I imagined coming up behind her, whispering in her ear, seeing the wisps of hair at the nape of her neck move with my breath. Man! I'm sure the Man had no idea when the magazine was ordered for the Native American spiritual awareness and cultural group. In anticipation of more ads, I flipped the page.

I recognized her instantly. I bolted upright in my chair, staring open-mouthed at a photograph of Cecelia in a studio, her hands upon a mass of clay. In the blink of an eye, I went through all the reactions of sudden shock: palpitations, shortness of breath, shaking hands, dry mouth. Disbelief, joy, and fear mixed together, ran through me. Man. I had to put down the magazine, give myself time. I stared into space, my mind blank. Then I picked up the magazine again and carefully read the photo caption: *"Pueblo potter-sculptor Cecelia Bluespruce, IAIA alumna (1975) and current artist-in-residence, mentors students in the Institute's studio. Bluespruce is one of many gifted artists who return to work with IAIA students on technique and personal style. 'An artist must find a center for his or her life and let art emerge from that,' Bluespruce tells students."* I looked at the photo again and noticed Indian students clustered on each side of her. Clad in muddied apron bibs, they intently watched her hands upon the clay. I flipped through the next pages, but there were no more photos of her.

I read through the article quickly, searching for information on her. There was none. The article focused on the curriculum of the Institute of American Indian Arts and its reputation for graduating stellar artists. In a colored display box, Cecelia's name was listed among the school's roll call of distinguished alumni.

For weeks on end, I reread the article, searching for clues to Cecelia's current life, and combed back issues to see if I had missed anything in previous months. I thought of her as an artist, as a teacher, tried hard to imagine her art. I studied the glossy color photo, though, as photos go, it did not reveal much. The angle of the shot was from below, the lighting from above and behind, so that shadows fell on Cissy's face while her work was illuminated. She still looked the same, like she'd been suspended in time, though both she and I were tipping past forty. Strands of her long, dark hair, loosely tied back, fell like rivulets down the sides of her face, which displayed the calm intensity I remembered about her. I couldn't make out her eyes clearly, only their shape, but I could see her hands smoothing the wet, glistening clay. With her sleeves rolled, her face hidden in shadow, she seemed vulnerable and young.

After a while, I wasn't content to look at the photo only during library hours. I tucked the magazine into my prison fatigues and took it back to my cell. When the magazine was confiscated in a shakedown, the incident was written up and included in my jacket with the notation that I gave the pig, Sanders, "a threatening and hostile gesture." Sanders had it out for me. He hated "mud people," spics and Indians, and was looking for an excuse to get me. Sure, I gave him the finger, but that was behind his back; he couldn't have seen, and for sure, he couldn't have heard what I called him in my mind. I know better than to let the pigs know what I'm thinking and feeling.

When Sanders found the magazine, he was triumphant. He flipped through the pages and opened it up to the page with the Indian model. He stared at it. Then he twisted the magazine around and thrust the picture in my face.

"Take a long look, chief. This is the last time you'll see this filthy squaw."

I snatched the magazine out of his hands and threw it in his face.

My act of defiance cost me a week in the Hole. When the library discovered I had "defaced prison property" by ripping out a page of what now became a "special collections book" as noted in my jacket, another week in the Hole was added and my library privileges were revoked indefinitely, though the Native Prison Project lawyers protested the entire incident. My bros helped me out by circulating the folded-up magazine page from one cell to the next for safekeeping. By the time I next saw it, it was deeply creased and torn from handling. I took one last look, committing it to memory: small hands on clay, gritty look of determination, hair falling across high cheekbones, eyes like a doe.

Then I flushed it down the john.

She must be living in New Mexico now, I figured, gone home. My sole thought in the Hole had been to reach her. I was especially careful in the next few weeks not to jeopardize my standing, concentrating on regaining lost privileges. With the help of the sponsor for the cultural group, a liberal, low-level administrator who loved the oppressed, I was allowed a three-minute phone privilege supposedly to call my ailing mother. I called long-distance information and on the first try, scored a number for Cecelia in Santa Fe. She was using her maiden name.

Did she have an old man? If a male answered, or a kid, I would know.

With trembling fingers, I dialed the number and dropped in coin after coin till the operator was satisfied. With one hand draped on the battered payphone as if it were a good friend, I listened to her phone ring, a pleasant, soft *brrring*. The plastic phone receiver grew slippery in my hand. After three rings, I figured maybe no one was home or maybe they were running to the phone from the bathroom. By the fourth ring, I heard the phone being picked up. My heart beat so loud I could hear the rush of blood in my ears. "Hello?" Tentative and soft. "I'm not at home. Leave a message and I'll get back to you as soon as I can." I hung up, then just as quickly as I'd put the receiver down, I picked it up again, redialed, dropped in my coins, listened to the rings and the message again. I hung up, sleepwalked back to my cell, ignored my bros' calls from across the block, laid on my bunk, and played back the message in my mind.

She said, "*I'm* not at home." I, singular. She lived alone? She must or would she not have said "we"? I played with that idea until I convinced myself I must be right. I listened again to my mental recording of her voice. She sounded more mature, more serious now. Of course. Teachers were always serious. If she wasn't home, she must be at work. Teaching, of course. "*Leave a message and I'll get back to you as soon as I can.*" In those few words, hope, almost gone, revived. More than anything, I longed to call back and leave a message, but I knew I wouldn't ever be able to go that far. I replayed the tape in my head till my heart ached; desire filled me, the right way it should be, a man for a woman.

Those two phone calls lasted me for months. Feeling a false sense of confidence, I decided to call again, to hear fresh the voice that was fading from my memory. At the last moment, before I picked up the receiver to dial, the thought struck me, what if she answers this time? I became so unnerved by the possibility I had to go back to my cell and ponder it. What would I do? I spent another two months deciding I had to hang up if she answered. When I returned to the payphone, I was so clumsy in my anticipation, like a starving man who, when given food, throws aside the spoon and slurps the soup right from the bowl. I put the coins in too quickly and the operator would not process my call until I dropped in two more coins though I had already dropped in the exact amount.

I heard a short ring followed by an ugly tinny sound. A recorded voice informed me that the number I dialed was no longer in service. I hung up before the message played out. For a minute, I stared at the grimy wall above the phone, then lifted the receiver and called information for Santa Fe. For Albuquerque. For Taos. Even Gallup. Those were the only places I knew in New Mexico. But the operator's response was the same each time: no such listing.

I punched and kicked the wall, beat the receiver against the phone box, not caring that the pig was approaching. I spent another week in the Hole for my outburst. But it was worth it. I found her voice again there. *"Leave a message and I'll get back to you as soon as I can."*

Between midnight and dawn, when the prison din has died down, I am alone, *truly alone.* I revel in the stillness, enjoy a short respite from the zoo atmosphere of cons caged like animals and the constant hassling of the pigs. It is quiet except for the sounds of the pigs in their rounds on the count, the rattle of keys and chains, the pant of the dogs they bring in, the sounds men make in sleep. Often, I do not sleep. I relive my life, all that I can remember from my earliest memory to the events that led to my imprisonment.

Only the days of my childhood and adolescence have remained singular, sharply focused. Pure. All other memories have been altered. I have examined them from every aspect, changing my life story so the outcome becomes different, better. I have done this so many times I sometimes have difficulty remembering the actuality of moments past; they get buried beneath desperate wishes. *If only Cecelia and I never parted paths. . . . I never met Viola or if I did, I do not fool myself that I love her. . . . I work harder at college, do not forfeit my scholarship. . . . I major in poli-sci, maybe even go to law school, become the fancy-pants punk project lawyer on the other side of the table out to save the disempowered. Or whatever. If only I do not make the choices I did, do not get busted. If only people remember me! See me as a warrior so that the sacrifice of my life means something, so that my family is proud of me. If only . . . I am not me.*

In the darkened confines of my six-by-eighter, lives rotting around me, I lie somewhere between the past and the present. Staring beyond the darkness, I remember the night sky in northern Nevada, where I grew up. I travel into its blue-black depths, whirling past stars of incredible beauty. They shimmer and sparkle like pieces of ice. I whirl past them, back into myself. The hard bunk beneath me turns to the lumpy ground in back-yards of government employee housing where I spent long-ago summer nights; the hot, suffocating stillness of my cell becomes the feeling I had when I burrowed deep into my sleeping bag to escape mosquitoes. I come up, draw in deep breaths of cool, grass-sweet air. I hear the *swish-swish* of the rotating water sprinklers left on overnight by the BIA agency grounds-keeper, crickets in the lilac bushes singing, the lone bark of a dog across campus.

Sometimes, I yearn for those days till my jaw hurts from grinding my teeth so hard. I yearn to wake to see the morning sun filtering through the leafy canopy of oaks and pines that were abundant on the agency. I yearn to be innocent.

I love Cecelia. Seeing her photo in the magazine made me realize that. I love Herman, too. That guy, he was funny, loyal as all hell. Later when all this trouble came down, he tried to help me. He couldn't do much, but I respect him for it. I sure as hell wish I knew where he is now, what he's doing. Even Jewell was all right. Man, she could get mad as hell quicker than anyone I ever saw, like some of these cons. She'd get all offended at the smallest criticism. She could dish it out, but she couldn't take it. But like I said, I love those guys. They were my friends.

Dreamcatcher

CECELIA—JUNE 1996

I looked out from the protected shade of my booth at the Blue Corn Indian Art Show with a practiced detachment, an expression on my face that revealed nothing. My eyes looked above the row of booths across from me where other artisans sat, like me, in a measured space we had paid no small sum for. We anticipated a weekend of wrangling and bargaining with tourists, collectors, locals, and Indian people who love nothing more than a hot piece of fry bread, some Indian dancing and drumming, and a good buy to brag about. We set out our wares, pottery, paintings, sculptures, jewelry, drums, or whatever other art form, arranged attractively on tables covered with Pendleton blankets, shawls, or linens. The appetizing smell of coffee, roasting chile, and frying hamburger filled the air.

My booth was smack-dab in the middle of the show. By the time people got to me, they still had money, had done enough comparison shopping, and were ready to buy. The looky-lou's were weeded out, having seen enough to be able to say, I was there, and they were lured away to the food booths or the entertainment, an Indian rock band at the moment.

The Indian art shows hosted by individual pueblos throughout the summer were my favorite art shows. The shows boasted that only handmade and authentic Indian art was featured. In a state that fed on tourism and the exploitation of Indian culture, such a declaration had become necessary. Each year I reconnected with artist friends, longtime customers, and old classmates from the Institute, and we marveled that another year had passed and we were getting older but no richer.

This June the Blue Corn show was situated above Santa Clara Pueblo in a flat clearing in the juniper- and sage-covered foothills of the Jemez Mountains. The morning had passed in a blur of faces, questions asked and politely answered, the across-the-table exchange of currency or credit cards for my clay work, which I carefully wrapped in tissue paper and released to the world. I had already made well above my expenses and had every reason to be happy. A special artist reception was being held tonight. Everyone was excited, but I felt empty and cold inside. My fingernails were bitten painfully short. I sat on my hands and stared at the rain-washed sky, a clean, fresh blue; fluffy bits of clouds like bolls of cotton hurried past.

The brisk movement of the clouds, their shadows sweeping across the ground, loosened my memory.

My dream last night came back to me, the herd of horses streaming across the sky, leading with their noses, their manes and tails whipping behind them like wind-driven trails of clouds. There was something desperate, urgent about their movement. Waking up, I spoke the name that first came to mind. Julian.

A whisper escaped my lips. *Julian.* His name rang in my head, stirred something deeply buried. I massaged the bridge of my nose, closed my eyes to shut off the memories brought on by speaking his name. Too late; the moment stood still and I was sucked into it. As if I had violated the name of the dead—called forth a memory from a deep grave—all the years that sat uneasily between us rushed at me, the distance closed, and there he was before me as I last saw him.

All the sensations of that September, the cool air, leaves beginning to turn, smells of pine sap and tree bark, the shift of the sun lower in the sky, the naïveté of our youth, our sense of timelessness where our future stretched before us endless and filled with grand possibilities—all these rushed at me. I stepped into the moment willingly. I remembered his hair beginning to touch the collar of his shirt, such a sign of rebellion back then, the slight trace of hair on his upper lip, his head cocked to the side, watching me. Almost feeling his arms coming around me, I opened my eyes.

For all practical purposes, Julian was dead to me. I had made no attempts to find him, to make inquiries about his whereabouts. I went on with my life. At least outwardly.

Inwardly, I was a prisoner of time, unable to move past those years of high school. I had my secret, which weighed heavy in me so that every attempt to move forward kept me in the same place.

It occurred to me, perhaps I had dreamt of Julian—and exactly how the dream related to Julian I didn't know—because Jude had called me yesterday at my home in northwest Albuquerque. The house, signed over to me by my dad for my studio when he remarried, wasn't much, but I loved the way the tall casement windows let light flood in. I hadn't intended to move in, but it was easier having studio and home in one. I had yet to change the utility billing to my name.

I was pricing my clay pieces in preparation for this show, deliberating the work I had put into each piece, deciding on a value for my effort. I wondered whether I was asking too much, perhaps too little. I thought about who might buy it, then hike up the price, resell a piece of Indian culture, a piece of my soul. I thought about Grandma, who sold a whole table of pottery for $20 to supplement Grandpa's farming and sporadic wages. Sometimes, I'd pull off the sticker I originally placed on the bottom of the piece, stick it to the table, and write another. I took each piece, wrapped it in a swathe of bubblewrap, and carefully nestled it in a box filled with plastic packing foam. Absorbed in my task, annoyed that the phone rang and I had forgotten to turn on the answering machine, I snatched up the cordless handset and tersely asked, "Yes?" then quickly tried to backtrack when Jude identified himself. Jude usually called on weekends and on special occasions such as holidays, Mother's Day, my birthday. At those times I gave him the cheery little pieces of myself I carefully saved for him between calls. I heard the strain in my own voice as I tried to pretend a happy surprise as if his mid-week call didn't signal something I should worry about.

"Don't be ridiculous," I had said to him. I continued to wrap storyteller figures, propping the phone on one shoulder. "I'm never too busy for you. What's up?" I placed a piece in the box, rustling the foam bits as I nestled it in.

"What's that noise?" he inquired.

"Plastic foam. I'm getting ready for the Blue Corn show up north."

Wrapping another piece, I listened to his apologies. "No, no. I'm not too busy. So what's up? Do you need some money?" The receiver almost slipped off my shoulder. I raised my shoulder awkwardly to cradle it against my ear.

"You won't get mad?" His question was casual but serious, I knew.

"About what?"

"I've been thinking for a couple of weeks now, well, actually since Father's Day, and even before that, really." He hesitated. "Well, I was wondering about my dad? Where he is? If—" Hearing the uncertainty and a slight tremor in his voice, I stopped packing and raised my hand to steady the phone.

"Jude. You know, I've told you before that was impossible."

He quickly assured me, "You don't have to get involved if you don't want to. I can ask my mo——," he stopped short, perhaps to spare my feelings, and smoothly went on, "Aunt Virgie for help."

"That's not the problem." I clutched the phone, pressing it against my ear.

"What is it?" His voice was calm, the question reasonable. He had obviously prepared himself to understand, had probably been preparing himself for a long time now. My eyes flew to the double-framed photos of him on the shelf above me. On one side, a studio portrait of a baby boy laughed openmouthed, not at me, I knew, but at someone behind the camera, probably Aunt Virgie. At six months, Jude leaned forward, balancing himself with chubby, dimpled hands perched on his outstretched legs, his eyes like shiny little blackberries, his dark hair a thick patch on his head. My baby. The other frame contained a recent photo of Jude, twenty-three years old, his eyes gazing thoughtfully off camera. There was no telling his thoughts by his expression, which was neither troubled nor smiling. After several years of drifting, Jude just now seemed to be getting things together.

"Jude, why are you asking?"

"I just have to know."

I looked at the table filled with pots and figurines I had yet to price and pack, smoothed my hair with my free hand, and found a tangle of discarded price stickers meshed in the ends of several strands. I realized I hadn't brushed out my hair or showered even, and it was already late afternoon.

I crossed the room and sat down in the one chair free of boxes and supplies. "I can't give you a name."

There was a short space of silence in which he was probably evaluating the matter-of-fact way I had spoken.

"You mean . . . ," he cleared his throat, "you don't know *who*?"

"I was young, much younger than you are now." Eighteen to be exact, I thought. Eighteen and stupid in love. I ran my fingers through the tangle of hair and price stickers, pulled them out, and balled them, along with strands of hair that had adhered to them.

"What's that supposed to mean?"

I heard the choked hurt in his voice and I felt a familiar guilt and sense of inadequacy rising in me. I imagined his eyes narrowing, going hard and shiny like watermelon seeds. When he was a young boy, he'd often pout like that when he was with me, staring moodily from under the brim of his sports cap pulled low on his brow, a sullen expression that bewildered me, then later exasperated me as he grew into a brooding adolescent. I did what I thought was best for him, leaving him in Phoenix with my Aunt Virgie, who raised him. Still, I felt guilty. I was hard-pressed to leave off work and school to visit him, but I did make the effort. Damn it, that counted for something. "Of course, it does. He just doesn't understand," Aunt Virgie would pat my shoulder.

When I didn't respond immediately, he pressed me. "Mom, are you going to tell me who my father is?"

"This is so unexpected!" So unfair, I wanted to add. "I put this behind me a long, long time ago. It's hard for me to talk about it. In fact, this might not be the time." My voice was projecting a firmness I didn't feel, a maternal authority I had never exercised with him.

"Mom. Just tell me. Do you know who my father is?"

His question raced through the 500 miles of desert between us; his anguish rang crystal clear in my ear, resounded in my head, pierced my heart. I squeezed my eyes shut. A choked "No" escaped my lips. There. I'd said it. "No," I repeated. "I'm sorry, but I never wanted to have to tell you this." My eyes opened to my storytellers on the table. Engrossed in story, they sat with mouths open in little **O**'s, their eyes carved slants, a multitude of small clay children enfolded in the crooks of their arms, seated at their feet. Their mute presence reassured me. Words came to my lips easily.

"I don't know your father's name."

Jude fell silent.

"I'm sorry. I was so young." My voice broke. "I just don't know who." As I spoke, my heart pounded in my ears, my chest. I wondered if Jude could detect my lie.

"How could that be?"

I was silent for a moment, frantically searching for an explanation. Then: "Think about it. Jude, I don't know what else I can say. I told you I didn't want to deal with it—especially not over the phone."

We listened to each other breathe, struggled to reach out and comfort one another, but in the end our own pain shortened our reach. In the space of the moment it took to draw a deep breath, we moved farther apart than the physical distance that had always separated us.

"Cecelia, I'm sorry I asked. I just needed to know." He often called me Cecelia, but this time it hurt, salt in a wound that had never healed.

A familiar dull ache deep within me, in that place that was beyond the physical, grew.

"I know," I assured him, although I didn't really. I was desperate to soothe him. "You need some money? I'll send you some right after the show. Maybe we need to spend time together. Why don't you come stay with me the rest of the summer?" He didn't say much after that, mumbled that knowing something was better than knowing nothing at all. Or words to that effect. Somehow the conversation mercifully ended, and I hung up.

I sat staring for a moment, dazed, somewhat frightened. Abruptly, I reached over and turned on the answering machine.

I continued to price pieces, my big pots, small bowls, storytellers, sculpted figures. My children, my works of art, perfect. I wrapped them carefully, cushioned them in boxes of foam, occasionally running my finger around a rim, holding a pot in my hands, feeling its walls, remembering the damp coils I had built up, then smoothed together. Sometimes, I remembered details of the day I had made the piece—the weather, what was playing on the radio, my mood.

At one point, I looked down in surprise at the seed bowl in my lap. I did not know how long I had held it without conscious awareness of what I was doing. The bowl was painted but not yet fired. It was large, widest at the center and flattening up to a small opening. I hugged the bowl, felt the fragility of its thin walls, the hollowness of its center. A pleasant earthy smell rose from its dark interior. Using a yucca brush, I had painted thin, evenly spaced lines around the width of the bowl from its base to the rim of its small opening, then more lines of equal spacing down the length of the bowl. The intersecting lines formed small blocks, and I had painted in every other block. I was pleased with the resulting patterns, which drew one's eyes two ways: First, to the bands circling the bowl like coral snakes. A second glance drew the eyes up the longitudinal bands, which narrowed as they approached the rim. I remembered setting the pot aside for days, debating which perspective I would emphasize.

Out of the blue one day, I picked up the pot and began drawing more lines, jagged like lightning, diagonally across the unpainted blocks up to the rim. I began one lightning streak and saw it sweep up from the base around the wide center and across the broad, flat top to the rim. When I finished that first line, a soft sigh of satisfaction had escaped me.

Recalling these details, I concentrated on the coolness of the bowl in my arms. Holding it brought me a strange comfort. This pot won't ever be for sale, I decided, getting up to set it back on the shelf. I stretched my stiff arms, massaged the ache in the small of my back, rubbed my neck and shoulders.

Packing took an inordinate amount of time, exhausting me. I placed my boxes of pottery next to the box I never unpacked, which held all those things I needed at an art show to transact business—calculator, credit card machine, business cards, pen, money bag, paper bags, tissue wrapping paper, covering for my table, a blanket, an umbrella, and a plastic tarp. Next to the boxes, I leaned my folding table and chairs, display case of art award ribbons, water bottle, and Lil' Oscar cooler. I went to the bedroom and tossed clothes and toiletries into a duffel bag.

When I was finished, I sat in the dark, leaned back in my chair, closed my eyes, and took a deep breath to ease the tightness in my chest. I worked hard to push unwelcome thoughts out of my mind. Finally, I rose, red-eyed, and lay on the bed in my clothes, falling into a fitful sleep. Then I dreamed horses.

They streamed up from the horizon, agile and smooth, a herd of them, at least seven, across the concave, moonlit sky above me, powerful and beautiful in their movement. I watched in awe as the horses wheeled in the night sky, their hooves striking the air, their coats sleek and multicolored. The wind was strong, cool, and stinging on my cheeks and ears. Without warning, the ponies scattered in different directions, gone as suddenly as they had come. I stared at an empty sky, frightened, straining my ears to hear a sound I thought I'd heard. I woke, my heart beating wildly, speaking hoarsely into the early morning. *Julian.* I heard a distant wailing of an ambulance racing through city streets. I allowed the thought: *Julian. The father of my son, Jude.*

My son, Jude. Mothers with their babies in strollers, holding the hands of older children, moved past my line of vision. My heart ached with the lie I had told Jude. A young boy, cornsilk blond with bluest of blue eyes, stopped at my table. His eyes sought the smallest piece. "How much is that?" He pointed to a storyteller.

"One-forty," I said.

"Is that more than this?" He opened his hand to reveal a sweaty fistful of coins.

"A lot more."

His face fell. "I just got this much and I want to buy something."

"Michael!" A blond woman rushed forward. "I'm sooo sorry," she addressed me, her hand clutching her chest. She turned to the boy. "Let's not touch anything, son. If you break something. . . ." She widened her eyes. She put a firm hand on his shoulder and turned him away, steering him down the row. "Let's go find your dad before *he* does any damage. This stuff is way too expensive. We'll stop by one of those stores where you can buy something Indian for a dollar." Michael turned his head, watching me as he moved away, his eyes tender blue and watering.

I watched Michael and his mother move down the row and fade away into the crowd, only vaguely aware of others stopping before me, idly examining my work, commenting to one another on the workmanship as if I wasn't there. Maybe they sensed I wasn't present entirely, at least not mentally. I stared right through the crowd in their shorts and Southwest prints, straw hats and caps, their skins tanned to the texture of dry leather, wearing chunks of turquoise and silver on their wrists or around their necks or wrapped around their waists. I stared till I saw my grandpa's cornfield, rows and rows of tall green plants, corn tassels swaying in the wind, the perfect place to play hide-and-seek in the evening. I wanted to huddle down, hide there.

My thoughts shifted when an Indian woman entered my line of vision. She wore a long-tailed maroon shirt over textured stockings of the same color. Her thick black hair cascaded down her back. She moved fast and determinedly through the crowd like the horses of my dream.

I suddenly knew what I would add to my bowl with the lightning streaks, the bowl I would never sell. Seven horses circling the rim.

In the early years, whenever a stray thought of Julian entered my mind, it was always followed by the vengeful wish that he could never get past me, never forget me. Even when he thought he had long forgotten, there, like a wisp in the corner of his eye, would be my disturbing presence. And he'd hear tell through the Indian grapevine that I was doing well, real well, without him. As the years passed, though, desire for revenge got old. What did it matter if he couldn't forget me? I was still done wrong. Still alone. And, truth be known, I wasn't doing all that well, not if you measure success by peace of mind.

Jude's phone call brought that home to me.

Ever since seventh grade I'd had a crush on Julian. He was just a regular stupid Indian boy back then, full of hateful teasing in front of others, throwing spitwads at me on the bus, thinking he was so clever, showing off, when he was just a smart-ass, he and his sidekick, Herman, the two of them smelling like dried sweat, hair dressing, and some metallic odor, maybe from their dirt bikes. But somehow I knew in spite of behavior to the contrary, he secretly liked me. The times we found ourselves alone, his sudden shyness was so sweet I could forget all his previous bad behavior. He'd be searching hard to find something to say and eventually ask something lame like, "What's that thing?" pointing to the lip gloss hanging from a strap around my neck. "A 'Slicker,'" I'd say, knowing he wouldn't know what that was. "Lemme see." And he'd lean close and take it off my neck, open it. "Looks sticky." He'd put it to his nose to smell, and I'd smash it into his face. Then we'd be fighting over it, laughing and yelling, and he'd smear it all over my mouth just to have the excuse to be close. Indian boys liked to do things like that, I noticed, never being direct, wasting a lot of time beating around the bush. Julian and I fooled around like that, always waiting for *something* to happen between us. We never told anyone else, which was unusual, especially for me, 'cause Jewell was my best friend and we told each other absolutely everything. Except when it came to Julian. I never told Jewell about Julian, not a word, even later. By my senior year in high school, when I finally had given up all hope that something would happen—Julian had jerked off all us Indian girls when he became a hotshot varsity basketball player—it suddenly did.

But all that was long ago. Far away. Not even here in "New Maxco," as some Indians pronounce it, but at the Nevada Indian agency at Stewart where we grew up, a place that no longer even exists as we knew it. The boarding school has long been closed, some of the government employee housing torn down, the agency land returned to the tribe to whom it originally belonged. Sometimes I wonder, did it ever really happen? But that's nonsense because after all, there's Jude.

I can see her. Young. Vulnerable. Frightened. Moving through her daily schedule out of habit, not purpose, because she was so distracted by worry. She left classes without hearing the lecture and rode the city bus back to the room she shared with an aspiring visual artist, a fellow student at the San Francisco Art Institute. Sometimes she overshot her stop, then had to walk blocks past shop windows she didn't really see, past people of all colors and nationalities who didn't see her. When she was first in San Francisco, she loved browsing the shops filled with exotic stuff, imports, one-of-a-kinds, drug paraphernalia, counterculture necessities such as silk-screened T-shirts, posters, incense, and the like. The smells were intoxicating. Now they were nauseating. Classmates who would have become friends if she let them joked and laughed around her, sipped iced coffees and café espressos, talked art and politics, rehashed last night's party or talked up the next one. She smiled and nodded, but felt only the fear in her stomach and the morning sickness, too, a growing certainty that, yes, she was pregnant and hadn't heard from *him* in weeks. He was never in when she called and his roommate was increasingly becoming embarrassed and irritable with her long-distance messages.

Then came the letter that sent her into shock. Her hands shook as she read the words. Her eyes stared, unbelieving, then she placed her hands across her belly, protectively, instinctively, the letter still in one hand.

I can see that young girl, her long hair wild across her tear-stained face. In the middle of her pain, she reached within, drew herself up with a strength she didn't know she had. Her college friends never knew what happened to her, why she didn't return to the San Francisco Art Institute after the first semester, that girl from the Southwest desert who loved the smell of the ocean and eating cups of shrimp on Fisherman's Wharf, who loved the Chinese restaurant where the owner yelled at his customers.

She submerged then reappeared as my clay-formed storytellers, my unconventional works of art that purists sometimes derisively refer to as *contemporary* pottery.

The storyteller's mouth is agape, but no one has heard her story.

I can feel her deep inside me.

My cousin, Marli, stood behind the tanned guy with the professional air and 35-mm camera hanging from his neck, her head peeking over and around his shoulders. She held a wrapped mutton burger in each hand and she used them to wave at me. I smiled, indicated with a nod of my head for her to come into the booth, then turned my attention back to the customer. The man, casual in his polo shirt and khakis, was closely examining the designs on one of my storytellers, tenderly holding the figure in his hands, turning it around at various angles, asking thoughtful, provocative questions, the kind that art connoisseurs ask, the kind artists love because you can go on and on about your work. Texture. Shape and form. Color. Energy.

Marli tried to maneuver around him to enter my booth, but he inadvertently blocked her each time, gesturing with his arms extended, talking animatedly with his whole body. Finally, resigned, she stood off to his side, mutton burgers in hand, to wait out the conversation.

Grateful for the chance to talk seriously about my work, I expounded, which in turn sparked more questions. It had been over a year since I taught art at the Institute, a year since I had opened my studio to devote myself to my work. I hadn't realized the depth of my isolation. With every answer, he looked at me, then at my pieces with increased appreciation. The man, fortyish, nice-looking, made a tactful inquiry into my marital status, embedding the personal question amidst an art one. Did I exhibit in galleries, or did I have my own studio? You do? Where is it located? Your husband—does he have a hand in your business?

Marli shifted weight from one foot to the other. I glanced at her. She wore an amused look. I looked back at the man, saw him watching me intently, realized he now seemed more interested in me than my work. I dropped my eyes to the table, embarrassed and mortified. I hadn't meant to encourage anything. I had a grown son, after all, whose unhappiness, along with my own, I had momentarily forgotten in the midst of my avid discussion with Drew. That was his name, he'd said.

"My son will be coming to stay with me this summer, so I don't know that I will keep regular hours at my studio," I told him matter-of-factly. He seemed taken aback for a moment at the mention of "my son."

I continued in a brisk business tone, "Are you interested in any of the pieces I have here?"

He straightened and reached for his wallet. "Yes. I want this one." He indicated the one he had been examining. "And may I have one of these?" Without waiting for an answer, he picked up one of my business cards. He removed a charge card from his wallet and handed it to me. I couldn't help but notice he wasn't wearing a wedding band, but what did that mean these days? Marli slipped by him, placed the food down, and sat in the folding chair next to me.

"Sorry I can't help you," she said, indicating her greasy fingers. "I'm afraid I might get grease on something." She rubbed her thumb on her fingertips and reached for a paper towel.

"You might not want to wipe that all off," Drew addressed her. "A Diné client of mine told me mutton grease is an Indian aphrodisiac. Said he'd dab some behind his ears and women would follow him anywhere."

Marli and I looked at Drew in surprise. Then we laughed. "My name is Drew Kamore," he said to Marli, holding out his hand.

Marli introduced herself as my cousin though she didn't tell him her name. "You work with Diné people?"

"Among other tribes. I'm with the Southwest Native Prison Project in Santa Fe. My clients include Native prisoners from tribes all over the country, some of whom are Navajo. Some of them are quite artistic, and I encourage them in that area." He said this last statement to me.

"Where you from?" Marli asked as I worked the card machine, then handed the form to Drew to sign.

"Arizona. I grew up there but actually my family is from up north. I'm descended from—" It sounded like he said *Squish-squash*, but I knew he meant some tribe. He handed the form back. I tried to discreetly evaluate his features for Indianness. Well, okay, maybe. His eyes were generic nondescript brown and so was his hair, but his skin did look too well tanned for a white guy. Guess that little ponytail could be taken for something more than Yuppie style. And yeah, well, there was something about him, at least he wasn't blond. He caught me staring. I handed him his purchase wrapped and bagged, and thanked him.

He slipped my card into his shirt pocket. "My mom and aunt will be coming to visit New Mexico later this summer. If possible, I'd like to bring them to your studio?" He looked at me hopefully.

"Sure. Call first to make sure I'm home—my son and all."

"Will do. Enjoy your mutton burgers. Nice meeting you all."

We watched him move away, then Marli pulled out the food, and we ate quickly before the fry bread and pieces of mutton grew any colder. Between bites Marli told me she had heard of this Drew guy, nothing bad, worked hard to set up his prison program, seemed to be committed, and yes, he was part Indian.

"Is he one of those who suddenly become Indian overnight?"

She shrugged. "Far as I know, his rap rings true. Bet he calls you with or without his mom and aunt." She shook her head. "Mom and Auntie. That's a new one."

"Could be it's the truth."

She gave me a pitying look, the one she gives me when she thinks I'm being naive. I shrugged.

I was grateful for Marli's company. She had brought me food and now saved me from my own dark thoughts. Marli taught an assortment of courses on Native American themes at the university in the American Studies Department, which I can't believe is actually an academic department and not a Spiegel catalog. Her dissertation, which she is trying to get published, was on Pueblo social and political resistance, a topic I try not to get her started on. We don't see each other often enough, so when we do, we make up for it, packing our conversations full, leapfrogging from one topic to the next.

"So Jude is coming out this summer? Great."

"I hope so. But I don't know exactly when." Jude hadn't actually agreed to come at all, but I kept that to myself. Since I had spoken it aloud, it now seemed a done deal.

Marli went on about what a fine young man Jude was, what a fine job I did raising him. My family seems to be in strong denial about my mothering, and I have done nothing to dispel their misconceptions. That way, we're all comfortable. I frowned at the remaining piece of my "burger" that seemed to bear more resemblance to a burrito than a hamburger. I wadded it up in its wrapping and tossed it in a trash bag.

"Did you come up by yourself?" I couldn't keep the surprise out of my voice, and I looked down the row half-expecting to see a male purposefully heading in our direction.

She seemed embarrassed by my glance. "Actually, I came up with Auntie Reena. Her car is in the garage, so she asked me to drive her up. She wanted to get here by eight this morning, but early afternoon was the best I could do."

Her answer surprised me further. "Where is she?"

"She's checking out the contents of each and every booth. All the way up here, she told me the best was probably gone, *already snatched up* this morning, she emphasized that, and she wasn't going to waste any time when she got here. I couldn't tell if she was ticked off at me or not." Marli shrugged.

I nodded. Auntie Reena was a serious buyer at Indian art shows. She had turned an old family home into a curio shop that was a modest success as a reservation business. Posted signs announced her shop to be "Indian owned and operated," featuring "authentic Indian-made art." Most artists don't like to work on commission or sell wholesale so she depended on art shows as her source of goods.

"She won't be going anywhere without me so I decided to get something to eat and find you. She'll come across us in a while." Marli dabbed at her mouth with a napkin.

"Auntie's not your usual choice of company." I lifted my eyebrows ever so slightly.

"Is this your not-so-subtle way of asking about Arnie?" She smiled, then looked pained. "Well, he's history. I'm not even going to tell you what he did. It's so jacked. Gawd, Cecelia, it's awful. I don't know why I do this to myself over and over."

Arnie had been the latest in a long series of poor choices. It got to be where I'd whisper to Marli after meeting her new guy, "Seems like I've met this one before," and she, always hopeful, would pretend not to hear. But Arnie I had particularly disliked. He made a lot of jabs cloaked in humor and prided himself on his muscled physique. He had a habit of looking at himself in windows, mirrors, anything reflective, a conceit grown from his time at the gym, lifting weights before floor-to-ceiling mirrors.

"You know what I thought about Arnie. Can't say I'm sorry it didn't work out. He was such an extreme health freak, it was un-Indian. Remember what he called fry bread? *Heart attack food*."

We laughed. "Can't say I'm sorry, either," Marli said, bravely.

"Same old story?"

"Same old story."

I debated restating my usual advice, but seeing Marli's downcast face, I merely shook my head sympathetically.

"What am I going to do now?" Marli wondered aloud.

"Forget men."

The words popped out unexpectedly.

She smiled wanly. "You're so sensible." She waved her remaining piece of fry bread at me. "Is that what you've done?"

I wished I could forget. Not men in general, just one in particular. I snapped my fingers. "Hey! I just remembered. There's a reception tonight for the artists. No speeches, I promise. Why don't you stay for that? It'll be fun."

"Well . . . what about Auntie Reena?"

"We'll talk her into it. Heck, you should just stay the night. My room at the motel is a double."

Marli nodded in agreement, her mouth full. She reached for her napkin to wipe her hands. "You gonna be the one to convince Auntie?"

"I'll give it a try." She had wiped the fingers of one hand with the napkin and was moving to wipe the others when I stopped her with a hand on her arm. "Wait! Put a little bit of that grease behind your ears; see if it works."

I woke to find Auntie Reena over me, shaking my shoulders, calling my name softly. "Cecelia. *Hita*. Wake up. You're having a bad dream."

I blinked in the bright light of the motel lamp, which she had turned on. Reena was wearing my nightgown. Her arms, larger than mine, filled the sleeves. She reached for her eyeglasses and then sat down on the other bed.

I sat up, my heart beating fast. Marli lay in the same bed as I and she rolled over, pulling the covers around her shoulders.

"I heard you mumbling and moving around on the bed. I knew you were having a nightmare." Her voice was still edged with sleep, but she seemed concerned.

"Nightmare?" The word came out so soft, I had to clear my throat and repeat it. "It was the same dream I had last night."

"Oh?" She leaned closer, yawning.

"Yes. I was. . . ." I drew my knees up to my chest, covering them with the T-shirt I wore as a nightshirt. "I was somewhere outside, I'm not sure where, but it was on a hill at night. And the sky was so huge, so beautiful, purplish blue. Then out of nowhere, across the sky came these horses." I described for her the multicolored horses I had dreamed of the night before, wheeling in the sky then disappearing.

When I finished, she sat still for a second. Then she took a deep breath, so I knew she had been frightened.

"Do you know what they say when people dream of horses in the sky like that?"

She was so serious she scared me. I hugged my knees closer.

"What?"

"They mean death."

We looked at each other without saying anything. I felt goose bumps on my arms and was grateful for company in the motel room. I had convinced Reena that she could get a fresh start in the morning when artists put out new pieces and perhaps would be willing to give her a good price on the last day. She had reluctantly agreed, not wanting to leave her honey, Buck, her second husband, alone.

"For pity's sake, Auntie," Marli had told her. "Buck took care of himself all those years when he was a widower; he can last one night without you. You've got to get past that fifties' mentality."

After dinner, Reena decided she wasn't feeling sociable enough to handle the artist reception. So Marli and I went by ourselves, and I ended up returning to the motel alone later in the evening. For years, I had tried to introduce Marli to an artist or two, someone I thought would be a good match for her, but she had resisted my efforts to set her up. "I've got enough trouble without having to deal with a starving artist. No thanks," she said, shaking her head firmly, like artists were a diseased species. "Besides, they can be temperamental," she added.

I hadn't planned it but I couldn't have picked a better person to introduce her to than Rupert, my potter friend from Laguna Pueblo, an old classmate from the Institute. They hit it off instantly. Their eyes met and sparks started flying. They talked together easily as if they'd known each other for years. After the reception, a group of friends wanted to go gamble at the tribal casino. I begged off, told Marli to go ahead, gave her the room key, and returned to the motel while she rode with Rupert.

Auntie Reena clicked her tongue when I told her where Marli had gone. "Always someone new," she said. I was so tired from the day's work and the tension of the previous day and night that I had fallen asleep while Reena watched the TV news. I hadn't heard Marli come in at all.

"What time is it?" I asked suddenly.

Reena looked at the travel clock on the nightstand. "It's four in the morning." Checking the time reassured us and broke the tension. I got up and moved to sit on her bed.

"You think someone's going to die, Auntie?" I was cautiously skeptical.

She didn't answer right away, and when she began to speak, I had to lean closer to hear. "You know, the week before your mother died, I dreamed like that, only a black horse came down from the sky and began eating the flowers in my garden. I should have known, but it wasn't until later that I realized what it meant." She stared past me.

Reena was my mother's oldest sister, the one who watched over the family after Nana passed on. Sitting in my nightgown, her shoulders bowed, hands in her lap, her face soft folds, her usually styled, gray hair tousled, she seemed frail. I suddenly realized she was aging, maybe losing the strength that had taken her through tough times, a bad first marriage to a shadowy man from Laguna, raising four kids alone, then nursing her ailing mother and later helping me care for my mother in the last year of her illness. Most of the family thought of Reena as tough and hard-driving, and she was, but I had seen a side of her most people hadn't. The times she cried after taking care of my mother. She would be eating soup and the tears would come down silently. Other times she fell asleep in an easy chair, exhausted, then she'd get up and cook dinner for the whole family, refusing to sit down till everyone had eaten and the kitchen was cleaned up.

Since my mother's death, Auntie Reena was like my own mother. After we buried Mom, when we were tired from burial preparations and still in shock, though her death was not unexpected, she had said to me, "An artist friend told me that he grew from pain. He said he became the artist he never would have been otherwise. Use what has happened and turn it into art. You'll know how."

Her hand rested on the bed between us. I placed my hand over hers.

"Do you really think that's what my dream means?" I heard the catch in my voice. She didn't look at me. I went on, "I had the same dream the night before. When I woke up, the name that came to me was—" I suddenly felt embarrassed. "Julian."

She looked puzzled. "Julian?"

"Julian is Jude's father. Someone I knew a long time ago." Reena waited expectantly. I had opened a carefully guarded door and I couldn't shut it now. "I've never talked about him to you or anyone else. We grew up together on the agency. I thought I knew him, but . . . maybe not. He got involved with AIM back in its heyday with takeovers and protests— you know, radical politics and all that goes with it. I'm not sure exactly what happened, I only heard it secondhand, but he got in trouble with the feds. Got charged with something heavy, and. . . ." I faltered, then went on quickly. "He ended up in prison."

Behind her glasses, her eyes widened. I dropped my eyes, paused awkwardly. "Anyway, I never saw him after high school. I went stupid after I found out I was pregnant, was messed up in a lot of ways. Then I had Jude, you know, came home and got myself together." The words were bitter in my mouth. "I haven't thought of him in years. It's just that I had this dream that shook me, and when I woke up, the thought of him came to me so strong. After all these years." I hesitated. "Auntie. I never told him I was pregnant. He doesn't know about Jude."

I'm not sure why I never talked about Julian to my family before, but it was a relief to bring him out of the shadows. I took a deep breath. "But that's not all of it." I told her of Jude's phone call, his wanting to know who his father was, my lie to him.

"Do you think . . . my dream . . . Julian?" I asked.

She didn't say anything right away, then replied, "I can't say, but it's not something I'd ignore." She reached an arm around my shoulders, gave me a squeeze, then smoothed my hair back from my face. "You need to straighten this out with Jude right away. Poor thing. He should know about his father."

I stiffened.

"You should tell him, *hita*, then leave it to him what to do." She yawned. "We better get back to bed or we're going to have a rough day tomorrow."

Auntie was troubled, I could tell, though she was trying to downplay it. I was chilled when I got back into bed, but it wasn't something blankets could warm. I stared into the semidarkness, listened to the ticking of the windup clock, let its methodic tick hypnotize me. I was drifting off to sleep when Reena asked, "Were you awake when Marli came in?"

I didn't answer, just slipped away into darkness.

Communications

JULIAN—JUNE 1996

When I came to, an insistent electronic beep was sounding above and behind me. I was in a bed in a room somewhere, I didn't know where.

In the corner of the room, light leaked around the edges of drawn window blinds; otherwise the room was dark, night I presumed. I started to raise my head to look around. Dizziness and pain in my throat, hot and searing, caused me to fall back on the pillow.

Where was I? Out of the corner of my eye I could just see and hear a machine sighing softly, rhythmically. I touched my face and then my neck to find a tube at my throat, seemingly leading from the machine.

I turned my head slowly toward the sound above me, strained my eyes upward. A red light was flashing from the contraption that was beeping. I noticed a depleted IV bag hanging from a pole above me and tried to raise my arm to see if the IV was attached to me, but I was too weak.

I heard the approach of footsteps and saw light brighten the room as someone pushed open a door. I closed my eyes to feign sleep, but the pain coursing through my body was too intense. I twisted.

A nurse moved to the machine, silenced it, and quickly replaced the bag with a full one.

"You've been out a long time," she said, pulling out a cuff and stethoscope. She fitted the cuff around my arm and pumped her little ball. She held my wrist.

I tried to jerk my arm away. It was strange to see a woman, have her touch me. I opened my mouth to say something, but nothing came out.

"Take it easy," she said, her voice gentle. "My name is Peggy. I'm the nurse on the night shift. Been taking care of you for two nights going on three now."

Two, three nights. All I remembered was blackness.

"Doctor said someone gave you a crude tracheotomy. Don't know if he meant to, but he saved your life, the doctor said. Made it easy for whoever found you. You came in here to the county hospital with a makeshift tube in your throat."

She took the cuff off my wrist with a tearing sound that grated on my ears. She was working another medical contraption, which she placed in my ear, handling me with surprising gentleness.

"You got roughed up pretty serious. Don't know if you remember. The blow to your throat ruptured a jugular vein and formed a huge blood clot that blocked your airway." She motioned with her hand cupped at her throat. "Apparently, you also suffered a concussion, which is why you were out for a while. You're a fighter, guy. You came to just as if you heard me calling you."

Calling me? I faintly remembered a distant voice, female, I thought was my mother's. Or Cecelia's.

"Now don't try to talk. Look at me. Surely, the pain's intense? Just nod. Okay. I can give you something to make you a little more comfortable. I'll just check your chart. If you need anything, press the buzzer right there on the bed control panel."

Peggy left the room. She spoke to someone outside the door. I caught her last words, ". . . wake now." A deep masculine voice grunted a few words. She returned shortly and added something to the IV bag.

I woke a number of times when she came in to monitor my temperature, to suction my throat, to turn me on my side.

I couldn't believe her gentleness, the genuine cheerfulness and warmth about her. Even through my groggy medicated state and the pain I felt when the medicine began to wear off, I was conscious of her presence and the warmth she radiated. I began to relax my guard, and she folded into my dreams. They were busy and pleasant. In my dreams, I was of no particular age, neither young nor middle-aged. Peggy became confused with the bubbly cheerleaders I had dated during my glory days in high school.

When the first light of day came, Peggy was gone, replaced by a brisk, efficient, tight-lipped nurse. She didn't have to say anything to let me know what she thought of me. If I were able to speak, if I thought it would matter, I would have told her, "White lady, you make me laugh, sniffing around here like I'm scum. As if I couldn't get up and punch out your lights forever."

I watched the way she carried herself all stiff, like she had a broomstick rammed up her. She was nothing compared to the Indian Health Service nurses I remembered. Those IHS babes had bedside manners like a scrub brush. Their eyes were X rays probing you 'cause they knew you were lying, you weren't really sick, just wasting their time.

My laughter echoed inside myself. As if she could read my thoughts, the nurse turned frightened eyes on me. I smiled, closed my eyes. A little humor went a long way.

I was poked and prodded, taken out of my room for X rays and some kinda test, could be experimental for all I'd ever know. Beside my door I saw a pig parking his fat ass on a chair. He turned uninterested eyes on me. When he saw I was of good size, he sat up straight. I checked out my location good, noticed I was on the trauma ward at the end of a hallway, the nearest rooms vacant. They were keeping me away from all the other ailing, good citizens.

The doctor showed up to give me the lowdown. My condition was now stable, he said. The X rays showed that my trachea was fractured and would need surgery. The swelling in my throat could take up to two weeks to go down and nothing could be done till then.

He laid a heavy trip on me about the body suffering trauma, a hema-toma, concussion, continuing to be intubated, blah-blah-blah. At a certain point, like I was used to doing with the prison lawyers, I quit listening. Instead, I checked him out head to toe, wondered what kind of man was behind those glasses, if his wife was a nag, if she was good in bed, if he had ungrateful brats for kids, if he had reproduced miniature versions of himself. Somewhere, balding, bespectacled, anemic-looking kids were running around.

"Mr. Morning Star," the doctor raised his voice. "Was there something you didn't understand about what I said?"

I thought about it for a second, turned my mouth downward to indicate I considered it, and no, there was nothing that got past me.

"I asked because you seemed to be smiling." He briskly shut my chart and tucked it under his arm. He looked at me hard. I was busted like a silly schoolboy.

"I'll get to the point. As a consequence of the trauma to your trachea and voice box, I want to make clear that you possibly face the loss of your voice. We won't know for sure until postsurgery. You may regain full use. Then again. . . ." He paused dramatically. "Of course, we'll certainly do our best, but you need to know your voice box may be damaged beyond repair." The doctor looked me straight in the eye, trying to put the fear of God and man in me.

I looked away till I could tell my lack of response, my failure to show visible emotion, made him uncomfortable.

Slowly, I turned back to face him, gave him the full benefit of "the look." I opened my mouth. "I never had a voice, Doc. No one ever gave a damn about anything I've had to say. Why'ja people have to go and save my raggedy ass for?" At least that's what I wanted to say. In actuality, I was unable to speak a single, friggin' word. I motioned impatiently with my hand at my mouth.

Though voiceless, still, I got the doctor good I knew. There are more ways to communicate than through words. Maybe my it's-me-or-you look shriveled his balls. We both knew if worse came to worse, which one of us would survive. Or maybe my inability to speak, my Indian stoicism, hit the doc in his bleeding heart. Maybe it was the frustration I conveyed in the wave of my hand, the pain I could feel in my psyche, that unnerved him.

The doctor mumbled more medical nonsense, something about my not being able to talk so long as I was intubated, and jotted in my chart. I played along, nodded my head, dropped my eyes in deference to his medical mumbo jumbo, looked appropriately sobered by grave news. I'm not stupid. The doc was a man in a system that never favored me when I was free. Show him what he only thinks he's getting. Respect.

As he was leaving, I made signs at his back with my fingers as if I knew sign language.

My message? "Eloquent, ain't I?"

The thought of losing my voice forever, going around *dumb*, being forced to communicate with my fingers, scared and repulsed me. Angered me, too. I did what I knew best to do in these circumstances. I retreated. Being among civilians was a threatening experience. I no longer knew the social nuances, was socially backwards, a bad-ass. And that's not who I really was inside. All the nurses except for the night nurse seemed to be scared of me. I was a con, after all, but to make matters worse, I was without speech, a savage. The skinny one on the day shift acted as if I might pull out a tommyhawk, tie her to a tree, do things to her that would taint her, make her unacceptable to her own kind. As if in my pain, attached to a respirator, I was even interested. Thoughts like these could make me smile, but mostly I was despondent, becoming less and less myself.

On summer nights, we would sleep out in someone's backyard, at least five or six of us guys, wrestling, roughhousing, telling dirty jokes, sneaking around the BIA agency campus late at night just to see how the stillness felt. Usually we'd just wander around the well-lit campus in the damp coolness, pick green apples from the trees in the center court, stop to sit on the steps of any one of the dormitories vacant during the summer, and eat the apples with salt; then we'd sneak back in the yard, lie down on our sleeping bags, which we arranged like radiating spokes on a wheel with our heads toward the center, pull out cigarettes we pilfered from some grown-up's pack, and light up.

Someone, Herman usually, would start in about the time he walked home late at night and heard noises in one of the deserted, boarded-up dormitories on campus. That would start the round of ghost stories, like the sound of footsteps and the typing and scraping as if furniture was being moved in an old, abandoned office building on campus. Must be the rare BIA employee who couldn't stop working even after death, we would nervously laugh. Some stories were from TV or the movies, or the tribal ones we heard from our relatives of werewolves, witches, water babies, the hoofed stranger, bloodcurdling war cries heard at night only at certain times of the year on ancient battlegrounds, dead relatives sitting in the backseats of cars. The tribal stories spooked us the most because we believed in Indian spirits more than mad scientists and transparent ghosts. They shared space with us. We'd spook ourselves to the bone till we could hardly breathe and the night darkness was thick with unseen presence, till Tobie's little brother, Bennie, who always had to tag along with us, started to cry. Afraid that Tobie's father would come out and get down on us for still being awake, we'd give Bennie bubble gum and tell him it was okay, he was in the center and nothing could get him, although technically, he was no more in the center than any of the rest of us. Nonetheless, our words would reassure him. By then we were sleepy and we'd crawl into our bags and fall asleep to the hum of crickets and other noises, real and imagined.

But I'd always lie on my back for a while, staring at the sky, a dark, speckled blanket of expanding beauty. Sometimes, I'd awaken several different times in the middle of the night and see different constellations each time. I would stare till I was overcome with awe at the stark beauty and incomprehensible vastness of the universe. Sometimes, staring into the depths of the night sky would scare me like I might see something I shouldn't, and I would pull back into my sleeping bag. I knew from the different tribal stories I had heard that the stars were bears, sisters, dead relatives, coyote's eyes, mica dust. A busy, busy sky.

The whole agency, which included the administrative office, plant management, employee housing, student dormitories, and school building, was an oasis of towering pines and full-grown oaks and expanses of grass, kinda like a highfalutin prep school except the Indians bussed in from the surrounding states were wards of the government, not preppies, growing up with a pop bottle in their mouth rather than a silver spoon. And the grass, while watered and mowed regularly, was weedy or bare in places. Nonetheless, in the summer, the agency was green and shady and cool.

What made it an oasis was that, for one, the surrounding terrain was sagebrush and sand, dry and scrubby-looking, and two, the agency was designated a federal reserve. Neither city nor county nor state nor sovereign nation, it just *was*, existing apart in its own time and place and status while the rest of society went about its business around it. Ditto for the state prison located down the road. We couldn't help but notice that both the agency and the prison were situated outside the city limits of the state capital, Carson City, which was named for a famed Indian killer, or, according to state lore, a "frontiersman." It didn't much bother us to be in proximity to a prison near society's misfits, except now and then, when the prison alarm sounded that a con had escaped, we worried a little that he might seek refuge among Indians. But we didn't fret too much because Indians and prisoners have a lot in common.

Stewart was located in the eastern shadow of the Sierra Nevadas. In those very mountains the Donner party, emigrants heading to California, had gotten stranded in the snow in 1846 and had eaten one another to survive, then gotten the pass named for them. The Indians of the region had watched them and wondered what they were doing, but that portion was neglected in the history books we studied in school. Nobody ever asks Indians what they think of white people's doings. Anyway, there Stewart was, in the Reno–Lake Tahoe basin, right in the crook of the California–Nevada border where it makes the elbow turn on maps.

The snow fell thick and heavy in the fall and winter, but the government houses, dormitories, and BIA offices were toasty, heated by hard-to-regulate steam radiators that made it seem like summer inside. Going outside was like passing from a sweat lodge straight into a cold river, the experience uplifting. A number of Stewart students, especially those from Arizona, would pass between buildings without jackets or boots. I would say it was to heighten this experience, if I didn't know better.

A paved circular drive wound around the agency campus. It tripped past the BIA administrative office, tennis court, student dormitories, the auditorium, the two-story school building, the gym, and around the backside of employee housing. Mid-campus, a tree-lined street, like any street in Anywhere, USA, cut through the center, separating the personal lives of Indian and white government employees and their families from the less personal lives of boarding school students with government housing to the west, dormitory and administrative buildings to the east. The campus structures were either clapboard or solid rock. Indian builders had hauled rocks of all colors, shapes, and sizes, fitted them together into lovely mosaic designs, and produced beautiful, solid structures. Then they planted the trees that now stood silent witnesses to the comings and goings of students, staff, and campus kids. A web of side streets, alleys, and sidewalks connected the campus into an intertribal, biracial neighborhood.

Every August a fleet of Greyhound buses pulled into the campus with a belch of diesel fumes, the hiss of air brakes, discharging Indian students in front of the school building. Students descended the bus steps, their expressions reflecting a mixture of emotions—anticipation, uncertainty, hostility, anxiety, joy at seeing old friends. A few were unreadable, seemingly true of the stoicism Indians were said to display. Dormitory matrons, smiles stretched so tightly across their faces you knew they were forced, were on hand to greet the girls and usher them and their trunks to their assigned dorm. The boys' advisers, clipboards in hand, gathered the boys, equally vigilant to keep the sexes separated.

During our summertime explorations of vacant dorms, we found out some of the inside story of the Stewart students' experience in the discarded duty reports of matrons and advisers: the bed-wetting, sleepwalking, suicide attempts, pregnancies, runaways called AWOLs like they were army deserters, acts of defiance such as refusing to get up in the morning or make beds, talking back. Lighter moments were recorded, too. There were the girls' hair fixing and beauty sessions, the boys' bull sessions around the TV.

We had no words then for their stories. We just filed the information away in memory, glad we lived with our families. We knew that the land we were on, as well as the land surrounding us, was Indian land. There were voices all around us, in the land, in the blood soaked into the land that cried out for justice, in the trees and rock structures. Voices of long-ago boarding school students who once walked the campus, voices of the people who once hunted and gathered, voices of those who were dispossessed and then despised. These voices were with us and, on some level of consciousness, we campus kids, the children of BIA employees, heard them.

With the blue sky above us, the trees around us swaying slightly in the wind, the grass growing beneath us, and the land designated a federal reserve, we inhabitants of the agency were in a world of our own. I didn't know it then, but I do now.

My eyes were open but I felt like I had been dreaming, my physical reality displaced, my state of being fluid, moving at will in time. I found myself more frequently drifting like that. Peggy, the night nurse, walked in, pushing her cart of medical paraphernalia.

"Are you awake, Julian?" she called softly.

I gave an affirmative nod.

"Good. I would hate to disturb your sleep. Just checking to see how you're doing on your meds. Are you comfortable?"

The question was ludicrous. My face probably reflected the thought for she rephrased the question.

"It's been four hours since your last dosage. How's the pain? Can you hold out a while longer?"

My pain was constant but diffused. The back of my head was sore, my throat still burned like a god-awful scorching fire, the tube in my throat was uncomfortable, my hand where the IV tube was inserted sometimes ached with a coldness, and my body felt battered. But, heck, I was a man, I could take it. I was nowhere near the pain I experienced the time the pigs beat me in the Hole, three against one. I closed my eyes and nodded to indicate I could wait.

"I could pray for you if you don't mind."

I opened my eyes in surprise. Peggy stood bedside in her pink nurse outfit, a loose-fitting tunic and baggy pants. The outfit gave a rosy tint to her pale skin. Her plump arms looked strong enough to lift a man and soft enough to cradle a child. Peggy was usually full of cheerful banter, calling me *guy*, treating me like a regular person, a civilian.

The expression of grave concern in her face threw me, caused me to agree. She closed her eyes and her face went soft in the moment before she began to pray, calling on God in the name of Jesus. Her prayer flowed like a river, beautiful and powerful, taking me in its flow. She spoke to different parts of my body, lightly touched them, told them to heal and resume their proper function the way God intended.

I know the power in prayer myself, know how it can transform a man, make him humble. You can't hate when you pray. Anger, rage, resentment, they all dissolve, too, making forgiveness possible. Until I began praying during sweats, I didn't really know this.

Peggy went on to pray for a healing in my innermost being, that I would be made whole. She prayed for any needs I had, prayed for my family, for my loved ones. She prayed protection for me in prison, even for my attacker and any others who wished me ill. She prayed that though I was in prison I would find freedom in my soul through Jesus, that I would find rest for my weariness.

I hadn't expected to be affected by the prayer of a white woman. My chest suddenly swelled, then collapsed, and a dam behind my eyes broke. I looked up to see her looking at me like she understood. In silence, my body shook. I couldn't bear to look at Peggy.

She took my hand in hers and patted it reassuringly. I tried to say something, but my lips just moved.

"I don't know what you've been through, Julian. Maybe I don't need to know. But I can feel your pain, and I want you to know it's all right. In response to hurt, people go to great lengths to erect strong, impenetrable defenses. They hide inside their fortress, guarding their hurt, their false pride. I know about such pain." She didn't say anything for a while, just patted my hand until I regained control.

"I've got to check on other patients now. A man and wife are going to be brought up soon. They were in a serious car accident, so I need to make sure the orderly is getting a room ready for them. I heard the driver in the other vehicle didn't make it." She shook her head.

I tried to say thank you. It was important to me to say that to her, but with the tube down my throat, words were impossible. I made my hands move like a hand puppet was speaking.

She held her palm up, signaling for me to hold on. "I'll be right back," she said. She left the room and came back with a legal writing pad and a fistful of pens and pencils.

"Go ahead and write down what you were trying to tell me. I'll be by shortly to check on you again."

I picked up one of the pencils and wrote in a heavy scrawl, *Thank You.* The words hardly took any space on the page and I felt I should say more. I thought awhile and then wrote about the release I experienced in prison when I prayed. "Prayer has brought me both relief and oppression in prison," I wrote. "The oppression comes because my form of prayer is different than yours. Not different in content, only in form. We Native prisoners pray during a sweat ceremony led by our spiritual adviser who comes in from the outside."

I thought some more, wrote on, telling Peggy about Willie and how the first time he participated in a sweat, he broke down and cried like a baby. "He cried for forgiveness for what he did—shot his best friend in the face while he was stinking drunk. He blacked out and didn't even remember doing it. Following the sweat, he quit drinking and doing drugs in prison. In case you didn't know, that goes on regular as day behind bars. Willie's now a responsible, sober inmate.

"As one of the longest incarcerated Skins, and the only one with a high school diploma and some college education, I took the lead in the struggle to get us Indians our religious rights in the correctional center. That's why I suffer oppression. For doing something good! For wanting what is a constitutionally guaranteed right under the First Amendment and under the Religious Freedom Restoration Act.

"In these few days I've been here in the hospital, I've thought about the attack on me. I know I was set up, probably by the guards, maybe the warden. I'm alive and I'm not supposed to be, simply because as an Indian, I fought for my religious rights to grow my hair long, to have access to and use of a sweat lodge, sacred items, like our pipe, sage, and medicine bundles, for spiritual advisers to be allowed to come in and conduct ceremonies and counseling. After my written testimony was presented at congressional and state hearings, I was framed by guards for possession of drugs, thrown in the Hole, beaten by the guards and left without medical treatment. I'm considered dangerous, unstable, a threat to society. That's what is written in my 'jacket,' my file, though I am a model prisoner as much as I can be under the stress of being caged. I know about these lies because they were read aloud at my parole hearing held earlier the same day I was attacked. I was denied parole, told to come back in a few years."

It took me a long time to write what I did because I thought out each sentence before I wrote it. I could hear a commotion in the hallway, nurses and orderlies rushing back and forth, talking excitedly, but I ignored it. It was well into the early morning hours when Peggy came back.

"How's the pain?" she asked.

I was surprised. I had forgotten about pain during my concentration, but now I felt an edge to it.

"Ready for a dosage?"

I nodded.

As she added a vial to my IV, she told me it was a busy night. "First we rushed to get a room ready for the couple I told you about. We moved patients into other rooms to free a room for the two of them to stay together. Then we got a call from downstairs and they told us, Forget two beds, the husband didn't make it, but we'll send the woman up. She doesn't know about her husband, they said.

"Well, we waited, then they called twenty minutes later and said, Forget it. The missus didn't make it either." She sighed. "Then right after another, patients called for attention, one thing or the other, then an elderly gentleman went into cardiac arrest, which sent us into a tizzy. Sometimes it gets like this. Just frantic. The floor finally quieted. I'm sorry I couldn't get back to you sooner."

Her eyes fell on the notepad on the bed table. I handed it to her. As she read it, I watched her eyes dart back and forth.

When she finished, she placed her hand on my arm and said, "Julian, you are welcome. You've been through a lot, as I felt you had." She handed the pad back to me. "Yes, our practices are different. I'm a Christian."

I quickly wrote on the pad, "You are the first and only Christian I ever met that truly acted like one."

She read it and laughed. "That's a sad comment on Christians." Then she told me she came to God broken and hurting.

Peggy had once cherished a dream about being a nurse-midwife delivering babies into the world. She attended nursing school, struggled, got her license, then began working at a home birthing center where she delivered babies without a doctor present. Peggy loved it. "Such a joy to see little ones enter the world! I've got nothing against hospitals, but I believe birth is a natural event, meant for families to participate in. Hospitals didn't used to think that way. They downright opposed it. I did my best to make birth a celebration," she said.

Looking at her hands, I could believe she was a baby catcher. Her hands were soft and dimpled, perfect receptacles for a head and a bottom. Peggy had gotten married to her high school sweetheart, Lyle. They worked hard and saved to buy a house, waited impatiently to start a family. They hoped to have their baby born right in their own home. They tried hard to conceive for several years, tried everything, Peggy said, taking temperatures, lying on a certain side only, herbs, meditation. "Quit thinking about it and it will happen, people told us." When she said that, I could picture a younger, bosomy Peggy in bed with her own man, sweating hard, trying their darndest till the fun all went out of it. Anyway, bottom line: They went to specialists and Peggy found out she was incapable of having any children ever.

The news devastated her. Lyle, too. And life just kind of came undone then. Her marriage fell apart and she couldn't bring herself to deliver babies any longer. It was too painful. At one low point, she attempted to check out of life. That's when God revealed himself to her, she said. Jesus came into her life and she was mended slowly but surely. She switched to general nursing, eventually ending up in the trauma unit.

I recognized the storyline from the testimony of prison cons who had converted and started packing Bibles, doing what they called "fellowshipping," where they sang hymns and clapped like Girl Scouts. They'd tell me, "Jesus died for all people. White, black, brown, yellow people. He don't care 'bout skin color. He loves us all." I believe them. Only somebody forgot to tell those God-fearing, Manifest Destiny pioneers and missionaries. Peggy probably didn't know Christianity was used against Indians.

She said she encountered all kinds of tragedy on this floor and had a real affinity for people's pain. It's the ministry God called her to. I don't know about that, but she is the kindest person I've ever known and I can respect that. Later on, I tested her, tried to argue with her about God— what kind of merciful God lets Indians get slaughtered by so-called Christians?—but she said if she had to argue with me about God and Jesus then I wasn't ready to hear anything she had to say.

That Peggy! She shamed me with that. What kind of spiritual person argues about spiritual matters? Fighting for your religious rights was one thing; disrespecting beliefs someone else holds sacred was a whole different thing.

Peggy and I began to converse by paper. She'd ask me a question or two, something about my background, my family, then before she left her shift or maybe the following night, she'd read what I wrote, then ask me more questions. After a while, I simply wrote whatever came to mind, was writing more for myself than to answer questions. I used to be a strong writer in school. Somewhere along the line, I laid that aside. Peggy is smart about people. I think the woman knew what she was doing right from the start—therapy.

At first I wrote a lot about prison and what a hellhole it was. I vented all my feelings, but since Peggy was such a tender person, I thought all that junk might be offensive to her. She was somewhat naive, too, as I came to find out.

She told me one night, "Our American system of justice stands the best in the world. I don't think there's a citizen in their right mind who believes that prisons should be bed-and-breakfast hostels. Still, you know, people in positions of authority need to be informed abuses are occurring. A person takes it for granted that kind of stuff—injustice, treating people like human refuse, violating human rights—doesn't happen here in America." Surprised, I took in her flushed cheeks and indignation and held her gaze a moment. I realized she was trying to express empathy and outrage. Suddenly weary, I sank into the pillows propped behind me. The flat black of my hair, the duskiness of my skin, stood in sharp contrast to the white bedsheets. My lids closed; my mouth turned downward.

Her words, spoken so righteously, hung empty in the air between us.

Seeing my reaction, her eyes fluttered in stunned surprise. I'd say the lights flickered on, and she experienced a glimmer of understanding that she possessed a privileged status solely because of the color of her skin. I could almost read her thoughts as if they were flashing across her forehead like an electronic billboard. *This was a great country built upon godly principles! Yes, unfortunately, some injustices were committed, but that was in the past, what's to be done about it? My God, America had an underbelly, dark and ugly. The past is dead and gone. Wasn't it so? The sins of the fathers shall not be visited on the children.* Stunned and confused, her flush deepened and her mouth opened, but for once, no words came out. This was probably the first time she had ever seen herself white in relation to someone else's brown.

But the woman's heart was in the right place. Eventually, she recovered her composure to say, "My words were only meant to comfort. On this ward I see tragedy, intentional and accidental, in all shapes and forms. I take care of people, often women, beaten so badly their face is one purple blotch, victims of auto accidents, knifings, shootings, suicide attempts. I hear moans of pain, anguished cries of both patients and their families, obscenities. That's the downside. I also witness amazing acts of recovery, strength of will, courage in the face of adversity."

Right then, I decided to tell her my story. I figured, if anyone, Peggy could appreciate the tragedy in it. Before I could begin, though, I had to think. What to tell, where to begin. What could I trust myself, trust this woman, to tell?

There was already a lot about prison I had left out. The bitter disappointment and frustration of waiting and waiting for our spiritual adviser to assist us in a sweat, only to be told he hadn't shown up. Later, we found out the truth. He had come, sat waiting for hours, but the guards never called us. I hadn't told her about the closeness of the Indian brothers, how we used to be the low men on the totem pole until we stood up and demanded our rights. We get more respect now; still, it's a battle. The day-to-day bleakness. How sweats and purifications were good for a few days, but the stress of prison was so intense we needed them more than once a week, which sometimes we didn't even get. How I had never sought to be a leader. It just happened that I was the one with a vocabulary. Maybe I could never tell some things because of the horror, the shame of experiencing them. I had not even told Peggy what I was in for. She hadn't asked, either.

Peggy had told me about her personal pain. Could I do anything less? I sat for hours, thinking, deciding.

Sounds of Silence

On a Sunday afternoon, a "49" came into my office through the radio tuned to the Indian program on the university station. I was making a third frantic search through the papers and notecards on my desk looking for a quote. I stopped my rummaging to listen.

The song was typical of ones sung around a drum and bonfire at a 49, a post-powwow gathering infamous for one-night stands. In the song a lover cajoles his sweetheart not to cry by promising to take her with him when he returns to Canada.

"Ken-a-dah"—that's how the singers pronounced it. I smiled and turned up the radio. The pound of the drum filled my cramped office, vibrating the walls. In ragged unison the men sang out, *Darlin'!* I could see them bending over the drum, all tall, good-looking Canadian Indians, prominent facial features, hair dark as night, singing from the heart, meaning every word of it. The details all came through in the resounding pound of the drum, in the clarity of their beautiful voices. In the last round, trilling punctuated the lyrics like a prolonged cry of pleasure, like fingers down the spine.

When the song finished, the deejay said enthusiastically, "Oh yeah! Awesome. They must have all da fun up dere in Ken-a-dah."

I smiled again, reaching for the book before me. My friend in college, Clyde, had been a deejay hosting an Indian program in much the same vein. I flipped through the pages, my eyes skimming the print, plain and boring. I closed the book and pushed it away.

I rubbed my tired eyes and then stretched in the chair, rolling my neck to ease the strain. So many things to do. "Indian Car" started to play on the radio. *Please, Mr. Officer, let me explain. I got to make it to a powwow tonight. I'll be singing 49 down by the riverside, looking for a sugar, riding in my Indian car.* I stared vacantly at the wall, humming the song. Suddenly, without willing it, my gaze went right through the wall, twenty-two years into the past.

Dusk was overtaking the East Bay. A bluish cast from the streetlight spilled onto the parking lot as a car swung wide into a space. Light glistened on car chrome. Clyde jumped nimbly out of his car, a beaten Buick Regal with the front seat on the driver's side sagging toward the door from his weight. I got out, carefully arranging my folded shawl over my arm so that its long silk fringe fell straight and untangled. Drumming and singing carried faintly over the distance of a football field, over the rush of the nearby freeway.

Clyde stared over the top of the car, past the football field toward the powwow grounds. He stood big, a refrigerator of a man, dark and wild-haired. His sunglasses, smudged and greasy-looking, sat atop the tangle of his hair. Although it was drawn into two wrapped braids, wiry wisps managed to escape all over his head. Clyde looked imposing. He wasn't quite six feet, but he seemed well over that height. His belly flowed generously over his beaded belt buckle. I happened to know it was beaded, but most people didn't because no one could ever see it. His feet, wide and flat, were encased in scruffy moccasins. Most of the spring quarter, he had walked barefoot around campus so that the bottoms of his feet had become thickened, his toes spread out. However, after Professor Kovacs, whom Clyde deeply admired, had stared disapprovingly at his feet and asked if he was facing financial difficulties, Clyde began to wear the moccasins, which, except for the few beads on top, looked very much like his own bare feet. Clyde placed one moccasin on the rear bumper to tie the leather string. The bumper, pasted with stickers declaring THINK INDIAN and INDIAN PRIDE, lowered noticeably.

He straightened, breathing heavily. "Dang et. We missed the Grand Entry." He looked at me accusingly.

"Don't blame me. You're the one who had to have your hair done."

Clyde's dark face darkened further. He looked sheepish. His preoccupation with wrapping his hair had become legendary among his friends. It all began when he had joined the Berkeley football team, not as a player but as a water boy or towel holder of some sort, though he would never put a name to what he did. His grades fell enough to put him on probation, so he took a class in modern dance in order to raise his grade point average with an easy A. He hadn't expected to like the dance class, but it turned out he could leap and twist and kick with a grace gone untapped till then. He learned disco, the Robot, the Bump, the Moonwalk, and more. He took over the dance floor at parties. His hair was just barely touching his shoulders then, and wild as it was, it fell into his eyes and interfered with the graceful execution of his dance steps. Clyde's hair was barely long enough to form two stubs for braids, but when he covered the stubs with rabbit fur wrappings, he cleverly lengthened what was not there. Overnight, he achieved the look of long braids any AIM member would be proud to wear. Clyde must have gotten caught up in his own image because soon it got to the point where he wouldn't go anywhere unless his hair was wrapped, which required a hairdresser, a female, of course, because no male was going to be wrapping another guy's hair. The job largely fell to my roommate, Jackie, and me, and the two of us got our share of jokes for the role we played in helping Clyde with his "sacred wraps," as they came to be known. When he twirled on the dance floor, the wraps enlivened and hung on. He passed out on the couch more than once, legs sprawled, head thrown back, mouth open, sacred wraps intact.

He'd gotten so obsessed with wrapping his hair, I think, because he wanted to make sure no one mistook him for what he was: a genuine, 100 percent, real Indian. Clyde was half Pueblo and half Apache. He told me that having the blood of two traditional enemies flowing in his veins gave him no peace. One part of him wanted to plant corn and send down roots; another part wanted to roam, free as the wind. Further complicating matters, Clyde hadn't grown up on either of his parents' reservations, making him feel neither here nor there. Instead, he grew up in Reno, the biggest little city in the world. Having fixed his hair so often, Jackie and I were sure that his wraps had become his ties to his people, and we told him so every chance we got.

Clyde and I remembered all this in the moment we looked at each other over the hood of the car. His flush deepened, so that his face was rose-hued. He looked down at the wraps on his chest, lifted one at me, and said, "At least one of us looks good."

Clyde moved loosely beside me. His feet bear-slapped the sidewalk, his head and arms swinging in a peculiar rhythm the way they did when he was happy. He wore his favorite ribbon shirt, which was in need of ironing. Tiny sprigs of red flowers on a black background stretched around his bulk like wildflowers covering a hillside. Red satin ribbons on the back fluttered like the red flags on oversize loads.

Clyde was babbling about his film production class, his thumbs and index fingers framing scenes like a movie director. He was always into something new, like the time he decided clocks were a controlling tool of capitalism. It was a mutilation of life's sacred cycles and forces to chop them up into hours, minutes, and seconds, and he refused to tell time by the clock. He preferred the sun. When asked the time, he'd look at his wrist where there was no watch and say, "It is." During this phase, by the white man's reckonings, he was always too late or too early, never on time.

I didn't pay him any mind. I was caught up in the excitement around me. The moon was beginning to rise, a beautiful orange ball in a violet sky. The people streaming alongside us began to backlog at the admission gates. An old Indian man, graceful in his slow movements and distinctive in a Pendleton jacket, was giving the moneytakers hey-for about the fees, complaining loudly about commercialization and exploitation of Indian traditions. His wife stood beside him, jaw out, lower lip jutting, nodding her agreement. He glared into the crowd as he slipped his wallet into his back pocket, challenging anyone to object.

Clyde raised a closed fist to the man. "Tell it like it is, bro!"

The man scowled at him through thick glasses that magnified his eyes and intensified his displeasure. Clyde shrank back. The man turned away, back erect.

"I like your threads," Clyde called softly. People in line snickered. I elbowed him.

When we finally got in, we walked onto the field and stood beside the newly erected platform where the master of ceremonies presided over the festivities, microphone in hand. He bellowed, "Ladies and gentlemen, welcome one and all to the tenth annual Bay Area Indian Council Pow-wow! I am sure tonight's powwow will be worthwhile your time. O-ho! Before we get stomping here, let's hear a few words from our reigning princess, Pony Yellowhair, Miss Bay Area Princess! This is her last night as our Indian royalty." The singers leaned over their drums and pounded with a vigor that made their braids bounce on their chests; whoops and applause broke out among the ever-increasing crowd. A pretty young woman clad in white buckskin, bearing a beaded crown and a banner across her chest that proclaimed her title in gold glitter, stood beside the emcee, fanning herself daintily. She stepped forward, head down modestly.

Twilight was deepening, closing in around the people who pressed closer together on the field and in the bleachers. Within minutes, the sky turned purple, then black, and the moon slipped higher. Stadium lights hummed on, flooding the field, distorting colors. In its light, my white shawl took on a bluish tinge, its red flowers turning purple. Miss Bay Area Princess's dress, covered with elk teeth, shimmered. Her beauty became electric. She tearfully addressed the crowd in a heartfelt farewell. Most people were too excited to pay attention to her words, myself included. I had to sort through all the sights and sounds before I could focus on any one thing.

We had missed the opening formalities, the parade of dancers in traditional dress as they marched in single file for the Grand Entry and Indian Flag Song, which must have taken quite a while, judging by the number of dancers. This year's powwow was another record breaker. A thicket of dancers mingled around each group of singers seated around the six drums scattered around the dance arena, the bells on the fancy dancers jingling nonstop. A trio of teenaged girls, entry numbers pinned to their shawls, giggled nervously behind fans of turkey feathers. They twirled the beaded handles of their fans carelessly, popped their gum, and passed a can of Coke among themselves. From head to foot all three girls were adorned in beadwork: necklaces, bracelets, earrings, hair ties, leggings, and moccasins. They hummed with an energy barely restrained in fan waving but obvious in their faces. They whispered to one another behind their fans, pointedly looking over Princess Pony after each exchange. They smiled at one another, assured that their own beauty and poise could stand up against hers.

The emcee's voice sliced through the air. "Let's powwow! Oklahoma Two-Step, ladies' choice. Take it away, head drum!"

The three girls hastily conferred. Then they moved decisively toward young fancy dancers. All across the arena, couples streamed into position. They two-stepped out from under shadows of city buildings, swaying together like grass in the wind. Turning their backs on asphalt and grime, they moved like clouds toward the mountains.

The dance was elaborate and beautiful, snaking, circling, folding in and out of itself. It gave way to another dance, then another and another. I got caught up with the beat of the drum, lost track of time, track of Clyde, circled the powwow till I met up with Jackie.

The drumming and singing drowned out the rush of the nearby freeway. Deadlines, concrete slabs, blaring sirens, city lights receded. Even the football field and the running track beneath our feet faded from our consciousness. The lead dancers, stepping carefully, found a winding road worn smooth from dancing feet and led us all away from the city in a stomp dance. With every drumbeat, with every nimble step, with every trill and pierce of a bone whistle, the murmur of a river and the rumble of a distant storm emerged in our souls. Mountains, prairies, plains, and deserts sprang up. We could smell sweet grass, mountain dampness, smoke from campfires. Relocated, no longer shadows of ourselves, we all became fancy dancers, tiptoeing a thin line.

As dancers left the arena, a figure striding past stopped my head in mid-turn. I caught my breath as I realized it was Browning heading toward one of the drums. I hadn't admitted it to myself, but I had been looking for him all evening, only I had been looking for him to be dressed in his fancy dance outfit, not in the street clothes he now wore, faded Levi's and a T-shirt. A drumming stick protruded from his rear pants pocket. I turned to tell Jackie, but she had spied him, too. Her eyes danced. She motioned with her lips in his direction. We watched him move with fluid grace. "Browning," we said.

In a sprawling, aloof metropolis full of deep shadows, Browning had emerged a hero. When he wore his fancy dance outfit, he stood out in a crowd in his bustles and beadwork in a shade of blue straight out of a summer sky, a satin shirt that played with the light, beaded drops that dangled at the sides of his face and draped over his eyes. Representing the best of everything, he reigned as the champion fancy dancer in the Bay Area.

Best of all, out of thin air he spun dreams for those of us who needed them. Time and again, we watched him pour himself into dance with perfect timing. Light as a feather, his feet flew in step to the drumbeat, too fast for our eyes. The bells strapped to his ankles and knees jingled madly. A strand of blue fluff from the bustle on his costume whirled about him as he spun faster and faster till his feathers melted into a soft blur.

Though other dancers were equally skilled, they lacked the style and grace that distinguished Browning. In a spectacular display of showmanship, he'd stop in perfect time with the last beat of the drum, posed on one knee, arms outstretched. The contest judges scrutinized him, then penciled thoughtfully onto their pads, though the outcome was already known. His competitors conceded defeat, some unhappily. The women drank him in. Their hands reached out to touch him, but they touched their lips instead. Tourist cameras snapped and whirled. Even the kids stopped running around to watch him, their mouths hanging open, eyes adoring him until they ran off again.

He was known by name throughout the California and northern Nevada powwow circle, but few people actually knew him personally. He was elusive, a deep shadow disappearing in bright light, everywhere yet nowhere. Despite all the attention, he never flaunted himself, which would have ruined his style anyway.

Browning sat with the Sweetwater Singers directly across from Jackie and me. His eyes wandered over the crowd, eventually reaching us, stopping when they met mine. The emcee cut in.

"Let's powwow! 'Nother intertribal dance. Take it away, Sweetwater Singers."

The Sweetwater Singers beat the drum, and their voices rose. The dancers stepped into the arena and gave themselves over to dancing. Jackie flung her shawl over her shoulders. "Let's go dance," she said. Reluctantly, I agreed, feeling self-conscious. In company with the other dancers, I let the song flow over me, carrying me along in its rhythm till I was invigorated with the simple pleasure of dance.

"Whoo-wee!" the emcee breathed into the microphone. "Just look at that bee-you-ti-ful moon up there! They say white people in cities do crazy things when the moon is full. You know what Indians do when the moon is full, doncha?" He threw back his head and laughed.

He bent into the microphone, breathing, "Tepee creepin'!"

Singers pounded their drums and whoops broke out all over.

I broke off the memory abruptly and snapped off the radio. I couldn't believe I had let it slip in. A deep sense of emptiness, dull but still there, told me the memory still had power. A disturbing fact, but I couldn't think of that now. *Where was I?* The paper, yes. Submission deadline. Arnie, that big-time jerk! I wouldn't be here, trying to piece together a twenty-three-page essay from memory, if it wasn't for him. I hunched my shoulders, huddling over my desk, frowning to draw out serious concentration.

My thoughts for the paper refused to focus. Cecelia, stressed and unhappy. Jude as a chubby baby. Jude as a rambunctious boy full of riddles and smiles. As a young man gone quiet and somber. They had wandered through my dreams, my thoughts, all week long, almost as much as Rupert. I smiled.

What I remembered most in meeting Rupert was the sound of his voice with its throaty vibration. I could tell he spoke his Native language by the way he spoke English, softening the harsh consonants and conforming English to a different speech pattern. Even as I half-listened to him

congratulating Cecelia for taking Best of Show in her category, as they
continued talking shop, I watched his hands, smooth and soft-looking. His
fingers were long and slender, graceful. I could imagine his hands upon the
clay as he kneaded it into the right consistency, then took a small lump,
balled it in his hands, and rolled it into long coils that he built into clay
walls, smoothing them together with fingers dipped in water. Maybe he
sang while he worked, the whitish-gray clay coating his dark skin, a
smudge of it across his forehead where his hand had brushed.

As I was thinking this, he gestured with his lips, the way Indians do to
point out someone across a room, and said something to make Cecelia
laugh. He smiled at me, wiped the corners of his mouth with thumb and
forefinger, and folded his arms across his chest.

The phone rang every night at the same time since I met him. Rupert
and I spent hours talking, using fluctuations in our voices to flirt like goofy
adolescents. On the phone, breathing, laughter, silence, all took on shades
of subtle meaning.

Cecelia and Jude weighed on my heart; Rupert lifted my spirits. All day
I moved between the two extremes. On campus, I saw Jude look-alikes,
even some big Indian guy who resembled Clyde from a distance. It was a
mistake letting Clyde creep into my already crowded thoughts. He had
always had a knack for creating chaos without even trying.

My eyes lifted from the blue lines on the notebook paper, which had
begun to buckle. Stacks of library books, half of them past due, formed a
ragged front around me. Behind the books, file folders piled haphazardly
threatened to slide off the end of the desk and spill across the floor.
Miscellaneous memos and fliers, copies of journal articles, and late papers I
never should have accepted overflowed a large wire filing basket. I peeked
into one of the foam cups littering the desk. A small amount of greasy-
filmed coffee remained. Another contained coagulated chocolate milk.
Index cards dotted with clots of blue ink from a leaky pen were in disarray
from my search for a specific quote. I couldn't remember what I had been
looking for.

I plucked up the foam cups, threw them in the trash can, straightened
the index cards into one pile, smoothed my hair behind my ears, and

reread the first page aloud. Pitiful. I just couldn't re-create the original thoughts of my missing journal article. The current draft was more a collection of research notes and uninspired thoughts I had thrown onto the page in the desperate hope that they'd become a familiar road leading somewhere.

More determined now, I poised my pencil above the page. The telephone ringing in an office down the hall shattered my thin hold on how to rephrase ideas that had tangled together. I waited for someone to answer it, but, of course, this was Sunday; no one was in.

I scribbled over the mess of words and wadded up the paper. Last summer, my Uncle Two Bucks, making one of his sarcastic observations intended to keep me alert and humble, told me that English was a sneaky language. He was right. English wasn't a clear-cut, honest tongue. It was full of inconsistencies, irregularities, and bastardized phrases. When a Native came to rely on it like I had, thoughts could get lost, wandering soulless and expressionless in vicious circles. I had grown more cynical about this in a year's time. As far as English goes, I've been dancing with the dead, falling into open graves, picking at the bones and shards of my own ideas.

I picked up the phone, punched out Cecelia's number, listened to the first few rings as I silently read the titles of books stacked on the desk, and wondered if she'd be home. After a few more rings, I was ready to hang up.

"Hello?" Her voice was husky as if she had wakened out of sleep.

"Hi, Cecelia! How you doing?"

A pause on her end. She didn't seem to recognize my voice so I reminded her, "It's me, Marli. I'm supposed to be working, but—" I was ready to launch into the details of my distressing writer's block, the wretched week I'd had trying to stay focused, dealing with equally distracted students who tried to substitute b.s. for a discussion of reading they obviously hadn't done, all before I plunged into the real reason for my call. *I knew.* And the knowledge was weighing me down.

"Marli. What's up?" The demand in her question threw me.

"Uh . . . nothing urgent. Just thought I'd give you a call and see what's happening in your neck of the woods."

"I've got Jude on the other line." She sounded irritated and I wondered with whom. Me or Jude?

"Oh?" I waited for more details. When the silence was getting awkward, I asked, "Is he coming?"

She sighed long and heavy. "I can't talk. I'll call you back soon as I can. Bye." She hung up as I was saying bye.

The second floor, which housed the offices of both the American Studies and Religious Studies Departments, was eerily quiet. I stared at the phone as if it might tell me something.

I had never noticed it before, but silence is not pure; in fact, it's quite noisy. There's this buzzing, hissy sound to it that can start sounding like other things, television white noise, radioactivity from outer space, the roar of the ocean, synapses firing in the brain. My office, windowless and small, was only a scant career step above the offices assigned to teaching assistants in that I didn't have to share it. Bookshelves took up two walls, one behind me; the other, to my left, blocked free passage around my desk when I left the door open during office hours. A molded plastic chair for students faced my desk; an ugly green file cabinet to my right locked me in.

"This isn't an office. It's a closet," Cecelia had told me on her occasional visits. She knew American Studies was the only department willing to take me on. Nonetheless, she was skeptical, wondering what they wanted from me. "This is not a legitimate academic department, no matter what anyone says. It's la-la land," she'd say, stopping before closed office doors on our way down the hall, pointing out some of the courses taught by my esteemed colleagues: "The Psyche of American Cartoons"; "Gypsies, Tramps, and Thieves—Politics Makes Strange Bedfellows"; "Victoria's Secret: Repression and Female Sexuality"; "Fantasy and Fear in Flicks."

"This is worthy of study? If you had a kid in college, would you let him or her spend tuition money on this?"

I don't answer because I know she's just teasing.

"They're going to keep you in the closet till you teach a course on serial killers, you know."

Cecelia doesn't know it but I overheard everything she told Auntie

Reena about Jude's father, that Julian guy, the night we stayed up north in the motel. I'm not one to eavesdrop, but neither can I sleep soundly in a strange bed when the light is on. Her story blew me away. I had no idea.

I'm struggling with my own sense of betrayal that she never told me personally about Julian. False indignation rises, then falls flat when I think of reasons why she didn't, and I worry that I let her down somehow. Cecelia had always confided in me, but only to a certain extent, I know now. She's always been a private person, and that sense of privacy seemed to deepen after her mother died almost four years ago.

For two weeks I've been in shock, barely able to deal with the fact that Cecelia has a murky past, that she lied to Jude, precious Jude, about his father, a prison con no less, who I can't begin to imagine without my heart beginning to pound and my stomach knotting. I've held close to my perception of Cecelia as having herself together. Unlike me, she worked everything out, effortlessly it seemed. So she had a child out of wedlock at a young age. She got handed lemons; she made pink lemonade and then sold it. Her art career has moved steadily along a plane of ascension. And even on occasions when plans have gone awry, she has offered a thoughtful analysis of why something hadn't worked out, where the weak spot had been, what was to be done next. Calm as a deep pool of water. That's how I've thought of her. Finding out that all was not as it seemed with her was somewhat discouraging, unnerving even.

I hate to think it, but perhaps I didn't watch out for her, listen to her as closely as I should have, being preoccupied with battles on my own front.

I'm closer to Cecelia, in age and intimacy and circumstances, too, than to my much older sisters, who always seemed grown up and capable in my memory. I grew up both on and off the reservation, an adolescent during the social pathos of the late 1960s. I was the pawn in my parents' drawn-out divorce that never clearly was a divorce until I was in my senior year at UC-Berkeley. My mother surely underwent her own midlife crisis, suddenly moving to Phoenix, shocking everyone. Since I was nine, I spent winters in California with my dad and summers at Isleta with my mother. My mother never wanted me to leave at summer's end, but I knew I had to take care of my dad. In the end, my mother finally got her wish when I came home after college.

I find it hard to be conventional, to follow social patterns dictated by others. I don't know why. I've busted past forty, setting off all the alarms what with still being single and without a child. Perhaps in the broader, fragmented American society, this is easier to get away with. Not in my extended family, which is ever-extending. My sisters are now grandmothers, my nieces are mothers, my cousins and second cousins, too. Some have been married and divorced twice, compounding family relationships with stepchildren and in-laws/out-laws. They wait expectantly, impatiently, for me to add to the tribal enrollment, to fold into the kinship scheme with my own offspring. For my part, I've published a few articles in journals only other academicians read, and struggle for tenure. Like love and marriage, publishing and tenure don't come easy to me.

Cecelia was the only one I could talk to about all this. She, too, grew up off the reservation, which gave her a different perspective of things, and she remained single, too, though she escaped the social flak since she had a son.

Cecelia grew up on a BIA Indian agency in Nevada where both her parents—my maternal aunt, Judy, and Uncle Roland—were teachers. She started art school in San Francisco the same time I was across the Bay at Berkeley, though I wasn't aware of our proximity to one another. She was there for one semester only before she went to stay with my mother, Virgie, in Phoenix while she had Jude. Then she came home, enrolled at IAIA in Santa Fe, and finished up with a B.A. and then an M.F.A. at the University of New Mexico. We really didn't know each other till we both came home. I had never given it thought before, but actually we don't know much about each other before then. We thought we left our pasts safely behind.

I pictured Cecelia as I had seen her two weeks ago at the Blue Corn Art Show, braving a thin smile, her slight shoulders bowed. "Give me a call, Marli," she had said as Reena and I left to return home.

Recalling the evening at the artist reception when she was awarded Best of Show in her category, I frowned. She was *there*, but she wasn't there. Later in the evening, she declined to go out with the rest of us—*Too good for us?* the others teased—and left the reception looking unduly tired and disturbed for someone who had just won an award. Now that I think of it, the signs of distress were there. I was just too accepting of her superficial responses to my questions of how she was doing.

She's done that to me all along! My mouth dropped open at the sudden realization. She had always smoothed over the hard questions I put to her, turned them around on me. No wonder I never caught on. I sat and marveled at her skill in hiding herself all these years, but after some thought, I realized she had gotten away with it only because I let her.

I redialed her number and listened to the phone ring on and on. The answering machine didn't turn on, nor did she respond to call waiting if she was on the line.

I hung up and redialed. Still no answer. I stared into space, hearing the hiss of silence. She wouldn't admit it, but she needed help in sorting out this whole Jude-Julian mess. She had to tell Jude the truth about his father. She had to help him meet Julian, connect with him. I felt sad for Jude, whose growth I had tracked, birthdays I faithfully remembered, school photos I framed. I was there for his first holy communion, cheered him on at soccer and basketball, attended his high school graduation. I had closely watched him from a distance. Sometimes, never intentionally, I confused Jude with another boy his same age, with similar circumstance of birth. *Cody.*

Forget the paper. I decided to drive to Cecelia's house to check on her. Never mind that the old guys in the department, tenured and musty, would be inquiring ever so politely about my scholarship. "In which journal?" they'd blink at me. After I answered with the name of a Native studies or women's studies journal, they'd sniff, "I don't believe I'm familiar with that publication." Old buzzards. They were watching and waiting for me to slip, so they could smugly shake their heads that women of color didn't seem able to meet the standards.

Well, I'm not ready to lie down and die. They didn't know of the long-standing resistance efforts of the Pueblos, the subject of my paper.

"Take this," I said, stuffing papers into my tote bag.

I creased the pages of my draft down the center, cursed Arnie for the negative energy he had radiated last spring when the paper should have been finished, and, worse yet, for the theft of my completed paper. Too often, love had failed me as miserably as it had my parents.

Arnie and I had gotten into an intense argument one evening after he burned our dinner. I had asked him to watch the food while I took a shower. He agreed, but when I got out of the shower and entered the kitchen, he was scraping pork chops into the trash can. He had been watching a game on TV and apparently got caught up in it and completely forgot about the frying meat. I didn't realize it at the time, but he had been drinking beer while he watched TV, and he flared up when I got mad that he laughed off his negligence. The frying pan was ruined, the house was smoky, we had no dinner, I was tired. The list went on. It turned out I was tired of a lot of things and I let him know all of them. He retaliated with a long list of his own. Guess he was tired, too.

"What are you going to do about it?" I demanded. He must have known I meant more than just dinner.

Without saying a word, he stormed out, grabbing the keys to my car as he left. He peeled out of the yard and didn't return with my vehicle throughout the night, not until the next day after I called him at work, at which time we got into another argument.

"I don't care what you do, Arnie. Just bring my car back," I finally ended the conversation.

He showed up that evening with his brother. Arnie drove up in my car, parked it, then got in his brother's car and left.

My car was a mess. It looked like he'd had a party in it. Both the interior and the exterior were coated with dust. Though the windows were down, the car reeked of stale cigarette smoke and beer. Papers and file folders I had left in the car were strewn all over, dirty with footprints. I noticed right away my camera and CD carrying case were missing. I was back on the phone with Arnie again, demanding he return my possessions. He denied taking them, insisting they weren't in the car at all.

"I distinctly remember leaving the CD case on the front passenger seat and the camera underneath the front seat."

"That was real smart." His voice was heavy with sarcasm. "I told you not to leave the camera or any valuables in your car. The heat's not good for the camera, and you just tempt someone to break in and steal."

Like I wanted his advice. "I can't leave my camera and CDs in my car parked in my own yard?"

"They weren't there when I took the car."

"I distinctly remember—"

"I didn't take them! They weren't in the damn car!"

It was an unproductive, frustrating call. I got so busy with classes and grading papers, it wasn't until days later when a friend offered to read my paper that I realized it was missing. I searched my bag, the papers in my office, and then at home. Then I searched again more thoroughly. Only when I couldn't find it did I remember it had been among the set of papers I carried out of my office and left in my car. Arnie! He had taken my paper, too! I called him again. This time, he didn't get angry, though he claimed he hadn't seen my paper at all. He seemed genuinely concerned, but he just couldn't be believed. It would be just like his mean-spirited nature to sabotage me with a smile on his face.

At least I had a copy on disk. To my horror, my office computer couldn't open the disk, though I tried repeatedly. The words on the screen, "Disk Drive Error, Not Reading Drive A," struck terror in my heart. In desperation, I appealed to the school's computer experts, but they said there was nothing they could do; the diskette was damaged.

"Access the document through your backup copy," suggested the young man with the gold earring stud in one ear.

Backup copy?

"Yes, you do have a backup copy saved on a second disk, don't you? And a copy saved on hard drive? Surely, a hard copy of your draft?"

No, no, no. He shook his head sympathetically. "You're not the first one," he said.

I left my office, exited the building, and walked out into the late afternoon heat. On the TV news, weatherpeople daily bemoaned the fact that the annual rainfall was well below average, despairing that we were in a drought. I stepped down into the sunken brick plaza, the sun beating on my head. Heat waves shimmered ahead. Feeling I was in a giant frying pan the way the bricks and cement of the plaza absorbed the heat, I looked around in annoyance.

I'm guessing that the storied buildings edging the plaza, which contained classrooms and department offices, including the one I'd just left, were supposed to be modeled after Anasazi cliff dwellings. They looked more like hideous cement cracker boxes painted adobe brown and other earth tones. The library, though, was a saving grace. A beautiful structure, Pueblo/Spanish adobe style, multi-storied with huge, paned windows, faux-wood vigas and balconies, it soothed the eye and always reminded me I belonged on campus as much as anyone else, no matter the politics of exclusion.

Reaching the other side, I climbed the first tier of steps from which slabs of cement spread into walkways in all directions. At the top of the second tier were more Southwest-style buildings. I trudged on. The campus architecture was a good example of the mishmash of New Mexico's much-touted, glossed-over, tricultural heritage, the coming together of three groups of peoples: the Pueblos, Navajos, and Apaches; the Hispanics; and the Johnny-come-latelies, the Anglo-Americans, who hate to be called that. The uneasy fit of the three cultures was often ignored as if pretending discordance didn't exist would make it disappear.

I thought that over as I left the campus, drove down Central Avenue, and headed into the valley through the downtown section with its towering commercial buildings, restructured streets, pedestrian-friendly civic plaza, and valiant historic preservation efforts, all part of the city's attempt to revitalize the civic center. Downtown used to be the heart of the city with thriving businesses, Sears Roebuck and J. C. Penney department stores, Woolworth's, Safeway on Fourth Street, the KiMo and Sunshine Theaters. Sidewalks were packed with pedestrians, the air thick with diesel fumes from city buses and the sound of air brakes. Smells of popcorn and wax on wooden floors were heavy in Woolworth's, while smoke and stale air rushed out the darkened interiors of small bars.

Downtown began to dwindle once a notion of "uptown" emerged and finally decayed with the opening of the first mall. It seemed like no amount of Yankee ingenuity was going to be able to turn back time and revive the area. Albuquerque—for that matter, New Mexico—had "progressed" into urban sprawl, overpopulation, and crime. Drought years made this more apparent when a precious water supply became more precious and political tempers flared over water and land use.

Superficial cosmetic makeovers were not going to mend the deep underlying split between native New Mexicans and outsiders, newcomers who came to the Land of Enchantment for its rusticity and rural charm and then proceeded to remake it into their own notion of the Southwest. Native activists and professionals and tribal people came to my classes to discuss such issues. Save the Jemez. Save the Rio. Save the petroglyphs. Such blind recklessness as if the natural world were a machine that broke down and could be fixed. Or was an inconvenience to be paved over.

Hispanic and Indian students in my classes freely made observations of that sort. Sometimes they burst out with pent-up emotion. I would see the uncomfortable shift of white students in their chairs, the flash of anger and resentment in their eyes.

I turned down Rio Grande Avenue and wheeled past Old Town, where New Mexico culture was simultaneously exhibited and exploited. I made a left turn and continued into a neighborhood of adobe homes. The homes on Cecelia's street looked like comfortable old shoes. The adobe walls had settled, creating deep cracks in the stucco. Cecelia's lawn was overgrown, weedy in patches. I stepped onto her porch, glancing down at the ceramic pots of bright flowers, slightly wilted. I couldn't see through the thick lace curtain across the window of the front door, charmingly Southwest with its turquoise paint.

I rapped on the door good and hard a number of times. Then I went around the side of the house, attached the garden hose to the spigot, turned the faucet on, and took the hose out front to the flowerpots. I was almost through watering when Cecelia opened the front door. With the doorknob still in her hand and the door partially opened, she looked out at me. She looked awful, dressed in an old jogging suit, barefoot, hair disheveled, no makeup on.

"Hi," she said weakly. "Geez, thanks for watering the plants. I forgot about them." She yawned and stretched.

"Hi," I said. "I'll be in, in a second." I finished watering and turned off the hose. When I returned to the porch, the front door was opened wide, Cecelia inside somewhere. The swamp cooler was on, and I shut the door behind me. Cecelia came into the living room with a hairbrush in hand.

We sat down on separate couches. The ceiling fan twirled slowly. She began brushing her hair, stopping to yawn. "I'm sorry. I just woke up, still sleepy I guess."

"I stopped by to check on you. I called and the phone rang and rang."

"You called again?" I nodded. "I must not have heard it." She looked around the room. "I wonder where I left the phone." She went into another room and pressed the page button on the base phone. We could hear a faint beeping somewhere. After repeatedly pressing the button and listening, we found the phone out on the back porch.

"Guess that explains why I didn't hear the phone ringing. I left the phone there after I finished talking to Jude. I went to bed afterwards." She put the phone back on the base.

"In the middle of the day?"

She sat down and resumed brushing her hair. "I haven't been sleeping well."

Looking at her closely I could see bags under her eyes. Her skin looked pallid and unhealthy. She was swallowed up in the bagginess of her jog suit as if she had lost weight. I got up, took the brush from her, and motioned for her to turn around. I began brushing the ends of her hair, then the length of it in long even strokes. After a few passes, the brush moved smoothly through, crackling with static electricity after every downstroke.

Hair brushing reminded me of Clyde and the sacred wraps. And something else. I spoke quickly to dispel the thought. "When I was growing up, I always wanted a little sister so I could brush her hair. I thought it was so unfair to be the last child." Cecelia said nothing so I continued,

"Sometimes I wish for a daughter whose long hair I could brush out every morning and every night." I made a few more strokes, suddenly sobered by my words. "I wonder if I would make a good mom?"

I placed the brush on the coffee table and sat back in the couch. Cecelia took an elastic hair tie and secured her hair in a ponytail. "Thanks," she said in a husky voice.

I looked at her face closely. She had tears in her eyes.

"What's the matter?" I leaned forward.

She shook her head. "It's just that time of the month. Lately, I've been having a real hard time, getting all weepy and depressed."

"Cissy," I said firmly, using her childhood nickname. "I know about Jude and Julian. I heard everything you told Auntie Reena. I didn't mean to listen in on anything private, but I woke up, and after a while, it seemed more intrusive to interrupt, so I didn't say anything. I'm sorry, but it happened, and I just wanted to let you know I know."

Initially, her eyes reflected shock at my words. She looked down and then into my eyes. "It's okay. I'm glad you know. I would have told you myself sooner or later."

We both relaxed and then she leaned over and hugged my neck.

"I appreciate your coming. I've had a real hard time. Haven't been able to work on anything, and I don't sleep well at night. I worry about the awful lie I told Jude and how I may have hurt him living a lie all this time. That's what drags me down the most. I haven't been the greatest mother."

I started to protest, but one look at her eyes glistening with pain stopped me.

"The other thing that bothers me is my dream about the horses. I haven't had any more dreams, not that I remember anyway, but what it could mean scares me. You heard what Auntie said?"

I nodded, yes. "Did you tell Jude about his father when you talked to him today?"

She shook her head. "I tried to, but I just couldn't. Not over the phone. I just told him it was an issue we needed to resolve together and that he needed to come out here 'cause I couldn't go there, what with my upcoming shows. He didn't want to. We were arguing about that when you called. He's got a good job for the summer that he doesn't want to give up. In the end, I got nowhere. I was so drained after the call, I crawled into bed, pulled the sheet over my head, and fell asleep."

"Let me talk to Jude. I'll give him a call this week and see if I can persuade him to come." I saw the alarm on her face.

"I promise I won't tell him a thing."

Her shoulders relaxed.

"And another thing. We're going to have to locate Julian, wherever he is." Her eyes grew big as saucers. "We have to, Celia," I said firmly. "For Jude's sake and because Julian deserves to know that he has a son." She swallowed hard, holding her hands quietly in her lap.

While Cecelia showered, I made a dinner of potato stew. I scrounged the refrigerator and found hamburger meat, half an onion, and some potatoes. My bachelor dad always swore by potato stew as the answer to all problems. It was simple but nourishing. He had that right.

Over dinner I told her what Arnie had done and how I was struggling to rewrite my article. She was sympathetic but not at all surprised by his actions. Afterwards, we sat in the living room, sipping iced tea. The color had come back into Cecelia's cheeks. In the evening light, she looked relaxed.

I put my glass down and drew myself up. "I've got to tell you something I've never told anyone else. I just buried it deep, thought it would go away if I left it alone. Just in the past two weeks, I realized pain doesn't go away if you ignore it. It follows you around like a ghost and shows itself in different forms. Like Arnie." I took a deep breath.

I began with Clyde and his sacred wraps and told what I had remembered so vividly earlier in the day, how we had made our way to the powwow in his beat-up old car.

"I think I know who Clyde is," she interrupted me. "Never knew him myself, but he was a friend of friends. He went to Menaul High School in Reno. I bet my old friend Jewell knows him. Where he's at, what he's doing. She still lives in Nevada and makes it her business to know every-one else's business."

Right, I'd forgotten that, going to school in Nevada, Cecelia may have known him. That's the way it worked all over Indian country. Someone always knew someone else by either blood, association, or notoriety.

"Yeah, he was a real card, that one."

Fancy Dancer

MARLI—1974–1976

All I knew of Browning was he was Shoshone from northern Nevada. Clyde was the only one of us who knew Browning personally. At least he claimed to. And for Clyde, Browning became a social asset. He quickly noticed how his parties were packed to overflowing when he casually mentioned Browning might be dropping by. Whole parties of nondescript people stood around, sometimes the night long, embroidering their mundane lives into fine-spun fabrications, waving cigarettes amidst low clouds of blue smoke. While engaged in red-eyed conversation, they had their senses tuned to the subtle change in group temperature that would signal his arrival. No one dared miss one of Clyde's gatherings for it seemed Browning always showed up when you were somewhere else. Just when doubts would grow as to whether Clyde was spinning yarn about inviting him, Browning would manifest at the height of the night, when his presence was difficult to confirm. Clyde always invited students from the colleges and universities up and down the peninsula. It was hard maneuvering through Clyde's crowded place to get to the bathroom, much less trying to find someone among the bodies of strangers parked on the sagging, cast-off couches in the living room or among the clusters of people gathered in tight circles. The next day credible witnesses always emerged to attest that, yes, he had been present.

Once, I refused to believe talk that Browning was present only to see him leaving a couple of hours later. My mouth fell open. I saw him heading toward the door, slipping his Levi's jacket over his shoulders and pulling out his ponytail from under the collar. Then his profile cut the night as he pulled the door shut without a backward glance. After that, I never failed to follow up on every reported sighting of him.

Clyde promised he'd introduce me to Browning just to prove he really was on a first-name basis with him. During halftime at the Oakland All-Indian Basketball Tournament, he'd actually led me to where Browning stood milling with his friends. Clyde called, "Hey, bro!" and Browning turned, smiled at Clyde, then widened his smile to include me. Clyde asked about the new player from northern Nevada and the talk instantly turned to basketball. All the guys jumped in, and the conversation got carried away where Clyde couldn't control its direction. When he finally got to work in a word, he said, "Hey, someone I'd like you—"

"Gotta go, bro." Browning spoke to Clyde but smiled at me, held my eyes a moment longer, then turned, moving away with his group, gone quick as the flashing of a white-tailed deer.

By the time of the Bay Area Indian Council Powwow in late spring, I still hadn't met him. I was intently watching the woman's shawl dance contest when Clyde appeared at my side.

"Hey. I'm making contact with people for my film project. I think you'll be interested. C'mon." He beckoned with his hand cupped.

I shrugged him off. No telling what Clyde was up to.

Clyde was not one to catch subtle turndowns. "Hey, now," he purred in his FM sign-off voice. "I think you'd really like to be in on this. Know whatta mean?"

He was already turning. "C'mon."

"I said no, Clyde. No. Get Jackie to go with you."

"My contact is someone you'd like to meet. Meet. Really like to meet." He raised one bushy eyebrow.

I turned away. Meet. Who else would I want to meet except Browning, and he was right here. Somewhere. I cast my eyes around to where he last stood with his friends in their fancy dance outfits, but his space was empty. My eyes darted around the singers and dancers. I turned back to Clyde.

He shrugged, muttering, "Wimen." He was moving away when I grabbed one of the ribbons dangling on his shirt back.

"You don't mean . . . ?" I searched his face, but, of course, I could see nothing there.

"Who else?" He blew on his fingernails and polished them on his chest. "I told you I'd introduce you." He threaded his way through the crowd. I followed.

When I caught up to him, he scolded. "See how you are. You have no faith in me." The tone of his voice was equivalent to a finger wagging in my face. "I seize a good opportunity, cut you in on my good luck, and you brush me off like I was a fly. There's the man. Up ahead. See?" He motioned with his lips.

I was speechless. Browning was walking ahead of us, crossing the open field, his ponytail bobbing. He stopped, turned slowly, and waited for us. I could see his lips curling into a smile. My mouth opened and closed. I looked up at the moon, so big, so silky, so round and orange.

"You owe me," Clyde whispered. He was laughing as we walked up to Browning.

"Marli here owes me a debt so big, why you could walk right into it, it's that big," he told Browning.

It's funny how a person can suddenly go blank. I couldn't say a word. I felt the breeze from the ocean and shivered. My hands were clasped, hanging low, my shawl over them.

Clyde introduced us. Browning took his hand from his Levi's jacket pocket and stretched it out. "Nice to meet you, Marli." His mouth curled around his words, his hand around mine. Silk fringe from my shawl caught in our clasp.

Male cousins always said handshakes revealed a lot about a man. Cold fish, sweaty palms, bone crushers, limp wishy-washy, grabbers, and feelers. His was none of these. His touch was electric. I looked into his fawn-colored eyes and saw my surprise mirrored.

Clyde was still going on, telling about my going to Berkeley, my major, and where I was from, embarrassing me with his gush. "I should also tell you Marli's married. To a real mean 'Pache guy, a relative of mine."

Browning's eyes widened. My mouth dropped.

"Married! Aiii! I just say!" Clyde's laugh bubbled from his belly. He raised his hands to cover his head as if he expected me to hit him. "Watch out for this one," he told Browning. "She's real mean."

Browning laughed. He smiled at me and hooked his arm. I slipped my arm though his, just like that.

"Yeah, we could do that, the Oklahoma Two-Step," Clyde said, hooking his arm for me to take. I ignored him.

We walked like that until it got awkward, making our way to the campground to Browning's van. I sat in the doorway, listening to Clyde work hard to convince Browning he was essential to the film he planned on the powwow experience. As he talked excitedly, his hands sometimes waved wildly in the air, framed scenes, or mimed the focusing of a camera lens. Once Browning's participation in the project was clinched, they chatted aimlessly of summer powwows and traveling and the best fishing and hunting. From where we sat, we could see the powwow field. Suddenly the field lights dimmed, then darkened. We could hear voices approaching.

"The powwow's over," observed Browning. He stood up. "I've got to go help clear the field. I'll leave the van open if you want to wait here till I get back."

"Yeah, man. We'll wait," Clyde answered.

I nodded agreement. Browning smiled, then tossed his cigarette aside. We could mark his progress back toward the powwow grounds by the voices calling out to him as he passed. I could feel Clyde's eyes on me.

"I know. I know. You told me. I owe you."

Clyde's laugh was a small rumble.

Clyde left before Browning got back, joining a group passing around tequila. I could hear Clyde's happy laugh in their midst. I wondered where Jackie was, if she'd show up at the 49. Already a drum was out. The song, "When the Dance Is Over, Sweetheart," carried to me. A lover promised to take his honey home in his "one-eyed Ford," his falling-apart Indian car. She would believe him, of course. *Way ya hi. Way ya hiya.* I tapped my foot, feeling more than seeing people round-dancing.

By the time Browning came back, a number of people had stopped by his van looking for him.

"You sure are popular. Lots of girls came by looking for you."

"Nobody I want to spend time with," he said, getting in his van, offering me his hand, pulling me in after him, and shutting and locking the door. "That should keep them away."

Browning sang in the dark of his van, his voice deep and clear. He had opened his sleeping bag full-length, and we stretched out, looking up at the night sky through the open sunroof directly above us. Moonlight spilled in along with the drumming and singing of the 49. We could hear laughter, raucous and drunken, could smell the smoke of the bonfire.

He pillowed his head with his hands and told me about how he'd been dancing since he could walk, maybe even before, he thought. He talked about his family, his parents and sister, a close, perfect, intact powwow family, about his love for dancing. The competition against himself to do better, always better, drove him. Plus, he liked winning money. He grinned.

He went on. I quit listening to the words exactly and listened to his voice, soothing and calm. A singer's voice. I could hear his measured breaths, became conscious of his nearness, his warmth. I suddenly remembered him dancing, crouching low, rising into a whirl, arms gracefully extended at his sides. My heart grew full and tender.

He grew quiet and looked at me as if he knew my thoughts; he pulled me close, held me tight, murmured in my ear.

"Are you really married?"

I laughed.

"Sure you don't have an old man? Someone who will come looking for me with a shotgun?"

Again, I laughed. I thought to ask him the same, but I didn't. In the distant background, the drumming and singing of the 49 continued, male and female voices mingling. *Way-yah-hi-yo.* He bent his head to kiss me. I closed my eyes and kissed him back, feeling our heartbeats become a single pounding beat. I saw us moving together in a solid rhythm just as if we danced around the drum.

Years and years later, I still remember what Clyde captured on film at that powwow: Browning prancing out to the arena, twirling his dance sticks. As the tempo increased, his silk, fringed apron flew out from behind, revealing a glimpse of gym shorts and muscled thighs. His legs splayed at the knees, to the side, then arced high to the front, to the back, toeing in, toeing out. His roach bobbed, his shoulders bent into the dance, dipping groundward, first one then the other, his bustles becoming a blue blaze; then he raised himself, head high, hooked his arm, and leaped into a spin that landed him right on the final drumbeat.

Browning eased into my life, settled into its rhythm and its pattern, as if that's the way it should be. Over two years later, all too soon, we were deep in August, over our heads in the pleasure of summer. Time had swirled past us. I wanted to grab the days, hold them tight, but they slipped away, water through my fingers. Around this time, my parents officially divorced. Surprisingly, it hit me hard though I had seen it coming for years. Right on its heels, my dad remarried without telling me, leaving me to find out on my own. I knew, historically, Indian families had been fractured by forces beyond their control. I didn't want to think of how much of what happened between my parents was self-inflicted. Bruised, I clung to Browning, vowing things would be different for me.

My mother had wanted me to come home after graduation. Probably she hoped I'd settle down and follow in my sisters' footsteps. I told her I had my own plans, which was kind of true in that I had a summer internship. The reality is I have never planned anything. I took things as they came, like Browning's gradual move-in. One of his late night visits turned into an overnight stay; occasional overnights turned to weekend stays, which in turn began to extend on into the week until the only time he wasn't there was when he was out of town. I didn't think of us as living together since only a few of his clothes and belongings were in my apart-ment, enough to establish a presence but not a residence. As a matter of fact, I didn't think about a lot of things. Like about how I paid the rent and all the expenses. How I never really knew where he was when he wasn't with me, what he did with his powwow winnings. Sometimes you don't ask questions if you don't want to hear the answers.

Unless he was on the road headed to a powwow, he was restless, a cat crouched, ready to pounce at first opportunity. I learned fast what being with Browning meant. We reach where we're heading, but we're never really where we want to be—that was always one powwow ahead. We rode the van hard, quickly outdistanced the demands of the city and what it took from our souls. After we reached and maintained a certain speed, it was smooth going, like riding the wind. The even drone of the engine and the hum of the tires on asphalt faded beneath the resounding beat of powwow music as we cut our way through tangled freeways and highways to reach indoor rodeo arenas, school grounds, or tribal land where we laid out entry fees, danced intertribal, camped out in the van, and then returned to the city, replenished, with just enough time to catch our breath before we were on the road again.

The powwow circuit was a whole new scene to me. After a while I recognized dancers and drum groups, emcees, and families. It had its own pattern, its own ritual. We formed some of our own, like brushing each other's hair. I loved brushing Browning's long hair till it crackled with static electricity. His hair was thick and coarse in my hands. Plaiting it was like forming ropes. If he wore it loose while dancing, it became a tangled mess which I painstakingly combed out inch by inch till I could run my fingers down the length of it. He did mine, too, brushing more gently than I ever did, lifting up my hair and letting it fall, nuzzling my neck, biting my ear. He didn't talk and I could sense his concentration. I never felt more loved than when his hands were on my hair, smoothing it, moving down my back, over my entire body.

Browning had left for Montana earlier that week, leaving me alone with my thoughts. I was grateful for the slowdown. Sitting alone in the kitchen on Saturday morning, I imagined him out in a grassy clearing in the midst of hundreds of tepees, hundreds of dancers, the sweet smell of smoke from campfires filling the air. I sipped my coffee, gazing out the screen door, wishing I could have made the long trip with him.

The times I didn't go with him, he traveled with his friends, most often with Goodwin Yellowhair, his best friend of ten years. Goodwin always came in second in relation to Browning's first, but he was good-natured about it. No one could be jealous of Browning. We all wanted him to win and to keep on winning.

Goodwin was a dangerous current running loose, the kind of friend people at home always warn about. He was beautifully brown, tall, with piercing black eyes that never rested. The first time I met him, he looked me up and down, then did it again. He stared at me full in the face till I looked away, which caused him to laugh, low and soft. Goodwin always kept me off-balance that way. Sometimes I would turn around to find him staring. He would look away, but sometimes he'd hold me in his eyes in a way that made me uncomfortable, made me wonder what was in his eyes. Browning seemed oblivious to his friend's behavior.

The morning that they were leaving for Montana, Browning leaned through his open window to kiss me good-bye. Goodwin sat in the front passenger's seat, staring moodily out his window. Suddenly, he thumped on the door and said, "Let's get this show on the road." Browning ignored him and kissed me again before putting the van in gear. As they drove off, Goodwin gave me one of his disturbing looks.

I was roused from my thoughts, poor company that they were, when Clyde rapped on the screen door. He peered through the wire mesh. Elated, I jumped up. I hadn't seen him for a number of months except in passing and I suddenly realized how much I missed him. No one could spin tales and poke fun the way he could. Clyde could make me shake hard with laughter till I wiped away tears. He was such a jokester, he could make people laugh even when he wasn't there. Just the mention of the "sacred wraps" busted people up. I missed his teasing ways, the way he made me laugh at myself.

After his intense filming of the Bay Area powwow, the capturing of moments on celluloid forever, Clyde found his niche. He plunged himself into editing his footage, reordering reality to his own design, producing a fast-moving collage of powwow scenes with an audio track of 49 and powwow songs. While the film was rough in places, his critics raved. It was Indian. Visionary. He got an "A" for the project and walked on air for weeks after, scripting everyday life into film scenes, yelling "Roll it!" and "Cut!" at odd moments. Clyde ended up majoring in film, making two more films. After graduation he was awarded a scholarship to Stanford's Summer Film Institute and was swept down the peninsula to Ivy League.

As I crossed the room, an odd sensation of having done this before came over me.

"Clyde! It's good to see you."

He stuck out his hand before I could hug him, so I cupped my hands over his, then gave him an awkward hug around his waist like we were doing a shuffle dance. He mumbled a greeting and shifted his weight from foot to foot. His face was troubled, his eyes guarded, casting about the room for a place to rest.

"Have a seat." I gestured toward a chair. He pulled it out and sat down gingerly on its edge, then waved away the coffee cup I took from the drainboard.

"Had too much already," he said.

"Coffee, you mean? How's it going with you?"

"Awww." He rotated his hand at the wrist, indicating so-so.

I sat back down and observed him over my cup. "Well, you look good anyway." His hair was now long enough to pull back into a decent ponytail, and he looked different with his hair away from his face. "How did the institute go this summer?"

He straightened. His face lit up briefly. "It was good. Not all that I expected, but it was good." He nodded several times, then studied his hands. He nodded again. "Yeah, it was good."

I tried probing the subject but only got more one-sentence responses. I teased him about the heeled, leather moccasin shoes he was wearing without socks. He smiled wanly. Good thing you came today, I told him, 'cause next weekend we have to move out. I babbled on about my job, telling Clyde the quirks of the staff and other interns, about Browning and the powwows we'd been to, throwing in the kinds of details he usually ate up. He merely nodded. I was baffled by his reticence and wondered if the Ivy League had gone to his head, got his nose stuck in the air. Finally, I gave up the small talk, sipped my cold coffee, offered him a cigarette from the pack on the table. He ignored it and played with the keys in his hand, shaking them.

"Where's Browning? Gone?"

I nodded. "For a week or more." I realized I hadn't asked Browning for specifics.

He looked around the room, then took a big breath. "I don't know how to tell you this." His face was serious.

I waited. He squared his shoulders, took another big breath like he was about to plunge underwater, then let it out so that his shoulders sagged. He rubbed his face and leaned forward, opened his mouth, then closed it again.

"Man!" Clyde pushed back his chair and walked around the room. He settled against the sink, his arms folded tight across his chest.

"What is it? What's it about?"

"Browning. Look . . . well, he. . . . Damn! I don't know how to say this except to outright tell you that Browning has another girlfriend in L.A. and they have a kid."

Clyde's words rushed me, hit me tight in the chest, and took away my breath. I felt my eyes widen, probably gone as wild as my heart. I searched his face, waiting for a smile to ease his tightened jaw, to hear him say, "Aiii, I just say!" Nothing changed. I couldn't tell what hit me harder—the news or the realization Clyde wasn't here for fun and games.

"This isn't what I expected from you." It was a ridiculous statement, more like an accusation. I wrapped my arms around myself.

He looked at me, then away. "I'm sorry to have to tell you, but, hell, I feel responsible. I mean getting you two together and all. I know you've gotten close with him, and I just had to let you know. I'm really sorry."

The room was closing in on me, squeezing me into a corner, dark and narrow. I fought against the suffocating feeling in my chest. Resisting, I straightened in my chair, recrossed my legs. My head lifted, my chin stuck out. I heard myself coolly asking, with just the slightest tremble, "Just how do you know this?"

Clyde came back to the table. He took a cigarette from the pack and tapped it on the table, end over end.

"This Indian girl I met at the film institute, Leanne, well, you see, it's her sister this concerns. Their family's been living in L.A. a long time now, you know, relocation, two generations. Leanne and I got to be friends; she's incredible—a real nice person, a good filmmaker, too." He said this with some emphasis, a trace of admiration, so I knew he liked her. "She was always talking about her two-year-old nephew, Cody, and how he was a born fancy dancer like his dad. We got to talking about powwows and the film I made, and she got interested, asked me questions. When I told her I filmed Browning, she was surprised, and that's when she told me Browning was the father of her nephew and her sister's. . . ." Clyde looked down at his hands and cleared his throat. "Her sister's old man. She was excited about the film. Of course, she didn't know I had any other reason for asking about Browning and her sister; I forget her name."

"Clyde. How can this be? Browning never said a word to me about anyone else, much less that he had a kid somewhere! Of course, I never directly asked about anyone else. Who would think! How could he have a kid and not tell me?"

He shrugged. "What can I say, girl? It happens." He threw the question back at me. "What do you say?"

I gave him a helpless look that surely indicated how sick I felt inside. "But . . . but you can't just walk in here and tell me this crap, just like that! Where's the proof?"

I looked at Clyde's hangdog face. Even as I asked, I stepped back, turned around, slow-danced in time.

At the 49 outside of L.A., I was leaning against the side of the van, watching people pass in the dark. Goodwin came to stand with me. He was drunk enough to stumble a bit, though with effort he could seem sober. I had never been alone with him.

"Where's your old man?"

"I'm not sure. Somewhere around."

He seemed saddened by my reply. We stood in silence for a while. The night air was warm, dry, intimate in its feel of closeness.

"If Browning weren't such a good friend, I'd tell you. . . ." He looked away from me, licked his lips, and contemplated the air.

"Tell me what?"

"Can I have a drag?" He reached out for my cigarette and held it carefully between his thumb and forefinger before he took the smoke deeply into his lungs. He exhaled a stream through his nose and mouth, then took another drag. He threw aside the cigarette, half-smoked.

"Hey!"

"Oh, sorry." His grin was lopsided. He slumped against the van, leaning his shoulder into mine.

"That guy has all the luck." I knew he was referring to Browning. Before I knew it, he leaned over and kissed me softly, a smoky-tasting, lingering kiss. I pulled away and Goodwin straightened.

"Sometimes things get all mixed up," Goodwin said sadly, addressing the ground.

I didn't say anything, amazed at my casual acceptance, my recklessness.

"Browning trusts me."

"He does."

"He's my best friend!"

I nodded.

"I don't trust myself." He shook his head at his shoes. A silence wrapped us. People continued to pass around us, laughing, calling out to one another.

"I should tell you. You should know."

I stiffened, afraid of what he was going to bare from his soul, afraid he'd foolishly declare love. I looked around anxiously, feeling guilty, afraid Browning would appear any minute and assess the situation.

"I don't want to hear." My voice was harsh.

Surprised, he straightened and looked directly into my eyes, his gaze clear and sober.

"That's right. Always the last to know."

He saw my confusion and looked away.

"I'm sorry, Marli. Didn't mean to bother you." He seemed embarrassed and confused himself.

Over his shoulder, he called, "Don't hold it against me."

I watched him walk off, leaning slightly to his right, till I could no longer make out his figure in the dark.

I stood outside in the night for a long time after Goodwin left, lonely, waiting for Browning. I held his jacket against my chest, experiencing a fierce sense of possessiveness. I put it on, smelling Browning's scent all around me. There were very few stars to see. The night sky was overwhelmed by the city lights. A need to see the stars, to gaze on the moon, to see something genuine, lasting, seized me. At home, it would be the time of the *gaiyu*, cars parked in the plaza, rivalries among riders on horseback vying to pull out the chicken in the ground, laughing voices of people whose lives were interwoven with one another since birth.

I was puzzled by Browning's behavior while we were in L.A. He was nervous and distracted, drank too much, and then took off without telling me where he was going. Finally, I got tired of waiting and went to sleep in the van. When he returned in the early morning, smashed, all he said was, "Baby, I'm tired." Then he fell asleep. That day we were both irritable and distant from each other. In the fancy dance competition, Browning took second place to a local. All the way back to Berkeley he complained about biased judges. Impatient and annoyed, I snapped, "Browning, let it be. You got drunk last night. That's why you came in second."

When I unloaded the van after that trip, I found a box of Pampers, a woman's shawl, and a large beaded hair clip. I remembered staring at them, wondering when and how they got there. I couldn't even remember what Browning's explanation had been, something so vague and elusive it evaporated from my memory. Echoes of his mother's loud stage whispers, which I knew she meant for me to hear, came to me: "Did you tell her yet?"

"Are you sure about this?" I heard my voice quavering.

Clyde nodded, his face miserable. "Sure I'm sure or I wouldn't be here. Like I said before, I'm sorry to be the one to tell you. It seems pretty serious, Marli. Leanne says her sister and Browning are getting married. She didn't say when, but it sounds like her family is pressing for it, come hell or high water. They're planning an Indian-style wedding, big time."

Clyde continued to tap the cigarette on the table.

I tried to hold myself rock-steady to withstand the shock, but I could feel my defenses beginning to crumble. I didn't want to break down in front of Clyde.

"It's all my fault, Marli. If I hadn't introduced you to him, then we wouldn't be sitting here talking like this. Damn!" He broke the cigarette in two. Tobacco splayed out of the broken ends.

"Would you shut up about that? It's not your fault. Like you said, these things happen. Does it make you feel better to take the blame? How do you think I feel?" I swallowed hard. "Did you say anything to Leanne about me?"

Clyde shook his head, no.

I stared out the door, registering nothing.

"Marli? I don't know how else to say this, either, but I've heard talk that maybe there are others, like in Stockton, Utah. At first I thought it was all just talk, but now I don't know."

"Stockton, Utah? Where's that?"

"That's what Goodwin says. Maybe he ought to know."

After Clyde left, I sat for I'm not sure how long, staring. Slowly, the truth of what he had told me sunk deep inside. Misery seeped into my bones and developed into a deep ache.

I let myself imagine a son of Browning's. Cody. I immersed myself so much in creating his image, he became so real that I knew him. The tiny tot dancers were the cutest contest group. I could see Cody among them. A natural. A chip off the old block, even in his baby toddling. Again and again, my mind would turn and face the unwelcome fact that this child was the outcome of an intimacy Browning had shared with someone else, that this son was a part of Browning. Then my thoughts spun off in another direction. I imagined the most beautiful, most elaborate of Indian wedding ceremonies. Beaded white buckskin. Old Indian traditions revived. The blessings of holy men. Sacred pipe, sacred smoke. Honor songs for the newlyweds. I saw Browning's mother in her rippling white buckskin, eyes tenderly watching, her hand holding Cody's.

This image was painful. Browning's parents, a handsome, elegant couple, starred around at the powwows, she in white buckskin, he in northern traditional. They stood, two closely spaced, stately pines, bending ever so slightly and gracefully to listen to each other. His mother, slim and shapely, looked like someone used to admiring glances, like a former powwow princess who rode on the front hood of a car covered with a Pendleton, tirelessly waving a fan of feathers at parade crowds. With her first appraising glance, she assessed I wasn't princess material and never would be. "*Do you dance in competition, dear?*" She tolerated me if only to indulge her son, to amuse herself. She'd greet Browning with a kiss on the cheek, a whisper in his ear. For me, she had a frozen smile, eyes cold as ice.

Now she could have what she wanted for her son. I knew Cody's mother would be beautiful. I saw it in Clyde's eyes when he talked of the sister, Leanne. And she probably danced in powwow competition, too. Pure princess material. My imaginings swept away my ability to reason, enhanced my sense of betrayal.

I gave myself over to grief, which turned to anger at Browning and extended to someone who remained faceless, nameless. At the height of my anger I blamed myself, hated myself for being caught a fool, for being reckless and careless. I chased around in a circle, loving Browning, trusting him, then hating him, hating myself. Wanting him with a helpless, defenseless, senseless love.

I had made Clyde give me Leanne's phone number. Quickly, before I lost nerve, I called her and point-blank asked if what Clyde told me was true. At first she was cautious, then openly hostile and aggressive. She told me damn right, it was true, and I'd better leave Browning alone, quit being a home wrecker. She called me ugly names and demanded to know who I was, but I slammed the phone down. I was shaking, sick to my stomach at what Browning had done, at what I had been a part of.

Before he returned from Montana, I was packed and gone. I came home hollow-eyed and heartsick, and thoroughly scared my mother. Maybe if that was all to it, I could have gone on and eventually forgotten about him. But not long after I got home, my energy began to lag. For a while, I wrote it off as depression. But when my period didn't come for a couple of months, I figured I was pregnant. I can't say I was even surprised, although I had been using contraceptives. Like I said, I've never planned anything in my life.

Before I could decide what it meant, what I'd do about it, I miscarried. About ten weeks old, the IHS doctor told me. Probably for the best; early miscarriage usually indicates something is wrong with the fetus, he said. Was that supposed to comfort me? I was racked with guilt. For weeks on end, I had been raging internally against Browning, thinking all kinds of bad thoughts about him, about myself, and later, about carrying his child. I could hear my mother's words to my sisters when they were pregnant: "Think good thoughts. The little one is affected by them. Don't cause harm to your baby."

"During this time, I used to hold Jude on my lap for as long as he let me. Jude gave me such comfort, Cecelia. Holding him helped me deal with the pain, the deep emptiness inside. Cody would be about the same age as Jude. I think I can quit watching Cody grow up now. And I guess it's time to let go of my loss, my anger that really hurt no one but me.

"Last night when I was talking to Rupert on the phone, I said to him, 'I'm old and crabby. Can you put up with that?' He just laughed. Made me feel better about time wasted on losers."

Home of the Braves

"What you guys want to do?" Tobie asked. Herman and I sat on the steps of a walkway under the oaks that were beginning to drop their leaves. We watched him balance a spinning basketball on his finger then chase after it when it fell off and rolled down the incline.

In the evening hours following dinner, scattered groups of students sat on the grass in front of the student "Kanteen," a former BIA office converted to a student hangout that sold refreshments and had a jukebox and pool tables. Out of the open windows and doors of the Kanteen seeped strands of a rock 'n' roll song about an Indian reservation with pseudo-Indian drumbeats and plight-of-the-Indian lyrics. "Turn it up!" someone shouted. It was a popular song, having a little edge Indian kids could relate to. No one wondered what white boys with a goofy band name would know about Indian life. It was just understood that things Indian were "in."

We watched with mild interest as a group of Stewart boys strutted past. Their moves were deliberate and exaggerated, the forward bobbing of their heads, arms swinging, taps on heels clicking on the sidewalk. Just like at any school, students grouped themselves in different cliques based on interests, popularity, styles of dress, and, here, tribal affiliation. We were all at that age where everything matters, especially identity and peer acceptance. In this group, the guys wore dress shirts and vests, some fringed, black dress pants tight in the seat, and black, pointed "Beatle" boots polished to a shine.

Two Stewart girls, heads bent so their long hair fell forward to obscure their faces, moved self-consciously past them, giggling. One of the guys said something under his breath in his tribal language. Another made kissing sounds. They all laughed, deep rumbles from their chests, popped their gum and strutted on, leaving the strong scent of Brut aftershave in their wake.

"Aiii! Smooth guys." We would have laughed but we were long since inoculated against the social eccentricities of the boarding school students, having watched many classes strut in one end of the hallowed halls of Stewart Indian School and strut out the other, rolled diploma in one hand and a pop spiked with whiskey in the other. Drinking on graduation day was risk-free for seniors as long as they didn't get drunk enough to call the cops. A number of students had wild nicknames. Bambi. Hoss. Broomstick. Hairdo. Beans. Lovey. Bumblebee, interchangeably called Bzzz. Seventeen. "Seventeen?" Herman would say. "Must have been a very good year for him."

The girls—white blouse, black skirt, bare legs, black flats, split ends— moved past without taking notice of us.

"Hey!" Herman called to them. "This guy likes you!" He pointed at me. I shoved him.

The girls cast a glance over their shoulders, giggled, acted as if they believed him.

"His name is Julian," he called to their backs.

I slapped the back of his head. "Don't put it on me just 'cause you want that one," I pointed with my lips to Queenie, short, round and mean, who stood a short distance away.

Herman laughed. "Queen size. Your type, not mine."

Tobie came back with the ball in his hands. "Whatcha guys want to do? I mean besides ogle Queenie. It's still early." Tobie always used words like that, *ogle*.

Herman reached over and knocked the ball out of his hands. "Watch your mouth! Use dirty words like that and we'll have to scrub your mouth out with Lava soap. Let's go get a pop and then head over to the gym. Probably hardly anyone's there this early."

We walked down the sidewalk, Herman bouncing the ball, causing strolling couples to move around us. We went into the Kanteen through the front door, ordered our pops and headed out the back door. We met Jewell and Misha coming in.

"Hi, guys. Where you going?" Jewell asked, holding out her hand for my pop. I handed it to her, and she took a long drink.

"Ooh, yuck. Strawberry." She wrinkled her nose, handing it to Misha.

"Where's it look like we're going?" Herman responded.

She looked at the basketball under his arm. "Oh. Maybe we'll go play with you?" She turned to Misha, who gave a noncommittal shrug, returning the almost-empty can to me.

"We'll see," Jewell said, as if we cared whether she joined us. All the while they talked to us, they eyed the room, checking out who was and, just as important, who wasn't there. Finished using us as a cover, they turned to go.

"Where's your sidekick?" I asked, meaning Cecelia, but they kept going without answering, heading for the concession stand.

I drained the last of the pop, tossed the can into the trash barrel by the door, and took the ball from Herman. A large group of tough-looking girls who didn't take crap from nobody flooded in the door and we had to wait for them to pass. Right behind them sitting on the stone wall lining the stairs was Cecelia and that guy, the Indian school Casanova who went through girls like water. Cecelia was laughing, pushing him playfully. He extended his long legs before him, then placed his arm around her. He bent over and was whispering into her hair.

My eyes narrowed. Cecelia looked up at us. Her face lit up, a smile raising her high cheekbones and closing her slanted eyes. The guy, What's-his-name, James, followed her gaze and caught me in my expression, but he continued to grin happily, oblivious to my displeasure. Idiot. I could have popped him in the face. I faked passing him the ball, and his arms reached out instinctively.

"Ha!" Tobie laughed at him, darting his arm out to muss his hair. James leaned back out of his reach, pushed Tobie's arm aside, and motioned with his fingers for me to hand him the ball. I tucked the ball under my arm and moved down the steps two at a time. Herman and Tobie followed me.

"Hey! Where you guys going?" Cecelia called.

"Basketball," Herman said.

"Let's go," I heard her say to James. I looked back, but they continued to sit.

I was mad. Mad and confused at fourteen. The whole world was like that, one mad scene, college students shown protesting on TV, throwing around Molotov cocktails, storming buildings and getting it on with the pigs, heads getting busted, bodies dragged away. Blood everywhere. Confusing scenes of that faraway war in Vietnam. Hippies all freaked out on love and dope. Mad, everyone was going mad, freaking out. And I was mad at myself because I didn't know what I was mad about.

Tobie knocked the ball out from under my arm. He began dribbling the ball down the sidewalk, under his legs, doing fancy things with it. Tobie was a grade behind Herman and me, always showing off, talking big, trying to make up for the year's difference in age. He ran ahead a few feet, turned around, and posed to do a free throw. I made a hoop with my arms and he tossed the ball, arcing it in.

"Two points," he said.

The ball hit my foot and rolled away. I chased it, scooped it up, then started running, dribbling as I ran, running faster and faster, busting through couples walking hand in hand down the sidewalk. I didn't stop until I reached the end of the long block in front of the school. I turned around. Herman and Tobie were still back at the same spot in front of the girls' dormitory, talking to girls. I dribbled for a while then sat down on the planter at the corner to wait.

She shouldn't be going out with him, I thought. Guy like that is only out for one thing; he gets it and on he goes. By the time James graduates, I figured, if he ever does, he's so dumb, he'll have had every girl in school, even Queenie. Glancing down the street, I scowled. There was Herman trying to make it with James's last girlfriend. Used stuff. At least she had sense enough to dump James when she found out he was making out on the bus back to school with that Goshute girl.

I looked back down the street. Herman was still talking. With his good looks, which seemed to be a trait of his Shoshone blood, he had his way with girls. He was facing me. I hooked my arm over my head at him, motioning him to come. I got up, stretched my legs, turned the corner, and started walking slowly to the gym. I really wasn't much with the chicks. Never knew what to say to them and usually said something that ticked them off. The only girl I could talk to was Cissy, and even sometimes I pissed her off, but she never held it against me. Jewell wasn't the same way. She was high-strung what with all that different combination of Indian blood in her: Cayuga, Oneida, Pawnee, Ute, and to top it off, a smidgen of white. Her eyes would flash, she'd get so mad she'd start spitting and cussing, rolling out the insults, challenging my manhood: little white boy, sissy, mama's boy, pansy. Jewell would get so mad sometimes, she'd start crying in her rage and when we jeered at her, she'd stomp off, howling, refusing to talk to us for weeks. And I never knew what it was I said in the first place!

We used to play together, all the agency kids, the usual kids' games, hide-and-seek, softball, bike riding, roller skating, skateboarding. Now at fourteen, the girls weren't too interested in us. They started going after the Stewart guys, always older than us, even the ones in the same grade. They referred derisively to us as "boys," and only seemed to know us when they needed to bum something. I didn't like or trust the guys they went out with.

In front of the gym a large weathered sign, red lettering on a white background, declared, STEWART INDIAN SCHOOL, HOME OF THE BRAVES. A dignified chief in full headdress was painted in profile. The gym door was open. I could hear a basketball bouncing on the gym floor, then hitting the backboard. I stood in the doorway. Devon was shooting hoops with uncanny precision from mid-court. The little gofer, Buddy, was feeding the ball back to him.

I watched him for a while. He was good, *really good*. He handled the ball like it was a part of him he could will to do anything. Devon was in ninth grade, the same as me, though I went to the public high school in Carson City, and he, of course, went to the Indian school. He had arrived at the school the year before, a shy, gangly, pimple-faced kid, standing head and shoulders above kids in his class. Unlike other seventh- and eighth-graders, the youngest students at the school, who huddled together or dogged the footsteps of older boys from their reservation, Devon was a loner. But now he handled his growth well. He was confident, cocky even, muscular, and well coordinated. His pimples were gone, his complexion was smooth, but his eyes were hard, making him look tough, which he was. He was light-skinned, must have white blood, I figured. I heard he beat the daylights out of guys who made the mistake of calling him white boy. Not bad-looking, I guess. He had the kind of face girls go for, with curly dark lashes and full lips like Elvis Presley.

After a few minutes, I sat down on the bleachers near the door, placed the ball at my feet, and watched Devon bounce the ball in even measures, raise it above his head gracefully, and send it through the air into the net.

When Buddy fed him the ball again for the umpteenth time, he suddenly turned to me. "C'mon," he said, tipping his head toward the court. "Let's play. One-on-one."

I looked around the empty gym. Of course, he meant me. I stood, and he passed me the ball hard. My palms stung. I began to dribble and then he was all over me. Every time I raised the ball to shoot, he blocked me. Finally, I leaned into him with my elbow then broke away for a layup. He laughed.

"Sheez. Girls play better than you," he said, dribbling, facing me. He watched my reaction.

"Is that how you learned to play? With girls?"

"Shee!" He brushed past me and dropped the ball in with a neat jump shot.

I took up the ball. "This is how you look on the court." I ran, dribbling the ball, swishing my rear end. He grinned. I turned around quickly and took a shot before he could react. The ball hit the hoop and he reached up easily for it. He tipped it in.

We played like that for a while, him getting the best of me. He had it over me with height, handling, accuracy. I was dripping with sweat, and his face was just barely beginning to shine. The score was something like

10–38 when Herman and Tobie showed up. By then the other half of the court was already taken up.

"We'll play you," Herman said. "Me and Tobie against you and him." He pointed at Devon, who was dribbling the ball.

"Okay with me," I said. Devon nodded.

We wiped them out.

"Damn, he's good," Herman said when they finally called it quits. By this time, the gym was full, basketballs drumming the floorboards. Our place on the court was quickly taken over. Devon was farther down the bleachers, drying his face with the towel Buddy tossed him.

"You're telling me." My T-shirt was soaked at the neck and armpits. Herman's face was flushed. He pulled off his T-shirt and used it to wipe his face, then tossed it to me. Tobie was at the water fountain, running water over his head. He brought back a pop can filled with water.

"How's it feel to be on the winning team?" Tobie asked.

"Good," I grinned. It was true.

"Here comes Goliath," he said under his breath. Devon was approaching, but just before he reached us, he turned and paused, watching the group at the hoop we had used earlier. When they moved from under the hoop, he ran forward, dribbling, and did a layup. He stopped under the net, caught the ball, and tossed it to me. I followed suit. The younger boys stopped in their play, watched a few minutes, and then moved over to the hoop on the side of the court.

We did layups for a while. Devon, for the most part, was silent, occasionally laughing at Tobie's clowning. Herman picked up our ball and we began taking shots from different positions.

I figured it must be getting dark by now and glanced at the doorway to check. Jewell and Cecelia stood there. They waved. I jumped, let go of the ball, and it fell short. They giggled. Devon ran to pick up the ball and tossed it back to me. This time the ball swished through the hoop.

Later, when we were walking home after the gym closed, Cecelia said to me, "You guys aren't so bad. You going to try out for J.V.?" She and Jewell were dribbling the ball between them.

I was surprised. I hadn't thought about it. "Maybe."

"Herman?"

He snorted, but I could tell the question pleased him.

"Hey, where's your boyfriend? Romeo." I didn't mean to say it the way I did, meanly.

"James?" My question surprised her. "He had to go in. You know that the Stewart students have curfew."

"James, James, he likes the dames," Tobie began, singsong.

"Shut up, Tobie. Little punk!" Jewell took up Cecelia's defense, threw the basketball at Tobie. "Go on home. Your mommy's looking for you."

We had reached Tobie's house. The front porch light was on, revealing a porch littered with kids' toys. Tobie tossed the ball on the porch and leaped up the stairs. "See you tomorrow!" he called. The rest of us continued walking till we split up to follow different paths to our homes. Herman and Jewell turned west; Cecelia and I, east. We reached my house first, and Cecelia stopped, turned to me. "You should go out for the team, Julian. I bet you'd make it."

"I don't know. Maybe."

Throughout the fall, we continued to play basketball with Devon after dinner. Herman and I tried out for the junior varsity team at our school, Kit Carson High, and made it, piece of cake. I didn't know it till later, but Cecelia broke up with James before he had the chance to dump her for someone else. Maybe I didn't know that till way later because I got too caught up with basketball practice and games and my sudden popularity with the cheerleaders. Before I became a J.V. basketball hero and later a varsity one, I had been a nobody at school. My sudden rise in status went to my head, and I ended up doing what I have never understood. I began dating white girls much to the ire of Jewell and Cecelia and the other Indian girls at our high school. They "accidentally" bumped into my girlfriends a lot and intimidated them with hostile stares. They cold-shouldered me in the hallways at school though they knew me well enough at the agency.

I felt cheated by their cheap behavior. Indian girls can be mean when they get stirred up. I'd seen that in the Stewart girls, but I didn't think Cecelia and Jewell would react the same way. We'd always shared things in common—cigarettes, homework, lunch money, secrets. *Didja know Mrs. Redner is having an affair with Mr. Kickingbird? Don't tell!* They taught us boys how to dance, told us what French kissing was, climbed every tree and hill we dared them to. I remember once when Jewell's rascally bachelor uncle, Edgar, was visiting and supposed to be babysitting, we all got into a huge water fight, throwing buckets and bowls of water at each other—inside their house! Edgar outdid us, hiding behind corners, drenching us with bucketfuls. When Jewell's mother unexpectedly came home, we all fled the house, our shoes squeaking with water, Edgar leading the way. There was the time we behaved so badly on the bus, we made the substitute bus driver cry. She pulled the bus to the side of the road, and we all comforted her, apologized, and told her we'd be good from then on if she wouldn't report us. Another time in eighth grade, as a spoof, Cecelia and Jewell ran a campaign to elect Herman and me cheerleaders. They put up posters at school with cutout photos of our heads atop sexy women's bodies. We actually got some votes.

So many times like that we shared and now they were acting shabby.

Indians love basketball. It's a game for Skins. They love the team effort, the close relationship that develops between the team and fans, how they can cut loose, yelling and jumping, when the game is tight. A pride swells for Indian players. I knew this.

Basketball made me who I was at my school. But despite the praise of the coaches and the support of my teammates, deep inside I knew I had been separated from the group. I told myself as long as I had my main man, Herman, it didn't matter what the others thought. Herman and I were having fun. We were showing the town how Indians played basketball.

No matter that I was a star at the public school, I was only second fiddle to the Stewart boys. The only times Cecelia and Jewell came to our high school games were when the Braves had an out-of-town game too far to travel to. That irked me, but I guess I deserved it.

I remember one game in which I had played particularly well against one of our more serious rivals. Inspired by their attendance, I scored in the double digits. We totally humiliated the other team, which had a good Indian player that year, and paid them back for all the years of their smug confidence. At game's end, the crowd was ecstatic. My cheerleader girl-friend ran out to the court when the buzzer sounded. She threw her arms around my neck, bouncing on her toes, hanging on me. The other cheer-leaders were jumping up and down all around us.

I looked up into the bleachers across the gym, saw Cecelia and Jewell taking in the whole scene. The look on their faces is something I've never forgotten—one of joy and pride, and at the same time, incredible sadness. I abruptly pulled away from my girlfriend, went to the locker room, showered, dressed, and went to a party where I slammed the drinks down one after another. All the praise I got from my teammates and coaches was empty. Herman thought I was celebrating our win. I was trying to drown an unnamed feeling.

The time I injured my knee in a fall during my senior year and was out for a week, the coach told me I didn't have to make the trip for an away game. I should rest my leg instead. I went to a Stewart game that night, the first one I'd been to in four years.

The Stewart gym was packed. Every square inch of the bleachers, both the lower set and the balcony, was filled. I squeezed beside some little kids near the stairwell where the visiting team from a small-town public school in the same AA league as Stewart also sat. The gym was hot and humid, but no one seemed to mind. Everyone was hyped.

As captain of the team, Devon came running into the gym first, wear-ing his silk warm-up jacket and pants, leading his teammates. A roar went up. He circled the gym and then led the team to the center court line. Buddy, the team manager, spilled out a bag of balls. Everyone started dribbling.

After a while, the Braves discarded their warm-up suits and began running through layups. The fans of the opposing team, the Mustangs, warily watched. Soon, they were poking each other, asking, "Why is that white guy playing with the Indians?" "I know!" "That's not fair." "He's big." "I thought they were all supposed to be Indian." "Yeah, that's not fair!" Soon they were all grumbling and muttering. It pissed me off royally. I leaned over and yelled loudly down the row, "Shut up! He's not white!

He's Indian!" Startled, they all turned their heads toward me, recognized the depth of my anger, then turned away, like nothing had ever happened.

The Stewart cheerleaders had been sent to a cheerleading camp the summer before in southern California. They now were a far cry from the cheerleaders of earlier years, who had been somewhat of a disaster on the gym floor. Their new routines were a combination of dance and acrobatics, their cheers fresh and hip, better than my girlfriend, Francine, and her team of cheerleaders.

The game was good, tense, the lead a constant toss-up. Feelings ran high when the refs' calls constantly seemed to favor the Mustangs, but the Stewart cheerleaders kept the animosity down. Near the end of the game, Cecelia and Jewell came down the stairs from the balcony. Surprised to see me, they motioned for me to stand with them. Cecelia stood behind me on the last step, her hands on my shoulders, using me to lean on. Her touch felt good.

In the last five minutes of the game, Stewart was leading by three points. The game seemed assured. But then the refs called a foul on Devon for interference and the Mustangs scored with two free throws. With a minute remaining, the public school scored again, leading the Braves by one point. The Mustang fans grew frenzied and began smugly chanting, "We beat Stewart!" Jewell and Cecelia were livid at their arrogance.

As the seconds ticked by, the Mustangs started stalling, passing the ball around their court, not risking a shot or control of the ball. The Stewart team seemed helpless to steal away the ball. Cecelia was almost crying. "Oh no. Oh no. Get the ball! Get the ball, Devon!"

With only a few seconds remaining, Devon suddenly slapped the ball away from a Mustang, grabbed it, and looked around to see if any of his teammates had broken away. No one had. Both teams were startled by the sudden steal, momentarily frozen. Devon dribbled downcourt. With no other choice, he stopped mid-court, jumped, and sent the ball through the air. Like in the corny movies, the ball flew in slow motion before our startled eyes. It made it through the hoop with one second remaining on the clock. Cecelia pushed off my shoulders and about went through the ceiling. Jewell was jumping up and down, laughing and screaming along with the whole gym, it seemed. "Can you believe it?" she was saying over and over. Then they were both gone, rushing out to the floor with every-one else.

Cecelia ran toward Devon. He must have heard her call for he stopped, turned toward her, slipped his arm around her, and leaned down to kiss her. The crowd spilling out of the bleachers and balcony blocked my view of them. I stood in place, stunned. When I caught sight of them again at the other end of the gym, Devon had a towel around his neck, and he gave Cecelia's shoulders a squeeze, a gesture so possessive I grew angry and jealous. I left the gym quickly.

Jewell was saying goodnight to some guy, who dropped her hand reluctantly when the boys' advisers turned their vehicle spotlight on them and gruffly said, "Let's get going, Max." Max waved off the patrol and turned toward the boys' dormitory. Jewell joined a group of campus kids milling about. They were laughing and toasting one another with pop cans. They handed one to Jewell.

"How long has that been going on?" I demanded.

She looked at me, puzzled. Then she handed me her can. I took a drink. It was spiked with vodka. I took another long drink and she yanked the can back.

"What are you all bent out of shape about?" she asked, taking a drink, looking at me over the can. She passed the can back to me.

The cool night air and the vodka calmed me. I nodded toward the gym. "Cecelia and Devon." I bent my head back and drained the can.

"Oh! Old stuff! They've been together since last September. How could you not know?" She exaggerated her surprise. "Oh, but I forgot. We don't hardly see you anymore. You're too good for us these days. You only know—" She cut herself short. But I knew by the flash in her eyes what she was going to say. "What's it to you, anyway?" Our eyes locked. Jewell's look was mocking, like she saw something in me to lord over. Her attitude pissed me off. I held her eyes as long as I could. Then, afraid she was seeing the hurt and confusion I felt inside, I broke away. She laughed that I looked away first.

"Good, you guys are still here." Cecelia spoke behind us. Jewell laughed again, looking at me knowingly. Maybe she was beginning to feel the effects of the vodka.

"Wasn't that a great game?" Cecelia was still flushed and excited. The whole group responded, everyone except me talking at once about Devon's last shot, about teaching those Mustangs—who do they think they are, anyway?—a thing or two.

"We're heading over to my place. We've got the trailer for the weekend! Can you believe our luck? My parents are gone. Gone! You coming, Cissy?" Misha asked.

"I don't think so. I told Devon I'd wait for him while he showered. Then he's gonna walk me home."

"You gonna come over later?"

She shook her head, looking back at the gym.

"Aw, come on. This is a once-in-a-lifetime chance!"

Cecelia acted as if she hadn't heard.

"How about you, Julian? Feel like slummin' with us bums?" Tobie asked this, a slight challenge in his voice. It had been years since Herman and I hung out with him—ever since we made the junior varsity team.

"Yeah, sure," I said. "I'll wait with Cissy and then be over."

"You better!"

The group left. We could hear their voices move down the street, yelling "Braves are the best!" and laughing wildly as the bus with the Mustangs passed by. Cecelia and I stood awkwardly in the night. The vodka had warmed me at first, but now I felt the cold. Cissy pulled her coat around her neck.

I finally spoke. "So you and Devon are together."

She looked straight at me, her voice a little edgy. "Yeah. Just like you and Francine."

"Yeah. Yeah." I toed the ground. "He's a good basketball player."

"The best." She didn't say it but I knew she was thinking it. Better than you.

So I said it. "Better than me."

She smiled. Devon walked up and put his hands on her shoulders from behind. "Hey." He nodded his head at me, leaned over Cecelia and stuck his hand out. I nodded back and gave him a comradely handshake. "Good game," I said. He put his arm around her, she leaned into him and they walked off down the street, past the post office and into the darkened night.

I stood for a minute, thinking. I could trail them home, spy on them. When Devon left I could wait a few minutes, but not too long, knock on her door, say I thought I'd see if she wanted to go to Misha's. With me, I'd say. Or I could go to Misha's by myself. Or I could go home, call Francine later, lie to her and tell her I missed her. The gym went dark. I heard the last of the Stewart team leave by the side door, heard the coaches and assistants calling goodnight to one another, their car doors slamming, motors starting, then their cars pulling out.

I stood there and stared up at the sky. The stars were like snow crystals, the sky blue-black. I drank in its beauty. Then I turned and went home.

For the rest of the season, I played ball with a vengeance. Still, I never got the newspaper coverage Devon did. He was the darling of the sports page. Photo upon photo of Devon dunking shots ran in the local paper, even began making the front page. Photos they ran of me were always wide shots including other players, our opponents, the refs, fans in the bleachers. I was running with my mouth open, my hair sweat-soaked, looking graceless in comparison to Devon's midair leaps. Even my best scoring ran second to Devon's. In my estimate, it came down to this: Devon was seen as defending the honor of all Indians. Poor things, they were fighting the odds. Everyone wanted to see the Indians get the upper hand at least once in a while. It made them feel good. I consoled myself: I played Triple A, Devon only Double A league. I had to compete against larger schools, so of course my competition was tougher. The difference between Devon and me was that I was the small fish in a big pond, Devon the big fish in a small pond. Not only that, as the representative Indian, he was thought to be on the endangered species list, conveniently vanishing, tsk, tsk. Rather than console me, that thought depressed me.

My team made it to the state finals but we narrowly lost the tournament. The Braves went to their state finals, too, and narrowly won. Devon was the star, of course, scoring the winning basket.

At the end of the basketball season, Francine lost interest in me. We broke up. Later, after it was officially announced I had received a scholarship to the state university, she tried to reconcile. I was in no mood. By mid-May the Stewart students went home for the summer, or in the case of the seniors, to live the rest of their lives. In the last weeks before our graduation, Cecelia walked around school vacant-eyed. I guess she missed lover boy.

Our high school graduation was more of a relief than anything else. That night, Herman and I, Cecelia, Jewell, and a few other Indian students in our class went to the graduation party at the lake. The white kids in our class got sentimental after a few beers, told us how much they respected us and a lot of other foolishness I was used to putting up with from teammates. I could handle it when it was just me. Being with the others and hearing how we were credits to our race, unlike, you know, those other kinds of Indians, was something else. The others took it with good humor. "Hey, Jack, have another beer! Isn't this the general vicinity of the Donner party's party?" "That's right! If Indians had named the pass, they would've probably called it Tastes Good, ain't it?" "Makes me hungry for an arm!" "Come on back, Jack. We were just kidding!"

I didn't drink much. Francine had overindulged and was crying around about me, carrying on real stupid. Cecelia and Jewell told her to shut up and beat it, or they'd make her sorry. She left, crying harder. After a few drinks, Jewell got real belligerent, wanted to find Francine so she could beat her up. Cecelia and I had to take her home, she got so wasted, started throwing up and crying about how we were her good friends and she'd never forget us. We left Herman behind and drove Jewell home.

I still had a six-pack so after we sneaked Jewell into her house, no easy task, we decided to go up to the Cross on the hill above the agency and finish it off. We sat on the hood of the car and looked down at the campus, just talking, reminiscing about the crazy things we all had done growing up together, wondering where we'd all end up. Herman and I were going to the state university that fall, Cecelia was headed to the San Francisco Art Institute, and Jewell was going to work full time.

Cissy finished her can of beer, tossed it behind her over the top of the car, then leaned back against the windshield.

"These are the best stars anywhere," she said dreamily.

I leaned back against the windshield, too, to watch. We spotted the North Star and the major constellations and made up our own patterns in the sky. Dizzy with alcohol, intoxicated with the feel of the night, I closed my eyes.

"Look, look, Julian, a shooting star! Quick, make a wish!"

I opened my eyes. "Where?"

She pointed. I looked in the general direction, trying to focus. My vision was fuzzy. "You're missing it! Right there!" I leaned over to see from her perspective where she was pointing. I looked up to see the last of it. At least I thought I did, a short yellow streak.

"Oh, yeah!" I looked down at her and she turned her head toward me, smiling. Without thinking, I leaned down and kissed her, softly, tentatively at first. She kissed me back and then we were lost in a long, blissful kiss that made me dizzy and incredibly happy. I hadn't planned this, hadn't even thought of kissing her till it happened. It seemed like a natural step we'd been heading to for a long time. When we broke apart, we smiled at each other. I kissed her softly again and again.

"My wish came true," she whispered, putting her arms around my neck, pulling me closer.

We stayed out there under the stars till just before sunrise.

Guess everyone got busy with their postgraduation plans, which is why no one, not any of our friends, was aware that Cissy and I began to go out together. I was working with a landscape company owned by the father of one of my basketball teammates. Cissy didn't have a summer job, but she took a course at the university extension office in town. We spent all our evenings and weekends together wandering the deserted campus, pretty much doing things we had done as kids, eating green apples from the trees in the courtyard of the girls' dormitory buildings, sitting in the grass with our backs against trees, smoking cigarettes and talking, walking up to the Cross, sitting on the steps of dorms, playing basketball in the gym. Simple things, but they were more fun the second time around. Anytime I wanted I could pull Cissy to me, nuzzle her, kiss her, touch her. She didn't behave any way close to my other girlfriends, which I had assumed was standard girl behavior. They were all for making out, but acted all uptight about it at the same time. Like Francine. After she pressed up against my chest, rubbing her breasts against me, making me think she was serious about getting close, she'd get mad if I slipped my hands under her blouse and touched her breasts. She'd smooth her blouse down angrily and pout, "I'm not like that." She did it over and over, maybe letting me go a little bit farther each time before she stopped me. It was tiresome fighting battles like that each time, not to mention confusing. Guys talked big about getting theirs, but I don't think most knew much more than me. The ones who did, like Herman, didn't talk. They just smiled.

It was different with Cecelia. She didn't play games. She just said, "I've never gone all the way with anyone. And when I do it will be with someone I truly love." Whoa. And she didn't have any hang-ups about touch. She'd just breathe in my ear, "Julian, I think we better stop." And she'd pull away, take up my hand, entwine her fingers in mine, and start talking like nothing had happened. More than anything, I wanted to be the one she loved in that way.

About a month before we were to leave for college, Cecelia told her parents she was going for a sleepover. Guess they assumed she'd be at Jewell's or Misha's. We slept outside in my backyard, my parents gone for the weekend. The radio was playing softly, and we lay in each other's arms, listening. The water sprinklers started up in a reassuring, rhythmic cycle. The moon was risen in the east. It was a beautiful night. She shivered as the air began to cool. I held her closer.

"I wish we were going to the same college," she said, her eyes on the sky.

I had thought of that, too. "You could transfer next semester," I suggested hopefully.

She just looked at me, and I knew it wasn't a possibility.

"I don't want to leave you, Julian. I'm afraid." Her voice broke.

"Of what?"

"That you'll forget me."

"I'll never forget you, Cissy. How could I?" My own voice faltered. "I love you." The words came out of me clumsy, but I was sincere.

She held my face in her hands and looked into my eyes. I don't know what she saw, but she seemed satisfied. Cecelia told me she had had a crush on me since junior high, had broken up with James because she thought I liked her, too, and was hurt when I chose white girls over her, which was one thing she could never be. She went out with Devon not because she really liked him, but only because he was a basketball hero, better than me, and she wanted to get back at me with the only thing she could do since I was "busy." The words spilled out of her. She had been looking up at the sky. Her eyes were moist when she looked at me again. "I love you, Julian. I really do. I'm not just saying it, and it scares me to love you, because I think you could really hurt me."

If I had thought I loved her in any measure before she said all that, then my love immediately increased to the nth power. I couldn't assure her enough of my love for her, so after a while I quit trying and just held her, stroking her hair. After a long while, as my arm under her was beginning to fall asleep, she turned to me and kissed me. She didn't stop me this time and we went all the way. I felt my love for her explode inside her, filling her, filling me, too, in a different way. I held her afterwards 'cause she cried, and I can honestly say I never had any intention of hurting her ever.

That night! Even now I can still remember the feel of cool air on my bare buttocks, the softness of her skin, how it felt against mine, the ripeness of our youth. Something happened between us that I can't explain. She got under my skin into my blood and coursed through my veins to my heart.

The last weeks before we left for college flew by, filled with emotion, with passion. We couldn't get enough of each other. I walked around on a cloud, dazed, bruised with love. When she left first for San Francisco, our good-bye was simple. We assumed we would see each other at Christmas break. She kissed me affectionately, a sisterly kiss, got into the backseat of her parents' car, and left.

Heaven's Blue Door

JUNE 1996

The bar was thick with blue smoke and conversation, Indian patrons packed tight like sardines, everyone out for a good time at Heaven's Blue Door. The joke was tired but still drew smiles if everyone was drunk enough: Oh my-y-y, t'ot I had died and gone to Heaven's.

The night was still young, the social custom well established: Everyone started off a night of bar hopping at Heaven's, moved on to any of several other choices, then rendezvoused for closing at Heaven's.

A handsome Indian couple sat close enough to make it apparent they were together, though the man with his thick shock of black hair was in conversation with everyone else in the bar. Every now and then he stretched his arm out behind his woman, squeezed her close, whispered in her ear, ran his hand down her back. Then he'd be back in conversation, teasing, laughing, hooking his arm in the air, motioning someone over.

They were easy to spot, so conspicuous. Lex gave a nod in their direction to Devon, who turned and scanned the bar, then frowned when he saw the couple. He shook his head. "I see she's got company." The two men watched for a moment, then moved into the crowd.

The woman, Darla, drew on her cigarette, seemingly indifferent to the man's caresses. She knew her don't-give-a-fat-baby's-ass attitude was what attracted him. The moment he thought she needed him, he'd be gone. He was whispering in her ear again, and she closed her eyes as if bored so that her long lashes rested on her cheeks. She pushed him away and smoothed her pink ruffled western shirt, then checked to see that its shirttails were smoothly tucked into her snug-fitting, raspberry-colored Wrangler jeans.

She looked up at the door across the way, then frowned. Her heart beat faster. She looked again, then stabbed her cigarette out in the ashtray.

"What's the matter, babe? You wanna cut out of here?"

"I thought I saw Lex."

"Where? Here?" He looked around.

"Over by the door."

"Don't worry 'bout him. He can't do nothing to you. You're with me." He took a long drink of his bottled beer, then pulled her close. "If he comes around, I'll take care of him." He spoke confidently.

She wanted to believe him, but took another look around before she put Lex out of mind and was laughing and joking, joining in the toast to Clifford and his championship bull-riding skills.

This guy was a lot of fun, which was why she was with him. He knew how to treat a lady, make her feel special. Unlike Lex. They were divorced six months now, tonight the first time she'd seen him. Word came to Darla of how he'd gone on a rampage soon after she left, shooting up their trailer, trashing out the place in his fury. His violent reaction had made her afraid, and she had gone to Reno to live with her sister and her family. But it had gotten crowded in their small house in the Indian colony. After four months, Darla knew she had to leave. She came back to Fallon, settled in, and formally met her new man at the Silver Spur, where she was waitressing.

She drank till she forgot her fears, felt them retreat like the memory of a bad dream. They danced. She knew he liked to dance with her. A tall, slim woman, almost as tall as he, she could dance western with class. He'd swing her around, then pull her close, their hips touching lightly. He was the best country-and-western dance partner she'd ever had.

He bent his head into her hair, smelling both shampoo and the smoke of the bar. Looking up, he saw that screwup, Lex Stevens. He sat with that other screwball, Devon Willis, the has-been Indian school basketball hero with the wicked scar down his face. Devon had been something at Stewart Indian School, but he wasted his talent in drink. After high school, he used to play decent enough in the all-Indian basketball tourneys, but he had lost his once-famous magic touch, was nothing compared to what he used to be. He'd heard, too, that Devon had served time in prison for armed robbery.

Lex was bad news. He didn't like seeing him in the same place Darla was. She hadn't said much about their marriage, but he gathered Lex was a regular asshole. She was afraid of him, he knew, could tell by how she suddenly tensed up when she caught a glimpse of him and gulped down her drink. He didn't want to scare her, so he didn't tell her of the handgun he kept in his truck.

Lex and Devon were watching them, too, obviously there for trouble by the looks on their faces. He danced Darla to the other side of the room. He'd take them both on if he had to, but when it came right down to it, he was a lover, not a fighter.

The band moved right into another song, slowing the tempo, an oldie, a classic favorite of the regulars. Darla sighed happily.

"Our song," she whispered.

He laughed and gave her a quick squeeze.

The night she met him, the band had invited anyone who knew the lyrics to join them onstage. To the delight of the crowd, she and Paula responded.

I don't care what's right or wrong. I won't try to understand. Let the devil take tomorrow, for tonight I need a friend. The audience whistled and clapped in approval. Emboldened, Paula removed the microphone from the stand. Then mike in hand, she sang, walking the floor, her steps uneven. The cord trailed behind her, and she reached for it with her free hand, tossing it behind her in a poor imitation of a Vegas headliner.

Darla stood alone, feeling foolish and upstaged. Without a second thought, she marched up to Paula, grabbed the microphone out of her hand, and sang the next line.

Yesterday is dead and gone, and tomorrow's out of sight. As Paula reached to pull the microphone away, Darla turned her shoulder on her, blocking her.

"You can't sing," she told Paula.

The crowd laughed, and Paula lunged to grab the mike. Soon they were struggling for it. The band played on, the members amused. The bar manager suddenly appeared, grim-faced. He snatched away the microphone and turned it off, leaving the two women on the floor, stunned. The band began a new song. At that point, Darla's present partner walked up, took her hand, and started dancing. The bar broke into spontaneous clapping. Later on that same week as a customer at the Spur, he recognized her and they'd begun their relationship, still in its honeymoon stage.

"You're just a regular knight in shining armor," she teased.

"No," he shot back, mocking himself. "A warrior on horseback. I do tricks."

As they moved across the dance floor, Darla thought of the stories her new man shared as they sat in the dark in his truck. This guy was so different from Lex that they could just sit and talk for hours about pleasant things. He knew all kinds of tribal stories he had collected from friends. The one she liked the best was about dancing.

> The tall, handsome stranger strode into a wedding dance, commanding attention with his silent entrance, looking neither to the left nor right. No one knew who he was, though he looked vaguely familiar, like someone's cousin's cousin. The bride's family thought he must be a guest of the groom's family, and the groom's family assumed he was known by the bride's side. He carried himself with grace and sureness, head erect, meeting all questioning eyes and answering them with careful indifference. Large turquoise stones, conspicuously old and heavy, dangled from his earlobes. His long hair was pulled back in an old-time style. He leaned against the wall, smoking a cigarette, a glint of amusement in his dark, slanted eyes.

> All the young, single women and even the restless married ones watched, ready to catch his eye, hoping to be the one he'd ask to dance. After a long time, when the dance was almost over, he asked the prettiest girl to dance. The other women sighed, tossed their heads, and pretended they didn't

care, but they watched enviously, seeing how he tenderly gazed into the depths of her eyes, and how he smoothly spun her across the room. He was light on his feet and she moved easily with him. Other women crossed their arms and shook their heads in disapproval at her reckless laughter.

The girl forgot who she came with, forgot that her sweetheart might have meant something to her, that he stood in the corner sulking. A woman letting her hair down, she danced on with the stranger, yielding to him. The songs became soft sighs, each dance a yearning. The stranger held her tighter and tighter till her boyfriend rushed forward, his eyes narrow slits. Before he could reach her, as the song was ending, screams and shouts filled the air. The band stopped. The crowd parted. The young girl lay lifeless on the floor.

In the confusion of the moment, the stranger almost slipped away, but he was stopped at the door by belligerent, red-eyed young men. Something about his movement as he stepped back from them caused one young man to look down at his feet. The young man paled and his eyes widened, causing others to follow his gaze. Once again, terrified screams broke loose, paralyzing the crowd. In the sudden hush that came upon the room, someone cried out, "Look! Look at his feet! He has the feet of a deer!" The stranger smiled, brazen and fearless. He pushed his way to the door unchallenged and walked out.

Later, his deer tracks were found beneath all the windows of the hall.

The story sent chills down her spine. Half serious, she'd asked, "Would you ever do that to me?"

"Of course not, babe. Who'd I dance with then?"

On their way back to their table, he leaned close to her ear and whispered, "Time to go."

"Let me go to the bathroom first."

"I'll meet you right outside the front door."

She was smoothing her shirt, checking her hips in the mirror when she heard some popping noises, then a commotion outside. Curious, she pulled the bathroom door open. People crowded the blue front door. "What's goin' on? What's happening?" everyone was asking.

Darla easily pushed her way through the people, who seemed to be frozen.

As she neared the door, someone came in running, shouting, "There's been a shooting! Call an ambulance!"

Darla stopped momentarily, then fear seized her. She placed her hands over her mouth, then rushed out.

She heard, "Don't go out!" Someone tried to stop her. She ran toward where they'd parked the truck under the sign pulsating *Heaven's Blue Door*. Eyes wild, she saw him on his back, a bloodstained front, blood pooling beneath him. He couldn't be alive, not with that hole.

She could hear herself screaming, flailing against whoever held her, "Herman!"

That Guy

On the long, early morning drive north to San Ildefonso Pueblo to the Indian Artisans Show sponsored by the eight northern pueblos, my eyes ranged over the passing landscape. I glanced down to the green valley winding along the Rio Grande, remembering my Auntie Lena's stories of making the days-long trip to St. Catherine's Indian School in Santa Fe by wagon, traveling along the river. We now complained about the hour-and-a-half drive from Isleta in an air-conditioned, comfortable car.

The freeway unfurled before me like a ribbon, down and over sandy hills covered with native grasses and shrubs, past red hills and mesas in the distance, through the Sandia, Santa Ana, Santo Domingo, and San Felipe Pueblo reservations and past the Cochiti Pueblo reservation. As I climbed higher in elevation, the road cut through volcanic hills that had been blasted or bulldozed open for the road. I moved past red and black volcanic rock, the record of geological changes. The steep climb slowed my car, and a vehicle zipped up behind and tailgated me. I moved over one lane, but not before I caught the driver's angry gesture in the rearview mirror, motioning me to get out of the way. He whipped past, showing Texas license plates. It figured. The luxury car disappeared around the bend.

As I passed through the exposed hills I recalled the geological time scale my grandkids and I had seen at the natural history museum. That was how Indian time went—in huge chunks, I decided.

Years ago, my nana used to reprove me and my sisters about always being on the go. "*Pedum bah!* Take it easy!" she'd scold. Funny how the old can so easily see the follies of the young. Maybe 'cause we've "been there, done that," which is what my cocky grandchildren say, as if they could know anything yet.

As I topped the incline, the sky loomed above me. My thoughts lifted into the clear blue sky, moving freely like clouds. I thought about my grown children and their problems, my youngest daughter, Carmel, now on her third marriage and counting, my grandchildren who know more about sex at ten than I did when I got married. I thought about problems in the school, in the tribe, about Indian gaming and the envy and anger it raised among non-Indians who didn't like the economic competition. I wondered what all this meant. My mind ranged far and wide as the miles passed beneath me till my worries became prayers.

By the time I reached San Ildefonso, my thoughts had settled and I was at peace. I parked in the grassy lot outside the village, got out of my car, leaned against the door, and took in the scenery with a deep breath. The mountain, part of the Jemez chain, rose serene in the cool morning air.

Peaceful and unhurried, I passed the Catholic church and entered the plaza, where the artists' booths and concession stands were grouped. As in the other pueblos, the plaza remained earthen, unpaved. Doors of the adobe homes lining the plaza stood open, and their residents occasionally stood there to watch the activity. Art show officials wearing nametags pinned to their colorful ribbon shirts dashed about, clipboards in hand, directing traffic, motioning with their arms at drivers. A few artists and their families were hurriedly unloading their wares, folding tables, and chairs from cars and pickup trucks parked haphazardly in the plaza. The booths of a lucky few were located under a large, old cottonwood tree, which provided the only shade. The smell of coffee was strong and inviting. I stopped to buy a cup at a concession stand and sipped it as I watched artists fussing over the arrangement of their work, making last-minute changes. One of my friends told me she spoke to her sculptures at shows, saying, "Okay, guys! Look your best."

A scattering of people, early birds like me, wandered down the rows of booths. I drew a deep breath, pleased that I could leisurely browse the booths, chat with the artists, make note of what I liked, and have time to decide what I most wanted without the pressure of having to grab it on the spot for fear if I didn't someone else would snatch it up under my nose. Perhaps I'd pick up a new artist whose work I'd carry on consignment.

In my handbag, I carried a slip of paper noting a specific booth number. I stopped, pulled it out, and read "Booth 375," written in the neat handwriting of my niece, Marli. She wasn't going to make the show till late afternoon, at which time she planned to sit with Rupert in his booth.

"Be sure to introduce yourself to him, Auntie. I told him you'll be looking for him. You'll like him, I know. Maybe we can all have dinner together before you drive back home." Her suggestion had been casual, but she watched my face closely so I knew she was eager for me to join them. She must really like this one.

From previous years, I knew the booths were organized in long rows, some running east to west, some north to south. On the northeast end of the plaza, Pueblo groups danced the Butterfly, Buffalo, or Deer Dance at scheduled times in the soft sand, their moccasins sending up dust as their feet touched ground. I had neglected to pick up a program as I entered the plaza. Without a map, there was no telling in which row Booth 375 could be. I'd just start at the nearest row and come across it whenever I did. The emcee for the event was announcing the sale of breakfast burritos, urging people over to the food booths. He joked about having a bad hair day and continued with countless announcements about raffle drawings, rules for taking photographs, parking vehicles, etc., etc. His voice quickly faded into the background as I began my rounds.

So many beautiful things! Pueblo pottery, both traditional and contemporary, silverwork, woven baskets, paintings, carved kachinas, stone sculptures, heishi necklaces. I wanted them all but I knew I had to be selective, choose pieces my customers would be likely to buy. My Indian customers wanted traditional work to give as gifts for a bridal dowry, items to complete traditional dress, something special and unusual for a retiree or a dancer, for Father's Day or graduation. Tourists visiting my shop liked faddish things. Right now, howling coyotes and Kokopelli figures were hot. Cecelia with her art training expressed disdain for what she called kitschy urgings. I was impatient with them, too, deliberately selective of the coyotes and flute players I bought. If tourists had to have them, then in my shop, they'd be ones I approved of. "You're the kitsch police," Marli teased.

I sighed happily as I examined a cross-stitched pillow. Nothing gave me more pleasure than to select items for my shop. Sure, I was picky. The woman behind the table chatted in the Towa language with her companion, probably elaborating on juicy details of an occurrence in their village. They were so engrossed in conversation, they paid me no mind. I replaced the pillow and moved on. Many of the artists had become my friends over the years and knew my preferences. They even told me they made something especially with me in mind, waited to see if I'd pick it out, and when I did, they grinned from ear to ear.

There were two items in my shop that were not for sale. One was a painting by my brother, Two Bucks, done during his years at the Albuquerque Indian School. Two Bucks took up house painting as his vocation and after high school never did another piece of artwork again, no matter how I urged him. Many people wanted to buy his painting of a pueblo scene, but I'd shake my head firmly, state proudly, "That's my brother's work. It's not for sale." Inevitably, people would want to know whether he had other work for sale.

The other item was a wedding vase given to me belatedly and rather grudgingly by my first husband's family. It was an old piece, handed down through several generations. The vase sat in its own custom-made showcase. I displayed it at the shop because after I remarried, I felt uncomfortable keeping it at home. I knew its value and its beauty, and on its own merits, it deserved to be showcased. When I saw customers marveling at it, especially the well-to-do, I simply said, "It's not for sale. Don't ask."

My first husband was from Laguna Pueblo, as was Marli's potter friend, Rupert. I was curious to meet him, to find out whether I might know his family. I went to the Indian school with a number of Laguna students and was courted by several, one of whom later became their longstanding pueblo governor. Perhaps Rupert came from the family of a former classmate. Cecelia and Marli ranted and raved over him. I wanted to see what the fuss was about, to assess for myself whether he was praise-worthy. I had my own concerns for my two nieces, each for different reasons. With Marli, I wished she'd settle down. Always someone new! Enough of this parade of fellows. I had repeatedly warned my younger sister, Virgie, Marli's mother, about letting her stay out in California with her father. Everyone knows about California. Not that Ernest was irresponsible or anything; it was that she should have been at home in the pueblo among her own people, not running around the country like a gypsy. Marli was headstrong, always wanting to do things her way. But maybe it was in her blood. After all, Virgie upped and moved off to Phoenix out of the blue, just like that, against my advice. Guess I didn't know everything. Virgie had done well enough in Phoenix, had supported herself as an artist, took in Jude as her own, bless her heart.

I sighed. Jude and Cecelia were heavy on my heart these days. Why hadn't I realized Cecelia was carrying a secret burden? When Cecelia came home to attend the Institute, I should have recognized it then. But I thought she missed the baby, and that time would ease that ache, that she'd realize leaving Jude with Virgie was the best thing she could do for him.

I put down the deerskin baby moccasins I was admiring. Just out of nowhere, I suddenly realized that Cecelia returned home at the very time I first became involved with Buckley and lost focus of everything else. I felt a stab of pain and sadness that the time of great happiness for me was also the time of great pain for my niece.

I had thought the haunting sadness that later settled on her was on account of her mother's sickness. Then her death. I should have known there was something more going on.

When I heard her full story about Jude's father, the disturbing dreams related to him as well as his disturbing circumstances, about her denial of Jude's request to know his father, my heart was stricken. Her careful avoidance of personal details from the past now made sense. In Cecelia, I saw my sister, Judy. The resemblance was strong. Judy had been the baby of our family, the one we guarded fiercely and pinned our hopes on, relinquishing her reluctantly to Roland, the only son-in-law who met with Nana's approval. Roland has since remarried with our blessings, including Cecelia's. We all agreed a wife, a companion, was what he needed.

Cecelia had a booth at this show, too. Same location as last year, she told me. Jude was sitting with her. He had driven up from Phoenix earlier in the week. The two of them had come by my place in their round of visits to all the relatives so Jude could say hello and everyone could exclaim over him. Such a sweet young man, tall, nice-looking, strong features. He bore scant resemblance to Cecelia. I couldn't help but wonder if he looked like his father.

When we were alone in the kitchen warming food, Cecelia told me they hadn't talked about it just yet. They would after the artisan show, she said.

"Don't be putting it off," I warned her.

By the time I had visited all the booths in the first few rows, my mesh bag was bulging. I stopped to think. Cecelia's booth was closer than my car. The practical thing to do would be to leave my purchases at her booth before I continued. They'd be safe there, or perhaps Jude could take them out to the trunk of my car. I glanced up at the number of the first booth in the next row. Number 354. Surely Rupert's booth was in this section. I could take a quick look since I was already here, satisfy my curiosity.

Each artist's name, tribal affiliation, and art form were prominently posted along with the booth number. A few booths down I figured out I was on the side with even numbers. The odd numbers were across the row. My eyes skipped ahead to Booth 375.

Stunned, I stopped abruptly, staring at the man sitting in number 375. It couldn't be! My bag felt like I carried rocks, and my grip on the plastic handle turned slippery. I felt I should sit down.

It was no mistake. I'd recognize him anywhere. There sat my ex-husband, Guy. I stepped back close to a group gathered around a jewelry case and stared at Guy, trying to figure out what I felt. Shock. *No, it can't be!* Outrage. *What's he doing here?* Incredulity. *Is it really him? I hope not.*

I closed my eyes, touched my forehead. I recognized something familiar about the situation, certain I'd been through it before, the morning air,

the people, the booths, the smell of frying grease, the bright sun, a be-
wildering sense of dislocation, voices around me—but when? As I struggled to remember a previous occurrence, what the outcome had been, the
feeling faded.

I swallowed, took a deep breath, and prepared to move forward.

The person behind me turned to leave the booth and bumped right
into me. "Beg pardon," he apologized. I barely glanced at him, a well-
dressed man with a mini-ponytail.

Guy was making change for a customer and didn't notice my slow
approach. He was the only one in the booth. I felt relief flooding me.
Surely, I had made a mistake, got the wrong booth. But there posted at the
front of the booth was Rupert's name, his billing as a Laguna Pueblo
potter. My heart sank.

Guy glanced up. I saw the surprise in his eyes, then with a quick blink,
he recovered his composure.

"Good morning, Reena," he greeted me as if it had only been yesterday
he had last seen me and not years.

Guy still looked much the same, only older, his face deeply lined,
puffier, perhaps from drink, his hair streaked gray. He held his hand out.
We shook hands briefly.

"You're looking good, Reena," he said.

"Thank you. I'm looking for Rupert," I said stiffly.

If he was surprised, he didn't show it. "He went to get coffee and look
around a bit. He shouldn't be long."

I glanced down at the pottery on the table. Marli was right. His work
was excellent. I touched the rim of a ceremonial bowl, traced it lightly with
a finger.

Guy watched my hand. I looked down. My wedding ring with its
cluster of diamonds was prominent on my finger. I withdrew my hand. If
he didn't already know I'd remarried, he knew now. Guy looked at me
expectantly.

"Rupert went to the Institute with one of my nieces," I said. "With
Cecelia, Judy's daughter."

"Is that right?" he marveled. "How is Judy?"

"She—" I faltered. "She died some years back, Guy."

"Oh! I'm sorry to hear that." He dropped his eyes and shook his head sympathetically before looking back at me. "You were always close with your family."

I cleared my throat. "This is Rupert's work?"

We both looked at the pottery on the table. "Yes. Rupert is my son, did you know?" He smiled proudly. "Sometimes I come to shows with him."

I thought I'd faint right there. "Your son?" I said weakly, my hand rising to my throat.

Embarrassed by my reaction, he was careful to avoid my eyes. "Do you 'member Alice? We went to the Indian school with her."

I looked at him blankly.

"Edwin's sister," he prodded my memory.

I nodded.

"She's Rupert's mother."

"I see. Well, tell him Marli's aunt came by. Perhaps I'll see him later."

"Marli is your niece?" I saw his eyes flitting like startled birds. "Whose—?"

"Virgie," I said curtly, turning away. By the time I reached the end of the row, I had it all figured out. Rupert and Marli were the same age. Marli and my daughter, Carmel, were born the same year. That meant Alice had been pregnant with Rupert at the same time I was pregnant with Carmel.

I walked quickly without seeing anything. *So many years later and I'm still finding out what a jerk he was.* Refusing to share space with Guy, to breathe the same air, I left the show.

It was odd how time used to pass so slowly. One season melted into another in degrees of change so gradual that I associated significant events in my life with particular seasons, with the slant and intensity of sun rays, with the presence or prolonged absence of rain, with varying qualities of light and shadow. Certain memories stood out like prominent landmarks, marking my path through summers and winters, droughts and downpours.

That's how it used to be, anyway. Nowadays, time, as well as the seasons, whirled relentlessly like the spin of galaxies in the deep ends of the night sky, pulling me against my will ever closer down into the center of a vortex, into the calmness of eternity.

September was ripe. The morning air was turning crisp, though the midday still burned hot. It was harvest time; the year, 1953, when Isleta Pueblo was a village encapsulated, oblivious to the world. What white people did or said was of little importance to the Dae-nine, the People. Community efforts turned toward picking the summer's crops from the outlying fields, roasting the corn and green chile, and drying the fruit, the apples, apricots, and peaches. Chiles were left hanging on the plants in the fields to turn red, then later strung into brilliant ristras that hung from vigas and porches. Tata rode his horse-drawn wagon loaded with watermelons, Indian melons, tomatoes, and chile to the highway intersection where he sat all day in the shade of an overhanging cottonwood tree, selling to passersby.

The men of the village were talking of hunting rabbits and deer, gathering firewood, joking about hiding out to avoid being caught by the war captains to serve as ceremonial clowns for the harvest dance at month's end. All summer long I had suffered morning sickness; by September, it had passed.

More than four decades later, the memory came washing back with the morning shadows, mercifully void of the pain it once evoked.

I remained in bed after Buckley had risen quietly in predawn darkness and left the house to begin irrigating his alfalfa fields. I didn't sleep after he left, just watched the sun paint the room in different shades of yellow till it lifted above the sill and left the room in soft shadows.

I smoothed the bedcovers. The house was quiet, filled with the kind of lonely stillness that descends on a home after children grow up and leave in search of their own lives, their own happiness, an elusive pursuit they may or may not secure. But God knows they try.

A soft escape of breath fluttered the threads on the bedspread with the raised imprint of Davy Crockett stalking a bear. Seeing Guy yesterday had agitated me. Thank heavens Buck was nothing like Guy, the father of my four grown children. Buckley was sensible and capable, solid, not only in his body, but in his character.

My marriage to Guy had had less substance. From the beginning I had carefully constructed my marriage to him into a delicate dream I smugly drew around my shoulders like a beautiful, silk-fringed summer shawl that I flaunted in public for all have-nots to envy. Wrapped in self-delusion, I had all too willingly ignored the obvious.

At first, I hadn't noticed that Guy was lazy. I had been too taken up with his easiness, eager to believe his promises that everything would work out if left alone. He pacified me with pretty words, with false assurances that together we'd open a curio shop *next week, next month, next season,* that my working to support us was only for a while. We wouldn't always live hand-to-mouth, scratching the dirt like pitiful chickens, he promised. We'd be one of the few to own an automobile, and it would be a fancy one at that. Just think, Reena, he said as he rubbed my shoulders, you'll be working in the shop as one of the proprietors instead of in the grimy back room of a trading post like I did at the time. "Proprietor" would roll off his tongue like honey, soothing my anxieties and fatigue. Guy had briefly worked at the Thunderbird Trading Post, too, but when the owner saw how buyers gravitated to him and sought information from him, he was told he was no longer needed.

While I tagged valuable, fragile Indian pottery, jewelry, and rugs hocked by Pueblos and Navajos, few of whom spoke English and who communicated by gestures, Guy spent most of his time, so he said, "making contacts" with potters and craftspeople, gathering inventory to supply our shop, an old family home, which my great-uncle was willing to lease us. Two Bucks had painted INDIAN CURIOS, TOURISTS WELCOME on the front, and added geometric designs around the windows.

Guy used to stretch out on our double bed with the creaky springs, shirtless, cinnamon brown, lazy as a mountain lion in the sun. He moved with the elegance of one, cutting the air as he swung an arm over me, pinning me to the mattress, humming in my ear. I would curve my own body snugly into his, ready, always ready, for a whirlwind dance.

I liked to study his perfect profile when he lay on his back staring at the ceiling, dreaming aloud in his soft-spoken, melodic voice. The ridge of his brow and the hollows beneath his eyes and cheekbones lay in soft shadows like the northern slope of a mesa. On their own, my hands reached out to him, my fingers moving gently down his nose, his chin, and down to his chest. I'd lightly trace the mounds of his nipples, trail down to his belly, taut as a drumskin, and back up again, over and over, as his chest gently rose and fell with the swell of his voice. He'd point with his forefinger at the vigas as if his motion could beckon his dream, *our* dream.

Excited by his own words, he'd slip out from my grasp and leap off the bed, landing graceful as a dancer. When he walked, he stepped lightly, arms swinging, moving with a restless hunger. To think that I had once been willing to share his hunger! It was now hard to believe, but I had wanted to stay locked in that pose with Guy, to remain that enviable couple moving with such fluidity and grace, cutting through the thick of gossip.

I was so willing to believe in him that our marriage could possibly have lasted even longer than it had except that I was rudely awakened by Guy himself. That act was quickly followed by the public humiliation I endured when the ceremonial clowns sang about me that autumn. My fall from grace overflowed the tongues and minds of the community. Rumor drowned truth, overtook me in its sweep. As white people say, I had been on my high horse, and when I fell, I hit hard ground, tasting blood and dirt.

Disquieted by thoughts of the past, I pulled at stray threads on the bedspread. I felt disloyal to Buck even thinking about my ex. But Guy's memory, encountering him face-to-face yesterday, had stirred buried emotions, demanded of me that I put the past in order, a gesture I felt I must make, like burning the clothes of the dead or discarding their possessions.

To begin at the beginning. But where was the beginning? What was real and what was imagined? What was the truth and what was a lie? The beginning and the middle and the end—reality, illusion, and delusion flowed together like the silted waters of the Rio Grande, the river that was now itself a lie to its own name.

I wet my lips, remembering the heat.

The story of the end went back at least to the evening in June 1953 when doings became too indistinct to separate.

Seasons

REENA—1953–1996

The June days that followed the longest day of the year were un-failingly dry and hot. The heat lingered in the house long past sundown, baking us like in an oven, affording no relief till early morning. I couldn't employ the old method of sprinkling the floors with water to cool the rooms since the earthen floors of my home had been covered with linoleum. The best I could do was to wet down the dirt in front of my home, which faced east, and sit quietly in my nightgown at the end of a long workday.

I sat on an old wooden bench, observing the long shadows cast by the setting sun, idly fanning myself with a folded newspaper. The smell of the damp earth brought some comfort, as did the distant rumble of thunder from the Manzano Mountains. A trail of low-bellied clouds had promised rain all week, but all that came each afternoon was wind and flying dirt.

The children—Maria, called Ria by the family, Lena, and three-year-old Bunky—earlier had gone across the village to Nana's. Judy, eighteen at the time, was taking them to the *gaiyu* to watch the young men show off on horseback in the plaza as they tried to pluck up the chicken planted in the ground. The sound of cheering and yelling occasionally carried from the plaza, wrapping me in solitude. Such events no longer interested me. Leave that to the young and to the idle. I debated whether to cross the village to bring the children home or leave them there overnight with Judy, who had more patience with them. Guy startled me from these thoughts when he rounded the corner.

I stared in surprise. He had not been home for two days. Now, he swept in like a cool breeze, a sight as mesmerizing as the blue of a flame. Despite the heat, Guy looked fresh and well groomed. His short hair was oiled and carefully combed back so that his hair fell into neat even rows. His best white shirt with the mother-of-pearl snaps was freshly laundered and ironed, and his jeans were sharply creased; his caramel-colored boots gleamed with wax. Had he gone home to Laguna?

Guy stopped before me and grinned, one end of his lip curling downward. Wordless, he pulled me up to him. Before I could voice the questions forming in my mind, his mouth was on mine. He tasted of berry wine, and smelled sweetly, innocently, of soap. He nuzzled his chin, smooth with a shave, against my neck and shoulders. I struggled to escape the tickling. Guy muffled my protests with hard kisses. The more I pushed away from him, the harder he held me. Finally, I yielded, and he took my hand, drew me inside the house. He latched the screen door, and led me to the back room where the whole family slept in beds neatly lined up dormitory style. He stopped beside our bed.

"Guy?"

"Shhh."

He bent to pull at the heel of each boot, then kicked each one off in turn.

He kissed me gently. Then he drew back to look me full in the face. I closed my eyes to listen to his whispers in Keres, the Laguna tongue, nothing I understood. Then he rained kisses on my face and neck till I forgot my questions and was only glad to have him home again, to feel his muscled back, and to be locked in his need for me. My hands slid up his chest to his neck, then onto his hair. I felt the tuft of hair at his crown that stubbornly refused to lie flat no matter what he did to it.

As Guy continued to shower me with kisses, he slowly inched my gown up till he worked it over my head. He let it drop carelessly from his fingers, and knelt to slip down my cotton panties. As I stood naked and expectant, looking down at Guy on his knees before me, I suddenly felt an overwhelming sense of power over him. But before I could savor the feeling, I lay on my back on the bed, Guy on top of me. The denim of his pants scratched my bare skin; the brass buttons pinched me. I pulled at his shirt front. The snaps popped, and his shirt flew open.

The room was slowly deepening in blue twilight as the sun slipped below the horizon. I could no longer see Guy's face clearly. He undressed quickly. Then he was riding me on waves of pleasure, at first moving as softly as clouds and then with a driving force, till I went soft and limp. It was always good with Guy, but the unexpectedness of our lovemaking and my silent compliance lulled me into a pleasant drowsiness. I sank under his weight into a dreamless sleep.

I don't know how long I slept. It was fully dark when I stirred. The night was hot and sticky. I extended my arm, feeling for Guy beside me. The bed was empty. I sat up, disoriented, wondering if night was falling or working toward sunrise. The crickets chirped steadily.

I sat on the bed edge. My gown lay in a crumpled heap on the floor. I reached for it, pulled it over my head. Moonlight spilled in the windows, illuminating my path as I walked through the middle room to the kitchen. The house was empty and quiet, the screen door unlatched.

I stepped over the front threshold expecting to see the glow of Guy's cigarette in the dark. The moon hung full and white in the east, a beautiful mother-of-pearl. Cool air penetrated the light material of my gown, sending a delicious chill through me. As I turned to go back inside, a movement down in Old Man Reyes's orchard below caught my eye. Someone in a white shirt was walking down the slope toward the apple trees. I thought to call out to Guy, but a sudden, odd thought stopped me. Was I awake?

I watched the figure walk a short ways then dip out of sight near the ditch. I caught my breath at what came out. It was a white horse luminous as the moon with a short-cropped iridescent mane. The horse pranced a few feet then tossed its head. Was I asleep? I fought against a tremendous weight to rise to consciousness, but nothing happened. I struggled to voice a prayer, but my mouth felt heavy with sand.

Dark movement among the trees caused the hairs on the nape of my neck to rise. I shivered, unable to move. A woman with long hair walked from out of the trees, carrying something in her hands. A rope? I strained to see better, to see details. My eyes watered with the effort. Then I was puzzled. Suddenly I saw clearly. The horse was no longer merely a horse, but a man in a white buckskin shirt who moved with a peculiar arch of the back, his gait swift as a pony's. I gasped. His long hair was unrestrained, flowing over his body; he wore some sort of Plains Indian headband with a plume that bobbed gracefully atop his head; the top half of his face was painted white. My heart pounded in my ears. Panic lodged in my throat.

The woman tossed the rope over the man-horse, pinning his arms to his sides. She straddled the arch of his back and rode easily in tight circles. With goading, the apparition pranced wildly. The woman's hair flew about her, tangling with the man's, but she held on, clutching, scratching at the man's face. Abruptly, the pair turned from the shadows of the orchard and crossed the open alfalfa field. In a blur of movement, the woman was tossed in the air; the buckskin shirt now stretched prone in the alfalfa, covering the woman. I heard no sounds, yet I had the distinct impression of hooves pounding the earth. Flying clouds streamed across the sky heading toward the moon.

I was back inside the house. I saw the latch of the screen door slipping into the hook, the front door shutting, and the bolt sliding in place across the door.

I woke to bright sunlight and to stifling heat in the closed home. I looked around. I wore my gown, and the bed was only slightly rumpled where I had lain atop the covers. There was no sign of Guy.

He came home that afternoon, drunk and disheveled, and went straight to bed, sleeping through the night. The next day he offered no explanation of his whereabouts, and I feared to ask, wanting to hear neither the truth nor a lie. The night before, what I saw, never happened, I told myself.

July brought no rain, but it did bring the realization that I was pregnant. By figuring the lapse in weeks, I just knew it had to be *that* night that I was impregnated. I wondered about a child conceived on such a night, worrying the thought ragged. Several times I almost confided in Nana, in my sisters. Instead, I kept the matter to myself.

The month dragged on. Many times it was all I could do to get up in the mornings, overcome by a distressing nausea that lasted until noon. Fatigue settled in my bones like silt. All I wanted to do was sleep.

The relatives gathered the weekend *Tata* butchered a pair of sheep. The yard buzzed with activity, with careless laughter and joking and feasting, and furtive bottle tipping among the men. Cousin Rosie, her youthful figure already rounding out, her chin perpetually jutting forward in self-importance, had been the one who pulled Inez, that two-bit tramp, out from under the table in the storeroom where she'd been doing Lord knows what with Guy.

"Right under her nose!"

"While she roasted sheep guts!"

"Can you believe it?"

"She's p.g. again, you know."

My face burned with shame at the clucking tongues and smothered giggles as I staunchly defended Guy.

In August just before the San Augustine feast, I was peeling potatoes for the evening meal when Cousin Rosie came to inform me of her husband's discovery. Rosie's chest heaved indignantly; her nostrils flared as she recounted how Ulysses, the undersheriff at the time—naturally the one to discover such indiscretions, she was quick to point out—had come across the two of them, Guy and Inez, down by the river in the apple orchard.

As I listened, I peeled potatoes with a viciousness. The skins fell off in long, curling strips. Rosie's mouth moved with great satisfaction over the details as if she was enjoying a juicy apple. Her full name was Rosenda but after her years at the Indian school, she went by Rosie. Nosy-Rosie, Guy called her because she was always poking her nose into his business.

"Just minding his own business, my man, on his way to the field when he hears these strange sounds coming from among the trees. He thinks that maybe somebody's pig broke out and is having a feast on the apples. *Tah-titah!* Well, let me tell you, it was something else, all right! They were. . . ." Rosie clutched the collar of her blouse tight. "Well, as a married woman, you know what things a man and a woman do when they're buck naked."

I struggled to maintain my composure. I stabbed the paring knife into one of the potatoes.

"Get out!" I yelled full-force in Rosie's face. Her face flamed red. She puckered her lips in indignation, and swallowed and reswallowed several times. She puffed up with the effort of containing her tongue. Then she stormed out.

A few feet from the door, she whirled and yelled, "Don't ever say I didn't tell you, Reena!"

I always rallied to Guy's defense, saying and doing things I'd otherwise never do, things that I didn't even know I was capable of doing. He drove me to it, clouding my mind with the vain ambition of becoming a Some-one. I desperately clutched at that dream, slapping the impudent faces of women who flirted with him. I even ripped the blouse off Ella Rose when she laughed in my face and said she'd been with Guy. Liar! Can't believe a woman like that. I closed my ears to Nana's warnings and insulted my own sisters when they hinted about his indiscretions. Peeping Toms! Bernice's baby was not Guy's. I shut my eyes tight and defended him with blind ferocity. Jealous Peeping Toms were all they were! Guy would be who I made him, not what others said he was. I was determined to accomplish that one thing at all costs, believing it was the only chance at happiness I'd ever have. I should have known the danger.

In September, in the brief lull between the harvest and the dance, we came near to opening the shop. Guy was shoveling clay taken from the riverbed onto the roof of the shop and packing it down with water to prevent leaks. I was planning to apply a fresh whitewash to the walls now that I was past the morning sickness. On a sudden impulse, I decided to take lunch down to Guy at the shop. I packed slices of headcheese, tortillas, and a can of purple plums into a paper sack and walked the short distance to the highway. I didn't see him on the roof, but maybe he was resting in the shade. As I neared the door, I saw the shovel standing upright in a partially sunken mound of earth.

The air was still, the buzz of horseflies loud. As I pushed the door open, I heard a woman laugh, a low, intimate murmur. My heart jumped. With a sickening feeling, I pushed the door open all the way so that bright light overtook the shadowed interior.

A woman squealed. As my eyes adjusted to the shadows, I saw a woman pull at a blanket to cover herself. Guy sat up, his shirt open to the waist, a wild look in his eyes.

"Reena!" he shouted.

Numbed, I looked at the scene before me. Discarded clothes, shoes neatly set aside, tangled hair. . . .

Despair rose up in me, then gave way to rage. There was no mistaking what was before me.

I swung the paper sack in my hand at the woman I now recognized as Inez. She wasn't even an attractive woman. Guy's hand reached out to stop me. I yanked the bag back, striking him on the mouth with the canned plums. The bag tore, spilling the contents. Inez scrambled, snatching up clothes as fast as she could. Holding them in a ball, she ran in a half-crouch to hide behind the counter.

Guy held a hand to his bleeding lip, now swelling purple as the plums.

I took in his crumpled appearance.

"You . . . you. . . ." Then I broke down, unable to speak, turned and fled.

By the time I reached home, my side burned, and I couldn't stop crying. I retched in the yard. I sank to my knees and gasped for breath. Nana came out of the house, wiping her hands on her apron. She was shouting but I couldn't hear what she said.

Nana helped me inside, where she made me lie down while she bathed my face with a cloth. She pieced the story together somehow through my sobbing.

Thin-lipped, Nana said, "I think *Tata* better do something about this."

When I heard that, I swallowed my pain. My sobs reduced to hiccups and then to a waver in my voice. Despite Nana's commands to stay in bed, I moved about the house, stuffing Guy's belongings into two cotton flour sacks, and called the neighbor's son to summon the tribal police.

Eventually, Eloy responded, and after listening to me, he toed the dirt. "I dunno. We don't do things like that." He spoke to the ground.

"Don't tell me that! I want that man off the reservation now! You go pick him up, and take him and *these*"—I thrust the flour sacks at him— "and drive him to the edge of the reservation, and tell him to get! Tell him to get back to Laguna, and don't ever come back. See if that mama of his will take him back now! You understand? What do you think this tribe pays you for but to protect us? Lord have mercy on us if we ever have a real emergency!"

My words rolled out of me with such authority and force, Eloy stared at me, dumbstruck. Nana joined me. She told Eloy to obey me, or she would report him to the elders and to the governor. Eloy reluctantly agreed.

By evening, Guy was back begging forgiveness. Eloy had driven him to Los Lunas, and after they shared a couple of swigs of peppermint schnapps, Eloy had given him money for a bus ticket to Laguna. Instead, Guy made his way back to the village.

"She's an evil woman, that Inez. You know that. Before I knew what I was doing, I . . . we . . . she made me do things I didn't want to! She's a witch. She must be!" Guy spoke softly, his eyes on his hands, repentant. "She's just jealous of you. Your beauty. Your goodness. She wanted to get at you through me." He looked up for a moment, his river-brown eyes indignant. In the light of the bare bulb, his face looked sallow. His lip was puffed, distorted.

"You know she has never liked you. She says that you think you're better than everyone else, that you're Miss High and Mighty! She was using me! Reena, believe me."

It sounded so plausible the way he told it, but that's how it had been all the times before when I was desperate to be convinced. He knew that personal criticism enraged me. Now I heard the whine in his voice, and I despised his cowardice, the way he danced around the truth, hiding behind another woman.

I picked up the cast iron skillet. Thickened bacon grease ran down my arm. "I'm not a fool! You're no good! Get out of here, you . . . you dog! Just like a dirty dog!"

I swung blindly at him. Guy leaped out of the chair. The grease made my hold slippery, and the skillet fell to the floor with a heavy thud, splattering grease across my feet. I heard the flat slam of the screen door.

I collapsed to the floor, cradling the mound of my belly, swaying in the intensity of my sorrow.

Ria, who had been watching little Bunky, appeared from the next room, standing uncertainly. "Mama?" she called.

I waved her away.

When the room filled with evening shadows, I rose and washed my face in the tin basin, moving as if I dragged deadweight. It was the saddest day I'd ever known.

Two weeks later, my story, with all its sordid details embellished, was sung in the dark into the curious crowd gathered around the ceremonial clowns. The people's pleasure at the clowns' chiding was as deep and wide as the river flow, silky as the feel of water on a hot summer night, and the telling and retelling of my story brought them equal pleasure. My domestic woes spilled into the night along with the follies of others.

They also sang about the one they dubbed "Tankcovers" because of his fondness for women's underwear. He was in the habit of stealing the best of women's underclothes off the laundry lines, even brazenly fighting with two women who caught him in the act. And they sang out about "Samson and Delilah." Frederick, whom they called Samson, had stolen his mother's old Indian pottery and with the money he received went on a weeklong drunk, bringing home skinny, washed-out white women. When the money ran out, the women disappeared. His irate girlfriend, Florentina, finding him flat broke and passed out, grabbed a pair of scissors and cut off his long hair, which was wrapped and bound in a traditional *chongo*. Then she threw his hair in the road. "Samson" lost his power with women after that, they teased.

To think I was exposed to such open ridicule! Those other fools were in need of social reproof, not me! Didn't people see that I was guiltless, that I had been the wronged party? The unjustness of the situation filled me with anger and despair.

Fury and hurt confused my judgment. I became sick with crazed jealousy when Guy took up with Izzie soon after I threw him out. I had always been wary of that woman even when I had cause for indifference to her presence. An air of haughtiness that knew no shame surrounded her. And her eyes! Her eyes were hard; not even her complexion, smooth as the porcelain dolls in the dime stores, or the seductive tottering of her hips could soften that discomforting gleam of malice.

Who could say exactly what caused Izzie's eyes to harden? She was a high-spirited girl. In defiance of the grandmother who raised her, Izzie had dropped out of the Indian school to run away with a white boy, the son of storeowners. She left the village, presumably never to return. After her young husband left for combat in Korea, people said the white grandparents took her two children from her. Whether they thought she was incapable of raising them or they feared she'd raise them as Indians, no one knew for sure. Izzie returned home alone then, her eyes sharp as arrowheads.

After her husband was killed in the war, Izzie received a belated settlement from the government or from insurance. Whatever the source, the money had been tied up in the courts by the white grandparents, who contested the settlement, feeling the children should be the sole beneficiaries. People whispered that the sum Izzie received was quite a bit.

Together, Guy and Izzie opened up the curio shop I had worked so hard to birth. Old *Meh-meh* Lemus was easily persuaded to put aside family loyalty when it meant quick money in the pocket, and for a small sum, he allowed Guy and Izzie to use the shop that Two Bucks had painted and I had furnished. I heard of how they laid pottery and kachinas atop Navajo rugs spread on the shelves that had been bought piece by piece with the sporadic leftovers from my paychecks. There were bows and arrows, trinkets for tourist children, postcards, and candies. Baskets hung from the vigas along with ears of Indian corn.

I heard of the Zuni and Navajo silverwork they kept inside the glass display case given to Guy and me by Mr. Jaramillo, our teacher at the Indian school, in gratitude for our regular visits to him during his sickbed days, visits that had been my idea and to which I had had to drag Guy. No doubt Guy and Izzie used the green cashbox with the hidden drawer that I had bought Guy as a special present.

Jealousy burned like hot coals in my bones and a desire for vengeance raged unchecked. Not only was my man stolen from me, but my dream as well. I fought back. First, I charged them with trespass in order to take them before the tribal council to get them evicted out of *my* shop, but the pueblo governor that year was related to Izzie, and I got nowhere with my complaint.

Meh-meh Lemus went deaf when I confronted him with his betrayal, but I pestered him nonetheless. Finally, exasperated by my persistence, he told me, "Who made me a judge over you and your affairs? Leave me alone! I'm too old for this."

I demanded that the parish priest publicly excommunicate Guy and Izzie from the Catholic church as adulterers. When Father James balked at the suggestion, I berated him, the father, the priest! "You're more afraid of what people will say about you than you are of God!" I charged.

"Who do you think you are, saying such a thing to me!" he exclaimed. My words must have saddened him for the old priest retired shortly afterwards, though without offering any rebuke to errant sheep.

I couldn't stand to see them together, Izzie acting as if she was Someone! I wanted to scratch out her hard eyes, to draw blood, and to wipe that insolent smile off her face. I wanted Guy, to beat him with my fists, to break him with my tears, and despite all, I wanted him back to collapse in his arms.

Ria and Lena, whom I sent to spy on Guy and Izzie, continually came back with reports of their success, which only weakened me further. Guy was prospering at a time when only Spanish people owned stores, when Indians were thought to be only dumb, ignorant, good-for-nothings. He possessed the natural talent for business that I had poured my hopes into. People had always wanted to buy from him. When he sat with *Tata* in the wagon selling melons and chile, they had always sold out. When we went to the Belen train depot to sell felt trinkets and small potteries, tourists pressed on him and bought all we had. This time, though, I had no part in his success. He wasn't mine.

In my pregnancy, I felt awkward and ugly. I carried Carmel low, and my belly swelled unbecomingly. Dark half moons lay under my eyes. My face was blotchy and bloated. My pregnancy hadn't started out well with all that morning sickness, and it worsened till I completely lost my appetite. In fact,

I couldn't hold anything down. Nana grew alarmed, fearing I had been witched, made to go crazy with love for Guy. It had been known to happen before, though that was long ago. Nana initiated a full-scale cure for me.

"Nonsense. This is all nonsense," Auntie Lena scolded me when she heard about the Big Doings. She sat beside my bed, smoothing her apron with her bony hands. The women had labored in the early morning, baking bread in preparation for the Doings, and Auntie had come straight over when the work was finished.

"The people are not saying nice things, *hita*." She said this while she studied her apron.

I looked up at the vigas, smelling the sweet aroma of Indian pies that lingered in Auntie's apron. Strangely, the smell did not nauseate me. I didn't ask what was being said. More than likely, the women were talking about how I had recently gotten into a screaming match with Izzie that turned into a brawl and how we had to be pulled apart by men.

Auntie smoothed hair from my face. Her lips moved several times as if she were about to speak; instead, she sat in silence, continuing to smooth the cotton apron over her thin housedress.

I watched Auntie's hands, dotted with age spots even then and covered with raised veins that coursed like blue rivers across the tops. I remembered the feel of those hands, cool on my hot forehead when, as a child, I cried after being severely scolded, or more likely, whipped with a willow or beaten with a broomstick by Nana for making some childish error like spilling bean juice on the stovetop, dropping firewood into the woodbox with a thud, or scattering a bucketful of chile on the ground when a dog chased me. Sometimes I was hit for no reason at all.

Auntie always held me till long after I quit sobbing, endlessly repeating into my hair, "*Tah. Tah.* There now." Then she rubbed salve on the welts, and gave me something to eat. Auntie had been the only one to visit the Indian school campus, frightening and lonely the first year. She brought Indian bread each time, and gave me a nickel for a treat. Auntie Lena herself was a graduate of St. Catherine's Indian School in Santa Fe, and she had great respect for the sisters and teachers, and for authority in general. Auntie believed all that the sisters had taught her about the church and

Jesus and the Blessed Mother, but she never dared express her deep faith in the church to anyone except the children.

I stared at the split in the thick viga above me, remembering the comfort that Auntie always offered. I wished one of Auntie's bowls of beans and red chile could smooth out my life again. I heard Bunky whimpering in the next room, and then it was quiet.

Auntie Lena finally broke the silence.

"Why are you allowing this? I don't think those Lagunas do that sort of thing, making people lovesick. Especially that one! He just has wandering eyes is all. If he'd keep his pants on, he wouldn't have half the problems he does."

Auntie Lena's eyes burned into mine. I thought then of Izzie and her eyes that rip and tear, and of the Mexican woman at the trading post where I worked, who was suspected of doing any number of wicked practices for a price. That one liked to touch Guy at any opportunity with her dark, heavy hands that smelled of herbs. I felt too weak to point out the possibilities to Auntie Lena. Those had been Nana's ideas, anyway. As for *that* night in June, well, I hadn't told anyone about that. Anyway, it might have just been a dream. A bad dream.

"You know yourself that no one witched you. You're just eaten up with wanting. *Ooh-the*," she turned her head away in disgust. "You want that one who's just like a dog. He can't control himself and runs after every woman. And to take up with one such as that Izzie!"

My head hung in shame at her words.

Seeing me, Auntie Lena's tone softened. "You know better than that. But sometimes we women make mistakes. I, myself, once did. Yes." She smiled, seeing my surprise. "But I ran the man off. I said to him, 'Oh you. You use me all up and throw me away like an old shoe. I'll show you. I don't need you!' I said that to him," she said, drawing herself up proudly.

"And your mama, too. She was first married to one of those wanderers. They're just boys who never become men. Finally, she could stand it no more! She went to her parents and said, 'You better find me someone else because I can't live with that one no more.'" Auntie threw her hands in the air with a look of exasperation, continuing, "They didn't used to let us choose our own husbands, you know. They said to her, 'All right, smarty. This time you choose your own. See how well you do!' Well, she did all right if you ask me! She married your father. Rooster, they used to call him because of the red in his hair. He was always a good man. You do the same thing. Don't give up your life for a dog! Get well. Be happy. You must think of this child inside you, and hope you have not harmed it with your thoughts."

Her hand, slightly damp, rested a moment on my shoulder. We lapsed into a silence as thick and heavy as if we mourned the dead. I noticed the worry around Auntie's eyes. As Auntie aged, her broad face had melted into soft folds; only now, the folds looked pinched. She held her rosary beads in one hand; her lips moved in inaudible recitation. She stopped and looked at me.

"Forgive him, poor thing! Forget him! He's not right in his heart to know what he's doing."

Auntie Lena was the one I turned to for help when Guy and I decided to marry. I didn't go home to inform Nana and *Tata* of our desire to marry or to get permission. Instead, I told Auntie Lena that we were to be married by a justice of the peace like some of our classmates who married outside of their villages, and that we were going to live in Laguna afterwards. Timid as she was before any elder or person of authority, Auntie Lena agreed to inform Nana and *Tata* of our plans. I caught the hurt in Auntie's eyes before she carefully lowered them to the floor. I knew the very idea of a J.P. wedding distressed Auntie greatly for she valued the sanction of the church and the blessing of the family on marriage. Before Auntie left, she shook Guy's hand and said almost mournfully, "Take good care of my niece, please, mister."

Guy and I went to Laguna after the brief ceremony. So proud and happy to be his wife, I purred with excitement on the bus ride. Once there, however, Guy's mother, Santana, and his older sister, Minnie, made no fuss over me as the bride, and didn't so much as offer us newlyweds a meal. Minnie flicked her plain brown eyes up and down me, taking in the white dress I had made in sewing class and my new white pumps, then dismissed me with a blink of pale lashes and a turn of her head.

I could understand but a few words in the Keres tongue, but the tone alone told me Santana was not pleased at being put out. Guy's father sat silent throughout the exchange, merely watching the women. Finally, impatiently beckoned by his wife, he rose from his chair to drive Santana and Minnie to the store to buy groceries. He paused briefly beside me and awkwardly patted my shoulder.

Guy and I sat in the windowless kitchen, feeling more than seeing the afternoon wear on. Finally, Guy rose and turned on the old brown radio above the sink. It crackled with static. The radio was tuned to a Spanish station. A song so plaintive and sad filled the room. *Mi corazón* were the only words I understood. Guy stood in front of me holding his arms out; I rose to enter them, and we turned slowly, my hot tears splashing on Guy's shoulders. He rubbed his hand up and down my back, then buried his head in my neck. We shuffled in tight circles, our dress shoes crunching on the dirt on the linoleum flooring.

I spent my wedding night sharing the double bed with Santana. I lay on the edge of the mattress, fearing that if I moved in, I'd slide toward Santana's stout body set like a rock in the bed. The thought of accidentally touching her terrified me. Guy slept on the kitchen floor alongside his father.

We returned to Albuquerque early the next morning, and so began my job of supporting us. We stayed for a short time at the home of our former teachers, Fred and Iris Jaramillo, while I cleaned homes for old, frail, white women whom I had worked for on weekends while at the Indian school.

The Jaramillos gave us the idea and encouragement to open a curio shop. Fred's brother owned a trading post on Fourth Street, where both Guy and I were given jobs, though Guy was dismissed within a short period of time.

"Know the value of what you have," Mr. Jaramillo told Guy. "You've got yourself a wife and a partner smart as a whip. Yes, sir. She's got plenty of horse sense, son."

Eventually, we moved to Isleta as I always knew we would. Nana and *Tata* gave us a one-room home in the village. I never asked Auntie Lena what she told my parents about our J.P. wedding, but whatever she said had soothed them, and they welcomed their new son-in-law.

"Oh no, Laguna is too far," *Tata* told Guy. "You stay here with us."

Our first year of marriage was our happiest. Guy, with Two Bucks' help, added on two more rooms to our home. I became pregnant late in the year. I always knew Guy was a flirt; he'd been that way during our school days, continually fluctuating between me and other girls. I had done the same. I figured he'd grow out of it, especially once he became a father. But as my waistline expanded, then rounded, and I grew increasingly touchy and fatigued, Guy's itchy feet carried him away from home. I tried as best I could to ignore it in the face of those eager to tell me what they saw and heard about Guy. I held my head high, and let it be known I would listen to no gossip instigated by those jealous of my happiness with a good-looking man.

Four children later it came down to lying weak and helpless in bed.

Nana entered the room, carrying a steaming cup. She scolded Auntie Lena for tiring me out. "She needs the quiet," she told Lena. In earlier years, Nana didn't seem to have much tenderness, but now she gently nursed me, bringing me bowls of *atole* and cups of boiled Indian tea, smoothing my bedcovers, brushing my hair, and shushing the children. She burned sage, and for extra assurance, lit candles in tall frosted glasses with pictures of the Virgin Mary. Never had anyone fussed over me like this.

She thinks I'm going to die, I realized. Suddenly, it seemed cruel to mislead the woman. I wasn't going to die. Auntie Lena was right. It was pure foolishness; no, it was downright stupid to carry on over a man who wasn't worth the trouble it took to keep him.

The thought hit me like cold water on a blaze. I broke into a sweat. I felt the dampness on my exposed skin, the clamminess beneath my gown, my feet cold and moist. My cheeks were wet with tears.

I sat up suddenly. A wave of nausea broke over me. I started to refuse the cup of broth Nana held out to me, then changed my mind. Nana stopped me before I could drink it all.

"Take it easy, *hita!* Don't try to get well all at once," Auntie laughed.

The community marveled at how soon I was back on my feet, attributing my health to the curing ceremony. I knew otherwise, that my strength had recovered the day of Auntie Lena's visit. Her words had cut to the heart of the matter as neatly as a willow whip on tender skin. Once I refused to feed the fire of my jealousy, it ceased its rage, and in a short time was cold ashes.

Soon after Guy left Izzie or Izzie left him, I was never sure which it was, I heard that he was living with Buttons. I was indifferent to the gossip. A few months later, he moved on to live with Sophie for almost a year. After Sophie's weak attempt to shoot him, he went back to Laguna. I heard of him every now and then. He lived with his mother in Laguna, painting pottery. Apparently the blaze died down in him, too. Either that or nobody wanted him anymore, used up as he was.

I resolved to go forward, to never look back. Yet I knew what devastation lay behind me: The sky was without color; charred tree trunks stood amidst blackened debris, and grayness stretched on a flat endless plain. And there on the far horizon, following me like the moon, was my pain. I consented to suffer it till it became a familiar and constant companion. It provided a strange comfort that not even children in my arms or the baby at my breast could equal. It made me strong and grow in stature though I remembered myself as a petite girl. It pinched my feet so that I quit ceremonial dancing even when the war captain came to my home and asked me to dance. My lips drew increasingly tight so that I forgot I had been a laughing, careless tease.

I determined that there'd be no further cracks in my public image, no more vicious gossip, no more smirks. I knew just how to silence wagging tongues. I fixed the most elaborate baskets for dances and doings, strictly observed all the ceremonial events, and held up my children as polished images of myself. The pious daughter of the village, I attended every gathering, doing, doing, doing, helping all, baking bread, comforting the grief-stricken, executing ritual, doing, doing, doing. I exceeded social conformity, becoming more *Dae-nine* in myself than all the people collectively were. I set a high standard from which to look down at others. None dared criticize such exactness.

But I couldn't erase all the signs. Long after Guy's affair with Izzie ended, the curio shop with its brightly painted front stood an empty shell to mock me. Graffiti covered the boarded windows, tumbleweeds grew thick as bushes, and plaster peeled off the walls. Amidst the neglect, TOURISTS WELCOME continued to blaze, reminding me I hadn't done things properly. I hadn't prepared the way.

After that I paid more attention to the words of my mother and other older women. As she vigorously rolled out tortillas, Nana admonished us, her daughters, "Don't be taken in by appearances. You can't trust people on their looks alone. Good looks mean nothing." She expertly flipped the tortilla several times and resumed her rolling, not pausing in her speech.

"Too much you are becoming like white people who look with their eyes without seeing." She looked up from her work to see if we were listening. "Oo-kem! Be careful! People can't hide what's in their heart though the crafty ones try. The truth always shows through. My daughters, pay attention to people's words and to how they speak. Watch their eyes and hands, and listen for the meaning in their words. They'll show themselves true or false." Nana nodded her head. "They can't help it." She told us this in our language, using the rolling pin to gesture for emphasis.

Virgie and Judy rolled their eyes at each other. But I already had learned the hard way that there was truth to Nana's words. I also knew how a woman could get so tied up by a man's fancy words, by his fast sidestepping.

Twenty years later Buckley dropped into my life as sudden as an apple dropping from a tree; the time was ripe. At the fiesta at Cousin Rosie's home for the christening of Rosie's first grandson, I expected only to pass bowls around the table, wash dishes, and maybe catch up on the latest goings-on. Instead, I had the incredible luck of being seated at the dinner table right next to Buckley. He was swarthy and full in his blue BIA police uniform. With his large frame, he naturally dominated the table.

I listened to him talk about the different reservations he'd been to in the Dakotas and Utah and Arizona. He spoke of tribal politics, social problems, reservation skirmishes, all subjects I had considered the rhetoric of radicals. I listened like Nana had told me to listen, and I heard his voice flowing like water. His words had depth.

The people nodded their heads at his words. The attending women fussed over his food, flirting with him with their laughter and attention; after all, he was an eligible widower. I felt a strong undercurrent pulling on me, drawing me to him, but I resisted, keeping my spine straight against the chair back. Buckley talked on about his retirement plans, of returning to farming and cash crops and investment capital. Rosie teased him about trading in the police cruiser for a tractor.

"I'm ready for the simple life," he responded.

I sipped my coffee.

"Chile rellenos, Doreena?" His voice rippled across my consciousness. He graciously offered me the bowl of "chile bombs," a special sweet dish of sugared minced meat, green chile, and raisins shaped into small ovals, deep-fried, and served in boiled sugar water. In accepting the bowl, my hand grazed his, and I looked directly into his eyes, seeing past the black flecks in his brown irises to their centers, dark and intense as cooled lava. I lowered my gaze to his lips and saw his mouth closing around my name, his lower lip full and tender as ripe cherries. His nearness loomed. He held my gaze, and I was unable to pull away, again feeling the insistent pull of an undercurrent. In that unguarded moment, I let go, feeling an exhilarating freedom in release as I slipped under and then emerged to a blur of voices. Staring into the bowl of floating sweets, I almost forgot where I was. I barely found the breath to murmur, "Thank you."

To my disappointment, he left the fiesta immediately after dinner, smacking a peppermint candy. But his shadow remained, trailing me into the spring, flitting into my thoughts unexpectedly, hanging on the edge of my dreams where he stood quietly singing in sweet blue light. He took a pinch of corn pollen from a small pouch and sprinkled it in a line before him. The pollen fell like flecks of sunlight. He sang all the while, his song indiscernible but simple and comforting. It was a song that hummed steadily through days and nights, transforming a dream to reality.

His name kept coming up in casual conversations, some new aspect of his personality taking me by surprise. Whatever was said of him, it was spoken with cautious respect. I heard he was as forceful as a summer storm: lightning, rolling thunder, and driving rain all in one. He drifted like cloud shadows or marched ceremoniously like dazzlingly white thunderheads. He kept people on guard, ever changing and unpredictable as the weather, ever constant and steady as the turn of the seasons. He flashed by on the highway in his patrol car, leaving fleeting images of his intense face that I studied at night. I thought long and hard, and listened to completeness.

By the time I saw him months later at a wedding fiesta, we had no need for words. From the doorway of the community center, I spotted him filling a pitcher with soda, his back to me. He spun neatly on his feet heading toward me to a nearby table. He stopped in his tracks when he saw me, and in a flash of perception, I saw the longing in his eyes, in his sudden lack of composure. He looked down at the full pitcher dripping on his shoes, and wiped the sweating container with his free hand. I knew he knew I knew. I smiled my acceptance of the fact. He resumed his advance on the table.

Buckley saw to it that I was seated quickly and then attentively waited on me, making sure my cup was constantly full, and that I was served steaming bowls of red chile and the customary chicken and rice, sending back cooled food to the kitchen. When I finished my meal, he handed me a paper sack, urging me to fill it with the candy, fruits, and Indian pies set on the table for the guests. I smiled warmly at him, clutching my sack, glad I had taken Carmel's advice and worn my red dress with the large belted bow on the waist, which smoothed the bulge of my tummy. Red was my best color. It created a flush in my cheeks and made me laugh. I grew full in red.

That evening at the wedding dance at the Manzanita Lounge, Buckley asked me to dance. We swayed like blue spruce in the mountain wind.

When the song ended, Buckley led me from the dance floor, regretfully saying, "I have to be leaving now. I have the night shift."

"Is that right? It must be hard to work nights." I smiled, surprised at how my voice fell softly.

"No, it's not hard at all," he said. "Actually, it's the shift I prefer. Quiet most times. I get off duty in the wee early morning hours, and on my way home, and the times I'm assigned to patrol Isleta, I always patrol your area."

I stared at him, remembering him filtering my thoughts, even in sleep. "Yes, it's a high crime area." I attempted to joke; instead my words were an icy blast.

"May I. . . ." He cleared his throat loudly. "I mean, would it be all right with you if I stop by to see you sometime?"

My head jerked up. I felt a flush creep onto my face.

Buckley added quickly, "I mean, sometime during the day, or the early evening when I'm off duty." In the mirrored tile behind him, I saw my eyes reflect a dark hunger. In a blink, they turned to the glossy sheen of well-used pottery polishing stones. I looked down so Buckley wouldn't see.

"If you'd like," I said in a toneless voice, neatly turning on my heels. From a distance I heard him call, "I would like to. Very much I would like to."

I felt my cheeks flaming. I veered toward the ladies' room, almost colliding in the doorway with girls too young to appreciate the merits of a man like Buckley. As I pushed past them, they stared at me with glazed eyes painted bright as peacock tails. In the mirror I saw them shrug at one another and saunter out.

"Merciful heavens," I laughed to myself. "I just may be the apple of his eye."

I glanced at the clock on the nightstand. The time had slipped by me. It was much later than it seemed. Buckley would be returning soon, expecting breakfast. Though I should get up, I remained in the bed, immobilized.

I felt nothing for Guy, not anger, not sadness, not an ounce of sympathy for his pathetic nature. A sense of relief, maybe, that I had washed my hands of him. One thing I knew: I wouldn't let Marli go through the same thing I did.

I sighed, flipping back the bedcovers. I never imagined that life was full of bends and twists. I didn't want to tell Marli about Guy, but I had no choice. Rupert could be just like his father. Even if he wasn't, the whole situation was sticky, sure to agitate the family elders. Marli and Rupert had no blood tie, but still . . . we were all family.

Or were we?

Two Bucks was the authority on family matters. I would go see him, ask him what I didn't even want to think: *Is Guy Marli's uncle, Rupert her cousin?* Relieved at having someone to consult, someone to shift the burden to, I rose. Why was it that just when you thought you were getting somewhere, you found yourself right back where you started?

Patty Hearst Did It

Even if Viola had never spoken a word at the first meeting of the university's American Indian Student Coalition, she would have still stood out. Her beautiful, sleek hair hung well past her waist and I remember she plaited it into a single braid, which she pulled over her shoulder. She wore dangling beaded earrings, a denim vest with an embroidered eagle on the back, and snug-fitting Levi's. Blue ink tattoos, homemade jobs, were etched into her hand and forearm. They were kinda cool, reminded me of the tattoos the Stewart students wore. She was a knockout, a natural beauty, but she sat there as if she was unaware of her looks, listening attentively as students introduced themselves.

When it was her turn, she stood without speaking till she had everyone's attention, the way tribal elders do when they have something important to say. She began addressing the group in her Native language. Then she translated her greeting, told us her name, what reservation she was from, a little of the historical struggles of her people, and how an elder had advised her to go to college, not to learn the ways of white society but to learn how to fight for her people. Her statements made those of us who preceded her seem lame in our rambling of names, tribal affiliations, high schools, probable majors. The people following her mimicked her pattern.

It was hard not to be impressed. She was so unpretentious in her delivery, clearly possessing a strong sense of who she was. Back then, there were plenty of phony-baloney Indian students bullshitting about their Indianness, plenty of AIM big shots shooting off their mouths about being warriors, preening in the limelight so you didn't know whether to laugh or take them serious.

Viola and I enrolled for the same anthro course. On the first day of class, we both were wandering hallways, maps in hand, looking for the lecture hall. "You looking for what I'm looking for?" she asked, laughing. "So embarrassin'!" Together we located the room and staked out our seats side by side for the rest of the semester.

Later when I saw her at the financial aid office, she came up to me and asked, "The anthro class, what did you think?"

I wasn't sure what I thought.

"These anthros are obsessed with puberty rites!" She sat down beside me, pulled her braid over her shoulder, and took the anthro textbook out of her bookbag, waving it at me.

Viola hated the book, the way Indians were lumped into broad categories and discussed like curiosities. She said the information about her people was wrong and she had already pointed out the errors to our anthro professor, who co-authored the book. He told her he respected her "opinion," but that oral history was not a reliable source, academic research was, then showed her the door.

"Typical," I said, shaking my head as if challenging authority was something I did all the time. I went back to my room and leafed through my copy. She was right. I wondered if I would have come to the same conclusion on my own.

Viola and I fell into these regular rap sessions that sometimes lasted for hours. We'd start out with our latest grievance with the anthro lecture, maybe Professor Wright's smugness with the fact that he did fieldwork at Zuni Pueblo and that gave him special license to make ludicrous observations about Indian people, like when Indians got mad, they wouldn't bathe. From there, we'd move on to larger issues that folded one out of the other. Grave robbing. Sacrilegious excavation of ancient ruins and burial sites. Museum display of sacred artifacts and human remains. Sacred space and objects. Disrespect of non-Western cultures. Ethnocentrism. Institutional racism. Government conspiracies against brown people.

I admired her confident manner of speaking. At the time, I was struggling to figure out what it meant to be an Indian, the politics of reservation versus urban Indian, living in two worlds, trying to put together all the historical shit that came down on Indian people, trying to figure out my politics.

Viola didn't need to wonder. She was politicized to the core, rock-solid certain of what she believed—that without action, Indian people didn't stand a chance. When I was playing basketball with white boys in high school, dating rah-rah girls, she was struggling to hold her own in school, butting heads with a racist principal, school district, and town, all of whom believed Indian people were no better than dogs. Her most important education, she felt, came from her family and tribal elders in the form of spiritual training.

As the semester progressed, I increasingly spent more time with her, discussing political issues affecting tribal people, grassroots politics, each time stretching beyond my base of experience. When Viola offered me a joint to smoke, I accepted it without hesitation. Marijuana made its rounds at dorm parties but I had always passed it by. This time, context made the difference: Sharing smoke was an Indian thing. I took a deep, manly draw and held it as long as I could. The smoke burned my throat and lungs, altered my consciousness ever so slightly with every draw. After that first joint, my thoughts became profound. I found myself speaking things that I must have already thought out, had stored inside me, just waiting for the right moment to voice. I waxed philosophical about institutionalization and the killing of the Indian spirit.

"That's it exactly!" Viola said excitedly. She leaned closer as if to tell me something special. Surprised, I held my breath. But she just slapped my knee, laughed that husky, sexy laugh of hers, and I joined her. We laughed uproariously, not even sure what we were laughing at to begin with, only that it was hilarious. I suddenly became conscious of her nearness, like her presence was all around me. Her hair was loose and when she threw it back over her shoulders, it whipped my arm.

"This is some powerful stuff. Man, my eyes get so red when I smoke." Her sunglasses were perched atop her head and she reached for them, put them on. The thought passed through my mind that she wore them almost constantly, even indoors. She glanced at me. "Man, Julian, you really look out of it. Your eyes are super-red!" She reached into her bag for eye drops, handed the vial to me, then took out a pack of cigarette rolling papers. I watched her extract one, reach her hand back into her bag, and sprinkle some pinches of weed into the paper. She tamped the weed evenly with a finger, rolled the paper expertly into a thin cigarette using her forefingers and thumbs, licked the glue, rolled the joint closed, twisted the ends, then handed it to me.

"Here's one for the road, bud." She patted my knee again, rising. "I've got to take off now. I'll be seeing you later?"

Bud. Yeah, we were buddies. I nodded at her.

"Take it easy." She walked across the stretch of grass, her long hair swinging like shawl fringe. Seemed like she floated.

I got spaced out there, just staring without seeing, my mind ranging like the wind.

Viola knew about Cecelia, referred to her as "your ol' lady," even asked about her regularly, casually. I thought of Cecelia, the letters she wrote weekly, the happiness I felt reading them, and my aching desire to see her, touch her. Then I thought of Viola, thought of kissing her. But no, we were good friends, a brother and sister together in the struggle, Viola always emphasized that. She wasn't into exclusive relationships.

For Viola, male and female relationships were just part of a larger political reality. She talked a lot about balance in the spiritual and physical world, and how white intrusion had upset the balance in the Indian world, screwed with the male role and stripped the women of their special status. There were signs of this imbalance in the physical world. The wolf, which symbolized the strength of the male, was nearly extinct. "Indian women have had to grow strong in order to keep the families together, but that's not how it was meant to be," she said. "Not until the wolf returns will the males resume their strength and power in our societies." When she talked like that, some of the Indian guys blew it off: "There goes Viola again." But I didn't.

My mind was tripping on that, on wolves and women, on how males in some tribes used to have more than one wife if they could afford it. Sounds

good to me, I thought. Then, suddenly the thought hit me, *You're disloyal.*
The revelation jolted me, shook me to the core. I looked around, paranoid,
like someone else may have realized my thought. No one was around that
part of campus at that time of the day. Evening was approaching, shadows
deepening. The fall air had taken on a sharp chill.

I got up, went directly to the dorm. My roommate left a note taped to
my reading lamp: "Cecelia called again! Give her a call, man." I did, but
there was no answer. Hanging up the phone, I felt myself step into a deep
loneliness that only she could fill. I hadn't answered any of her letters in a
while. I began a letter, pouring out my emotions. I grew sleepy partway
through, and when I awoke, moonlight was pouring in the dark room
through the open curtains. My letter was stuck to the side of my face. I had
slept through dinner and I was ravenous. I shook off my sleep and went in
search of food.

One of the national AIM leaders was invited to campus for an anti–
Columbus Day rally. Indian college student organizations throughout the
West were using the national holiday as a rallying point to bring attention
to Indian issues and concerns. The holiday was proclaimed a national day
of mourning for Indian people. We sponsored a one-day conference with
featured speakers and panel presentations by tribal grassroots activists.
Students and supporters wore black armbands that day to signify the day
of mourning.

Viola was one of the primary student organizers, bringing in tribal and
spiritual leaders from her reservation up north and around the state. You
could tell she wasn't in it for the glory. Unlike others, her walk matched
her talk. She rolled up her sleeves and did whatever had to be done to pull
off the event, even the shit work no one else wanted to do.

The national AIM speaker was something else. He came in all decked
out in a fringed leather jacket, bone choker, folded kerchief headband,
sunglasses with reflective lenses, talking rough and tough, eyeing all the
chicks. He exhibited that arrogant, macho, super-Indian attitude that gave
the movement a bad image among a lot of tribal people. But I must admit,
his speech was dynamite. I had never heard anyone speak out so boldly on
behalf of Indians like he did, calling an ace an ace, a spade a spade. He

raged against racism, injustice, the rape of mother earth, massacres, white-induced reservation dysfunction, cultural genocide. The white people in the audience, most of whom were sympathetic and supportive, were blasted. When the speech ended, they left, hair singed, ears burning.

After that event, I read between the lines of the anthro book more clearly and with a growing anger and resentment.

A local all-Indian basketball tourney was announced. Regional teams from northern California, Nevada, Idaho, and Utah would be competing for the trophy. The guys wanted to form a team to represent the student coalition. Nothing fancy, nothing serious, just a bunch of Induns playing out on the court, one of the guys told me. "Heard you played in high school. We could use you," he said. I declined. I had started out the semester playing intramural games with Herman and other guys from the dorm but that had fallen by the wayside. I didn't have the time or much of an interest in the game anymore.

"Hey, Julian," Herman said. "What's this I hear you don't want to join our team? What's with you, man? We need you."

"I don't know. . . ." I hedged.

He laughed. "What's there to know? You in?"

Since Herman was asking, I agreed.

Our team placed decently in the tourney though we didn't make the finals. Other teams had been playing together for years and were more serious about the game than us guys. I was somewhat frustrated by lesser skilled players—they tried, but, well, they couldn't seem to hold on to the ball or shoot with any accuracy. Herman clowned a lot and put the game in its proper perspective. But for me, the game wasn't the same anymore, not even with the chance to play against Devon and his reservation team composed mostly of ex–Indian school basketball stars. His team, the Warriors, won the tourney.

By mid-semester, Viola and I had a thing going on. No flirtations, no deepening attraction, no romantic nonsense, no talk of love. I mean, we were together all the time, putting more and more of our time into activism, getting involved with tribal struggles over water rights that pitted Indians against ranchers, sportsmen, and government agencies. We were so intense about the call, I guess it was inevitable that we shared the energy through our bodies.

Viola was always straight with me, I'll give her that. I don't think she could be otherwise. The main problem with me, she said, was that I wasn't the one. I guess I was too stupid to understand what she was saying.

Believing I must be in love with Viola, I wrote to Cecelia that it was over between us. With Cecelia, it was like we shared the same thought. No sooner did I think something than she spoke it. We'd always been that way and I had this eerie feeling even as I wrote the letter that she already knew what I had to say. I didn't stoop so low to compare Viola and Cecelia, but there were essential differences I didn't think about till years later. Maybe it was the difference between the physical act and an act of love.

Though I had cut her off, Cecelia was always with me like a ghost love. You know how people lose a limb to amputation and say they can still feel it itch but it's not there to scratch? There's a pain where nothing is supposed to exist? That's how it was for me. Cecelia was there without being there. I used to think what I would tell her about the issues I took up, think about what she might say about my activities. If I hadn't dumped her, she and Jewell probably would have come later to bust me out of jail. Or at least baked a cake with a file in it.

In that first year I knew her, Viola opened my eyes to a lot of political realities. At her urging I changed my last name from a generic American surname to an Indian one. A tribal name validated your Indian identity, she said. Names and naming were important, if not sacred, acts to tribal people. Why surrender such an important area to the white man? Why allow him to impose on a sacred realm?

Despite my parents' vehement objections, especially my father's, I legally changed my name to Morning Star, the English approximation of my grandfather's name before he was assigned a Christian name by boarding school teachers. The change was largely symbolic. If I really wanted to subvert political dominance, I should have retained my grandfather's name in our language, but adopting Morning Star was a radical enough move at the time.

My parents were totally bewildered by my politics, my hair growing past my shoulders, the grassroots people I hung with. In a lot of ways, we weren't on the same page. They were brainwashed by American propaganda into thinking America truly was the land of the free and the home of the brave, even for Indians. Like a lot of people of their generation, they were scared when radical Indians demanded what was rightfully theirs. Their fear was justified. Historically, renegade Indians were killed outright or imprisoned then killed.

My parents were just plain freaked out by the obvious changes they saw in me. They didn't know about other things. My scholarship was in jeopardy because of failing grades. Attending classes didn't seem so important when stacked against treaty rights. I was smoking weed heavily, scoring it by the pound, keeping my friends supplied. Viola and I were moving in together primarily to cut down on our expenses. Herman and I still were close, but our differences were increasing, creating strains. "Lay off that shit," he used to say to me about smoking dope.

Herman didn't say anything to me about Viola, but I don't think he ever much liked her, especially after she joined the local chapter of AIM and became more outspoken. He would just laugh her off when she started in on the warrior spirit of AIM, give me a handshake, say, "Later, bro," and leave. I never became a bona fide, card-carrying member of AIM but I was definitely sympathetic. A hardcore supporter.

I realized I wasn't in love with Viola when she moved on to California two years later with Al, a Lakota she had met at a national AIM meeting, one of the to-the-bone AIM guys who was in on action at the Trail of Broken Treaties and Wounded Knee II. Maybe my pride and ego took a blow when she told me, but I meant it when I told her I wished her the best. The guy seemed like a straight arrow.

By 1975, the curtains were drawing on the boarding school era all over the country. By then, most of the families I grew up with had either moved to other parts of the country or retired, my own parents included. I heard that Cecelia's parents had gone home, that her mother was not well. Almost overnight, the agency had become a ghost camp with the clapboard houses torn down and only the enduring rock structures remaining. The campus was still shady and cool in summer, though the grounds were no longer as well kept. The gym had gone dark and silent. Loneliness filled me to see the campus like that. With the last of my bridges burned down, I never went back.

I was still bummed by Viola's departure, by the hole I felt in my heart whenever I allowed myself to think of Cecelia, when I met up with Joe, a high school classmate I hadn't known well. "Indian Joe" we used to call him 'cause he was so quiet. He was still soft-spoken, but his words now took on an edge in his environmental activism against radioactive contamination of groundwater. He had the respect of both tribal people and non-Indian environmentalists, conservationists, and U.S. Fish and Wildlife reps. I offered my support and we began to work together. I was surprised by how much I knew about organizing a campaign, using the media, calling in favors, surprised by how many people I already knew who were willing to join the effort. Joe was the spiritual anchor, the main man I stood behind. If anything was going to get accomplished, I knew it had to be led by and involve the people most affected. They had to call the shots.

The work I put in during this time drew a lot of flak from mining corporations and high-powered citizens with vested interests, even brought death threats. But it also brought me deep satisfaction. I began to realize what we were fighting against, that the forces of hatred and greed were powerful. AIM people warned me to be careful. They also encouraged me to be strong. It was the only way.

My friend Hector asked a simple favor of me to drive his car across the state line to an AIM gathering. It was a large regional meeting, both a strategic planning session and a spiritual gathering. His old lady was there and needed a way to get back home. If I agreed, I was to drive down, hang loose, catch a ride back with her and the kids.

Side by side, arms across our chests, Hector and I leaned against the car as he gave me the lowdown on the gathering. Where it was, who'd be there, what was planned.

"They're serious about no drugs and alcohol, so don't take any in with you if you decide to go. They don't allow no loose weapons, either. The combination has caused some problems." He hopped up on the hood, patted his shirt pocket, and pulled out some smokes—regular nicotine—

then offered me one and lit his. We smoked, staring off at the junk in his yard, just shooting the breeze, talking about going fishing later in the summer, checking out the Sun Dance up in the Dakotas if his car held together after this trip.

"You thinkin' of takin' your ol' lady with you?" he asked.

"Ain't got an ol' lady no more," I said, flicking the ash from my cigarette.

He raised an eyebrow, and I told him about Viola splitting with Al.

Hector shook his head. "Shit. You're cut loose just like that. Well, one way to look at it is, you're a free man now. No obligations." He flicked the ash off his cigarette, was quiet for a moment. "Hey, man, I wonder if I can trust you with my ol' lady? You might be a little lonesome now."

We laughed. I told him I'd think about making the trip and let him know.

In the end, I decided, what the heck, I would drive the car to the AIM gathering, maybe get my head together. I didn't mind doing the favor, didn't mind at all when Hector told me I'd have company on the trip, some Indian guy I didn't know who wanted to join the sweat. "Be cool," he told me. "Be careful."

I was glad for the company during the long stretch through the desert and for the good weed the guy had. At this point in my life, I was sorting through my options, which basically came down to dropping out of college or hanging in despite my poor standing. It wasn't that college was beyond my ability. It just wasn't my priority. I was wondering what I was getting out of the white man's educational system, questioning whether I was just playing into the assimilation plot.

One thing I've learned is that nothing happens in isolation. Everything is interconnected.

In 1976, the fallout was heavy from the incident at Oglala the summer before when two FBI pigs got themselves killed. Everyone in AIM was on edge, fearing FBI infiltration, suspicious of one another. They knew the pigs were intent on wiping out AIM and Indian resistance. Like always.

Two FBI plants faking it as Indians had been uncovered, Douglas Durham, a pushy loudmouth, and a woman with a Hollywood-Indian name that she claimed had been given to her by the proverbial medicine man. These two did their best to smear the reputation of AIM in California by pinning the murder of a taxi driver on two AIM members. They set up the whole crime, using Indian people against their own, taking great pains to make sure the crime occurred at a so-called AIM camp, which AIM had officially disavowed because it drew mainly weirdo non-Indians, alkies, and druggies. The place had bad vibes as it was the site of numerous murders, and was near the ranch where Charles Manson and his women hung out. By himself, Durham did a lot of damage as he infiltrated the national AIM inner circle. He mistreated and turned off non-Indian AIM sympathizers and used and abused the media to make AIM look like rip-offs and criminals. Who knows who in AIM he may have identified to the FBI as ringleaders who needed to be eliminated.

During their all-out campaign, AIM leaders all over the country were arrested on various charges ranging from possession of marijuana to assault, which had been provoked or fabricated by cops, to false charges of murder. The charges were meant to intimidate, get AIM to lose heart and stop the work. Some AIM members were offered deals if they would sell out and testify in cases against AIM brothers. Even AIM sympathizers, Indian and non-Indian, were targeted, bullied by FBI agents and asked how they and their families would like to be buried.

AIM had made itself known as the defender of Indian land, treaty rights, sovereignty, and Indian pride. The movement grew out of the same pent-up, helpless rage and frustration that the Indian brothers come into prison with, the kind that blinds them into alcoholism and despair, then defeat. AIM wanted to break that cycle. It started in the streets of Minneapolis and in a matter of years, resistance spread throughout the country like wildfire. Indian people all over began reclaiming land and resources, resisting environmental exploitation, talking treaty rights and sovereignty. It even went beyond U.S. borders to the north and south. You can see why the government launched a conspiracy to smear AIM, make it look like a bunch of misfit Indian militants. Loose cannonballs. Dangerous renegades. A threat to internal security. Ever since the occupation of the

BIA building in D.C. in '72, AIM leaders were harassed and arrested across the country, driven underground. Some were dead.

The cop claimed he pulled us over for a traffic violation, though I know I wasn't speeding or anything. I suspect they already had the car targeted for a bust and looked for any excuse. The pig demanded ID from both of us. It turned out that my passenger, Gene, was an ex-con with a parole violation, which then caused events to take a heavier turn. The next thing I knew, the pig was back at the window with his revolver drawn, pointing it in my face, and he was ordering both of us out of the vehicle. He slammed me across the hood and had my hands cuffed behind my back when Gene took off. Before I knew it, it was pig city with every kind of cop car, cherries blazing, piled up around us. Well, it didn't take them long to catch Gene. The early media reports claimed we put up an armed resistance and said police officers feared the nearby AIM encampment would turn violent in response to our arrest. Yeah, right. Women, children, and spiritual elders, a large part of the gathering, were going to stage a shoot-out with heavily armed police. In the glove compartment, they found the dope and a pistol, and to my absolute surprise, in the trunk they pulled out rifles and ammo from under the blankets.

AIM hysteria among law enforcement was at its height then. I was roughed up, lost a tooth, had my cheekbone fractured so that now my face is a bit crooked. The second day in jail, the FBI showed up, told me I was in big trouble, facing some serious life-changing shit, they said. Some of the rifles found in the trunk, a .22, several 30-30 hunting rifles, and an AR-15 with an obliterated serial number, supposedly were stolen, and one, the AR-15, was linked to the killing of a prominent rancher in Utah whose body turned up on federal land. I didn't believe them. How could such a bullshit story come out of a favor to a friend? They told me they didn't believe my chickenshit story either. "We know you don't like ranchers," they said.

I was shaken, though I tried not to show it. I kept telling them I knew my rights and I wanted an attorney, but they told me I had watched too many TV cop shows, insisted they just wanted to "talk," nothing more. It didn't take long to figure out what they were up to. They weren't after me, though they knew all about my environmental activism. They wanted bigger fish, and they outright told me, although they later denied it in court, that if I were to help them catch the "real killer," charges of murder and illegal interstate transport of weapons would be dropped against me. The other charges, possession of an illegal substance and possession of an unregistered firearm, would be dismissed as well.

They intimated they knew exactly who the real killer was.

"If you do, why don't you arrest him? Or her?" I asked.

"You're a smart boy, Julian. Do the right thing," they said. "These people who call themselves your friends set you up to take the fall for a murder they did. They travel across the country first class, womanizing, talking big, raising hell, letting the little guys clean up their shit. Why would you protect such sleaze?"

I never doubted my Indian people, not then, not now. I thought I knew who they were after—a national AIM leader who lived in Nevada whose family they later killed.

"Okay, I'll tell you who did it." I took a big breath. The pigs sat up. I leaned forward and couldn't help but smile at their baited response.

"It was Patty Hearst."

My face got smashed into the table, and I quit trying to mess with them.

A red-faced agent put his face in mine. "You're nothing but a chicken-shit punk involved with a chickenshit cause, doing nothing but tearing down the country. You dumb-ass Indians are ungrateful for all the opportunities of America."

Even with the flagrant violation of my rights, I figured I had nothing to fear. I truly was innocent. True, I was guilty of a lot of things I never got caught for—transport of so-called narcotics across state lines when I knowingly and willingly picked up peyote buttons for use in ceremonies. That was freedom of religion. I had been with people when they obtained eagle feathers other than through the federal depository and supposed that would be considered an accessory. I smoked dope, grew it, sometimes sold it. I had defied orders to evacuate federal premises, participated in unlawful assemblies. I betrayed my girlfriend's love. But I never murdered anyone.

To my surprise and my attorney's, the agents testified that the fingerprint found on the rifle said to have killed the rancher matched mine. Gene, who didn't have to return to prison, testified that I had bragged about putting away the fat cat. I know, God knows, Peggy, I never touched that rifle, much less killed with it.

I was charged, tried, and found guilty in such rapid succession it stunned my parents and my lawyer. When the sentence came down and my name made the AP stories, the only thing I had to be grateful about was that my name change shielded my parents from public shame.

In Recovery

After I finished writing, I took a break. I had given Peggy the first part of my story, but not this latest installment. I'd let it sit awhile before I'd give it to her. Stirred by my recollections, I wrote a letter to my parents. My mother wrote to me regularly in prison, but I couldn't remember when I had last responded. Legal fees had drained my parents' finances, and now they live modestly back on the rez. My father is in ill health. Once a large man, he shrunk into himself. A proud man, what happened to me affected him deeply. I think that was pride he lost, not weight.

In the hospital a month now, the swelling at my throat had decreased. The doc said I was looking good and he'd operate in three to five days. My skin coloring had improved. It was no longer pasty-looking, but I did drop weight, my shoulders slightly concave, skin sagging on the frame.

When Peggy came in, she told me about how she had stood in her driveway that evening, keys in hand, gazing at the full moon. The features of the man in the moon were clearly visible. "Standing there with my mouth open, I felt just like a kid again. 'Hey guy!' I called up. If I was a wolf, maybe I would have howled into the night, it's that kind of moon. Made me feel good, infused with energy."

She did her nurse thing, checking me out, then glancing at my note-pad, she said, "I'm glad to see you're still writing. I enjoyed reading what you gave me. It was a good piece of writing there, guy. You had quite the rival in Devon."

Her words startled me, then I was surprised and pleased that she had even read it. I flipped my notepad to a blank page, jotted something quickly, turned the page for her to see.

She read aloud my words: "I saw Devon about ten years ago in the prison." She looked up from the page, raised an eyebrow.

I held my hand out for the notepad and again wrote: "He was in for armed robbery. We saw each other across the yard, but we didn't talk. He was only there for a short while before he got transferred to another facility."

She clucked her tongue. "How about Cecelia? What—"

Before she could finish her question, I pointed with my lips at the doorway where the new orderly stood uncertainly. Poor kid, he didn't have much going for him upstairs. He asked where was the supply of towels kept, he needed some to clean up the patient in O-five. She had already shown him the night before, I knew.

She gave me a shrug, told the orderly she'd be right there. I lifted one end of my notebook, a gesture to indicate there was more to my story.

The trauma ward turned busy and crazy like people were cracking under the pressure of the unrelenting heat wave. I had come in on the eve of it. Peggy said it was now in its record-breaking twenty-eighth day with daily temperatures averaging 105 degrees. An overflow on the maternity ward sent new mothers down to this floor. The beds filled up with moms and victims of freak accidents and criminal attacks, but I remained the sole occupant in my room. To top it all off, a crazed woman had attempted to steal a baby from the hospital nursery. All these hospital security guards flooding the floors were increasing tension rather than relieving it, Peggy reported. All worn out, she looked forward to the next three nights she had off. She would be making a transition to a day schedule, the afternoon shift.

Three days later, I was scheduled for surgery at 7:00 A.M. The doc informed me it would be a tricky operation. It had its risks as all operations do, not the least being the loss of my voice. First, he'd remove a bone fragment from my vocal cords, then repair my damaged trachea. Fly sure delivered one powerful kick for a faggot.

"Hey, Julian." It was Peggy's voice.

I stirred, briefly opened eyes that wouldn't focus, and returned to sleep for who knows how long. I wakened later to see a nurse, not Peggy, administer some pain dosage, then I was out again.

Another three days later, I was whispering, my voice hoarse.

"Hey, Peggy, I can talk. I sound like a frog." I touched my throat gently, avoiding the area where the incision had been made.

"Don't strain your throat trying to talk. How's the pain?"

"I live with it." I grimaced. "Gimme a mega-dose of painkiller."

Over the next few days, I continued to whisper. It was funny when Peggy started whispering back instead of speaking in a normal tone, a natural response, I suppose. As my voice gained strength, it sounded strange, not the same as before. It had become raspy.

"I misjudged the doc," I admitted to Peggy. "He's all right, did his medical best by me."

"Yes, Dr. Randall is excellent," she agreed. I didn't mean just his talent with a knife. I learned that the doctor stood up to prison officials who wanted me sent back to the prison, like now, like right off the operating table. I overheard the nurses talking about how the prison biggies had argued that I was a dangerous criminal and needed to be incarcerated for the public's safety. The prison infirmary could take it from here. Dr. Randall had gotten sharp with them, told them he was well aware of prison infirmary conditions and that for a full recovery, his patient needed the kind of medical attention their facility didn't offer.

"Dr. Randall told the prison administrator, 'I don't believe Mr. Morning Star is a threat to anyone. He has not demonstrated such behavior here on the ward. Intubation was discontinued this morning, and he is in recovery, still on medication, confined to bed. A posted guard is adequate for public safety in my estimation.'"

"Really?" the other nurse responded.

"Dr. Randall said he should have told them the patient was the one in need of protection, considering the severity of the attack on him. And if they had concern for the public, they ought to get a new guard. The one they have posted at the door is the kind of individual who looks lazy even when sitting. He makes you wonder about the waste of taxpayers' money."

"Yep, the doc's all right," I repeated, almost to myself. He wanted to keep me for another two weeks.

Peggy asked what came next when I returned to prison.

"Probably I'll be placed in protective custody, which is a laugh. If they want to get rid of me, there's plenty of ways. Or I could be transferred to another federal facility. You know, I wouldn't really give a sh—" I stopped short, looked at Peggy apologetically, then went on, "give a darn if it weren't for. . . ." I trailed off.

"Cecelia?"

I nodded, seeing beyond the room. My sense of regret was like a bottomless pit. Writing about her had stirred me up, made me wish I could tell her I was sorry.

"I made mistakes big time."

"We all do."

"At least I've had this time here with regular people." Being so socially inept and clumsy in social niceties, it was as close as I could get to telling Peggy thanks. She seemed to understand.

Lying in the hospital bed, all I have to do is think of prison life, and I can hear the clang of a metal gate sliding shut across the cell, feel the walls closing in. It comes back to me like I've never left it for a moment. Sicko guards. Beatings in prison. Murders, rapes, conspiracies. Mental anguish and torture. Prison can be a state of mind, you know, as well as a physical place of confinement and punishment. If you don't watch out, and you better, hope shrinks to a small dot, a faint smear on the wall, then fades.

I have to work hard not to let that happen.

I picked up a pen, adding an afterthought to my story:

At one point, I was dying. I could feel life seeping out of me like water leaking through a sieve. Flat on my back, I thought at first I was on my bunk in my cage. Then I felt the stirring of the wind, cool on my skin. I realized I was lying atop some kind of raised platform outdoors, looking up into the night sky. I could hear singing below me, Indian voices, mournful and sad, then a faint chorus of voices above me. As I watched, the constellations began to wheel overhead with dizzying speed, turning faster and faster till they became a white blur. I lifted into the night and began to move with the turn of the stars. An immense force sucked me toward its center. The pull grew more intense until I felt pulled into myself, becoming ever smaller, denser, insignificant.

Just when I thought I would suffocate, when my heart would be crushed, I suddenly felt a release and I curled up into myself. When I awoke to a blurred consciousness, bruises all over my body, blood dried on me, guards were carrying me out of the Hole to the prison infirmary.

"Man, what they do to you?" the con working the infirmary said to me.

Many of the Indian brothers who come into the pen believe the lie that until Indians become like white people, they're worthless, a pile of shit. Imagine that—to hate yourself, despise your people. All us Skins, incarcerated within or without, became separated from our true selves; we had to bring our selves back, or we'd either destroy ourselves or fade away into the larger society around us.

It's a struggle. It goes on and on.

They came to take me back about nine o'clock in the morning even though another eight days still remained on Doc Randall's hospitalization timeline. I realized I hadn't yet given Peggy the second part of my story. I handed the pages to the head nurse and asked her to see that Nurse Peggy received them.

As I was taken out amidst a circus atmosphere, wheeled out in a wheelchair by an orderly, two guards in front, one flanking me, and two behind, civilians craning their heads to see, I imagined Peggy's response later that day when she came in.

She'd get off the elevator, round the nurse's station, stop when she realized something was out of order, but it would take her a minute to figure out what it was: A guard was no longer sitting at the door to my room. She'd walk to the end of the hallway, turn into the room, see the bed empty and stripped. She'd stand for a minute, too surprised to move, staring at the bare room. Then she'd walk back down the hallway, check the patient board, and see "Morning Star" was no longer listed.

"Gayle, what happened to the patient in O-ten?"

Gayle would look up briefly from her computer screen, answering as she clicked the mouse. "The inmate? He was released around nine-thirty this morning, sent back to the prison infirmary. A whole entourage of prison guards came to accompany him like he was some big security risk!"

"But he wasn't scheduled for release."

"Apparently, the prison insisted on his return and put pressure on the hospital administration. Dr. Randall reluctantly signed the release though he wanted to keep him a few days longer."

Peggy would remain rooted to the spot. After a minute, Gayle would look up from her screen.

"Oh, Peggy! He left something for you. Some papers. I put them in your box."

Peggy would step behind the nurses' station to the slotted files. She'd recognize the yellow legal-sized papers torn cleanly along the perforated lines, my handwriting that looks like typeprint. She'd remember how I had become absorbed in my writing, barely glancing at her when she entered the room. "You're the busy bee," she had kidded.

She'd swallow, reach her hand forward for them. On the top corner of the first page, she'd read what I had quickly scribbled that morning: "Thank you Peggy for your time and attention. You're one helluva nurse, a true Florence Nightingale. JMS, #10105-702."

The Whole Truth

CECELIA — JULY 1996

I can't help but sigh every time I look at Jude. He's such a somber young man. I should be relieved that he now has focus; still, it worries me he's an old man before his time. He's studying computer graphics at a junior college. In high school, he wasn't much of a student, but now he was doing well enough. I just wish he'd lighten up.

He was taking in the view from my booth at the Indian Artisans Show at San Ildefonso Pueblo. We were located in the last row of booths facing north, the second booth on the east end, across from the adobe homes that formed one long line in the village plaza. Turquoise-painted windowpanes and door frames stood out brightly against the walls stuccoed in different shades of brown. Doors stood open, the interiors dark. One home had a porch with folding chairs and benches set out for the occupants who came out to watch the dances and eat watermelon. Our location was ideal to view the Indian dances scheduled every half-hour. Pedestrian traffic was heavy, too. The dancers in their colorful kilts, Indian shirts and scarves, and varied headdresses passed by. Other people drawn to the sound of the drum stopped to examine my work more closely and ended up buying.

Jude idly watched some kids fooling around on the porch then followed a group of senior citizens with his eyes as they passed, gabbing about visiting Indian friends in their home like it was some exotic thrill, and bragging about which artists they knew personally. I was keeping an eye out for Auntie Reena, who said she'd be by. It was already almost noon and I wondered where she was. Nia, the daughter of the heishi jeweler in the adjacent booth, sashayed past in a cloud of perfume. The tops of her breasts, two smooth mounds, peeked out of a low-cut denim dress with a lace-up bodice she had strategically left untied. An attractive young woman, she was making the most of her assets.

"Who's that?" Jude asked, suddenly alert. He watched her settle down behind the table covered with colorful heishi necklaces. Her mother spoke to her in the Keres tongue. She murmured a response. The older woman, dressed in the floral-print shift that women of her pueblo favored, white bobby socks, and red moccasins with thick white soles, seemed satisfied with her answer and continued to play patty-cake with the child on her lap. I was glad Jude had perked up, though I wish something else had caught his interest. Nia had a two-year-old daughter and a reputation as a heartbreaker. She noticed Jude watching her and smiled at him sweetly. Then she smiled at me before turning to fuss daintily with the arrangement of necklaces on the table.

"Two scoops," Jude said. I knew what he was talking about.

"That's Nia. I can introduce you if you like. She's not married, but she does have a kid. Right there." I motioned at the little girl sitting on her grandma's lap.

He seemed to lose interest. "Oh. Yeah, maybe later." He looked back out at the crowd.

"I'm glad you're here, Jude."

"You got it made, Mom. You just sit here all day, yakking with people, raking in the bucks. What the first two customers bought paid for all your expenses! It's been all profit since."

"This morning's been good, yes. But things could change this afternoon, tomorrow. It varies day to day, show to show; some shows, some years, better than others. You'll see. I just have to take it as it comes. Besides, you're forgetting all the work I put into making the pieces."

"Work? Pinching the clay around, then painting it?"

"Jude! It takes a lot more than that. You sit down with me the next time I'm working clay, and you'll find out."

"Uh-huh." He seemed doubtful about the prospect, but I got excited. Jude was good on the computer but maybe—I ended the thought there. I didn't want to get my hopes up.

He stretched in the chair, raising his arms in the air. "I'm going to go get us something for lunch before the lines get long."

"Good idea. Keep an eye out for Auntie Reena."

He walked around the table and down the row toward the concession stands. I saw Nia checking him out as he passed. Indignation filled me. Nia was such a, well, sexpot. She devoted herself to it, and my son deserved, well, better. Jude was an eye-catching young man, six feet tall with shiny black hair cut short and combed back, a pleasant arrangement of features. It was symmetry of features that made people good-looking I'd read in a magazine, and he had that along with strong features. He worked out, lifting weights, and his clothes, baggy as they were, looked good on him. Jude had my almond-shaped eyes, but the rest was all Julian. Would Jude be glad to hear that?

I gave a start to see Drew Kamore, the prison project director I had met at an earlier show, coming up the row. What luck—just the person I needed to see. Marli had suggested seeking advice from Drew about how to contact Julian. He spoke from a short distance as he approached with a companion, a light-skinned, pretty Indian woman. The two of them were overdressed for an outdoor art show, I thought, eyeing the woman's silk blouse and expensive jewelry.

Drew smiled broadly, his eyes sweeping the table, then resting on my face. Of all times for Jude to be gone. He turned to the woman and introduced us. She was a lawyer from the Northwest, in Santa Fe for a law conference, a session of which just broke, so they came out to the pueblo to catch the show.

"Hope you enjoy your visit, Denise," I said to the woman. Then to Drew, "I didn't get your card the last time I met you, and I've been wondering how to get in touch with you." His eyes lit up, and I rushed to explain. "I was hoping I could talk to you about how to locate a particular Native prisoner. Perhaps I could call you and explain the situation?"

"Of course. I'll be glad to help any way I can." Drew extracted a business card from his wallet and handed it to me. "Doesn't she do beautiful work?" he addressed Denise.

"I love it! The expressions on these storytellers' faces are so distinct. So lovely. Their lips are so delicately shaped and their cheekbones so prominent." She reached her hand forward. "May I pick one up?"

"She studied at IAIA," Drew told her. Impressed, Denise looked at me with admiration, then studied individual pieces. I was trying to remember if I had told Drew about my schooling the last time I saw him. I didn't recall doing so. The three of us chatted, Drew and I bantering as if we were old friends. Denise purchased a piece and I swathed it in layers of bubblewrap and put it in a box to safeguard it for her plane trip home.

"It was nice meeting you, Denise."

"Likewise. If you're ever in Yakima, look me up."

I nodded. "I'll be calling you soon, Drew."

"I'm looking forward to hearing from you." His eyes searched mine. Denise moved away, but Drew lingered for a moment as if reluctant to leave. She turned toward him to address him, and only then did he move away from my table. In a few long strides, he caught up with her. I watched till they passed out of my line of sight, then turned back to the passing crowd. I must have been smiling. A passing show official glanced at me, then gave me a wide smile, calling out, "Morning! Is it hot enough for you?"

Melvin, the silversmith in the booth on the other side of mine, responded, "No, it's not, Sam. She wants you to crank up the heat!" They laughed, deep throaty chuckles.

I picked up Drew's business card, read it, fingered the raised, gold lettering.

On Monday, after the show, before I unpacked my boxes to take inventory and wash the dust off pieces, I cooked Jude and myself a large breakfast. I rarely cooked full-blown meals, much less breakfast, but I actually enjoyed frying the bacon, eggs, and potatoes, mashing green chile, making orange juice and toast, and slicing cantaloupe.

"Whoa, Mom. You really went all out," Jude observed as he towel-dried his hair.

I laughed. "Guess I got carried away." I had overdone it maybe because I needed to perform some act of mothering. I knew I had put off talking to Jude about Julian for too long, and it was time to deal with it.

We stuffed ourselves and then, over cups of coffee, discussed plans for the week and gearing up for another show coming up in two more weeks. I let the conversation drift over inconsequential subjects before I put my coffee cup down.

"Jude," I began uncertainly. I didn't know where to go next. He looked at me, then down at the table when he saw I was struggling to voice something. His sensitivity touched me, enabled me to say, "Your father. You asked about him, and I told you I didn't know who he was. Well, that's not true." His head lifted in surprise, his eyes wide.

"I do know who he is, and I will tell you, but I want to explain some things first." He seemed to brace his shoulders. "I didn't tell you when you asked, I *couldn't* tell you, because, you see, your father wasn't just anyone. He was someone who meant a lot to me, and the hurt was just too bad when—" My mouth twisted with a remembered bitterness, but I went on, "When he wrote to tell me it was over. He had met someone else. I was young and just didn't know how to handle it."

Jude didn't look at me. His head moved in a barely perceptible nod. I continued, "The thing is, I never told him about you. He never knew I was pregnant, and I don't know whether that would have made any difference to him. I couldn't bear taking the risk of finding out. Maybe that wasn't fair to him or to you, but that's what I did."

Jude looked like he had the air knocked out of him, but I couldn't stop. I'm not even certain exactly what I said from that point on, but I did tell him Julian's full name, explained our relationship, how I left school in San Francisco and stayed with Aunt Virgie in Phoenix till he was born, then went to school at the Institute.

"It made sense to me then. I thought, just go on, do the best you can. Aunt Virgie offered to take care of you while I was in school. She urged me to go, not to worry. 'You've got to do it,' she told me. 'Don't wait till you're old like me before you do what you really want to do. Do it for the sake of Jude.' Everyone in the family said the same thing. At the time, Grandma

Judy's long illness was just beginning. She was too tired for anything. I knew she and Grandpa really couldn't take you in. They were so sad, so disappointed about my situation.

"Back then, people weren't so cavalier about unwed mothers like they are now. I never told them Julian was the father. I knew if they knew it was him, they would get him and his parents involved, insist on marriage, and I didn't want it that way. But of all the things I did, if there was one thing I could do differently, I would have kept you with me no matter how hard it would have been."

"My father's name is Julian?" Jude spoke in a voice of awe. "I always wanted to know." His mouth trembled with emotion. Then he took a deep breath and squared his shoulders. "Thanks for telling me." Tears filled my eyes. I dreaded telling him the rest. *Jude, your father is a convict in prison.*

Not telling Julian I was pregnant was my way of evening the score. If I had told him and he had said, "That's too bad, good luck," things would have probably gone along their same course, anyway. But he would be privileged with knowing. This way, I was denying him a chance to choose me, to give his child a name. I was angry. He had gone and met some la-de-dah radical Indian, probably slept with her right off the bat after all the cheap lies and promises he gave me about how much he loved me and how he would always be there.

After my initial shock had subsided when he wrote to tell me about—what the heck was her name? I can't remember—anyway, rage filled me. I tore up the few letters I had, photos of him, keepsakes like movie tickets and dried flowers. I threw the turquoise ring he had given me into the garbage disposal and turned it on, but after a lot of noise, all that happened was a few nicks in the band.

My anger might have been assuaged if he had called me, if he had asked my parents about me over Thanksgiving or Christmas. But he didn't. That's when I decided I'd be damned if I would tell him he had fathered my child. The most precious gift to come out of our so-called love would be mine alone.

Going into labor without Julian was the loneliest thing I have ever done. Labor was the culmination of my uncomfortable, frightening experience of pregnancy. Carrying a child was for mature women who were ready for the demands pregnancy places on the body and emotions. During visits to the IHS prenatal clinic, other Indian girls, deserted like me, some way younger, seemed frightened and ashamed; some stared defiantly with eyes heavily underscored with black liner. The married pregnant women, grandmas, nurses, and clinic staff looked at them with sympathy, sometimes with judgment. I hid behind a dated *Parents* magazine with coupons for disposable diapers and wipes already clipped out, acting as if my baby had come by careful planning. My heart ached in direct proportion to the increase in the size of my belly.

Both my mother and aunt told me labor and delivery were painful experiences, but nothing they said prepared me for the actual pain that racked my body. Over the hours, my contractions grew in intensity till at their peak, I felt my uterine muscles tightened into a band of iron, torturing me. I could see the stress in the faces of my mom and aunt, hear it in their voices as they tried to soothe me. Aunt Virgie was babbling on about how my Uncle Ernest used to drive her to the Indian hospital when her labor started, drop her off, and return three days later to pick up her and the baby without so much as asking what she'd been through. I could have cared less! I began crying, screaming, "I can't do this! I can't do this!"

When the Indian nurse came in to check me and saw me crying and twisting, she asked tersely, "Were you prepped for labor?" Scared silent by her brusque manner, I looked at her blankly. She shot an accusing glance at my mom and Aunt Virgie. "You are just wearin' yourself out," she said, disgustedly. "You won't have any energy left for pushin'. When the next contraction comes, I want you to take in a deep breath, like this." She modeled the breath. "Then let it out slowly. Begin to breathe with the contraction, slowly at first and then work up to a pant as the contraction intensifies. Your body will tell you. Then as the pain decreases, slow your breathin' again." She gave me a crash course in breathing techniques that pregnant women spend months practicing.

"One's coming!" I yelled in panic.

"Okay, deep breath. Look at me, honey. Honey, look at me!" she commanded me sternly. "Relax. Your face is all scrunched up. Breathe! I know it's hard, but try to relax. Breathe with me. Not too fast, now." Maybe she meant well, but her voice was cold. She walked me through the process, and I found my concentration on breathing made a great deal of difference. "Good girl. Now one of you," she glared at my mother, "come over here and do just what I did. You," she looked at Aunt Virgie, "can time the contractions. I'll be back shortly. It shouldn't be too much longer now."

When Jude was finally born, he just slipped right through my body. His infant cry pierced the air, then the doctor laid him on my stomach as she clamped, then cut the umbilical cord. Quieted by contact with my body, Jude seemed to be staring around in wonder. His body was wet and slippery, but somehow, my hands knew just how to hold him. I laughed in relief, in pure joy, in my own wonder, my heart full of love.

Jude's skin was a dark rosy tint, transparent enough to see blue veining. Downy hair covered his back and shoulders and his stomach seemed distended. His spindly legs were bowed, hands clenched into tiny tight fists, toes curled under. I counted all ten of them.

"You're beautiful," I told him, smoothing the silky pile of dark hair on his head.

I dressed with care for my meeting with Drew, putting on and discarding outfit after outfit. I wasn't sure exactly what I was looking for, but I knew I'd know when I found it. At last! Not too formal or too casual, a dress that said nothing. I wound my hair in a loose bun, letting a few tendrils hang.

I met Drew at La Placita restaurant in Old Town. Already seated at a table, he stood when he saw me and watched me walk the distance. He pulled out the chair for me and said over my shoulder, "You look great." The formality was nice, but it made me uncomfortable as I wasn't used to it. For years, I had been opening my own doors, paying my own way. He wore jeans and a dress shirt open at the neck, sleeves rolled up. I noticed other details—a fresh shave; the clean, masculine scent of aftershave; brown hair pulled tight into a small ponytail. Articulate and sharp, he spoke passionately about his work, the high incarceration rate of Native Americans disproportionate to the Indian population, alcohol as a major factor in crimes, working with inmate families, working the system, religious rights struggles. He mentioned an upcoming art exhibit by Native prisoners and a benefit concert to raise money to buy firewood for sweat ceremonies.

I let Drew carry the bulk of the conversation. My heart was pounding and my stomach churning throughout the small talk we made as we ordered and waited for our plates. When our food arrived, I picked at mine. I didn't know how I was going to explain my situation to someone I felt increasingly attracted to.

"So you wanted some advice concerning an inmate?" Drew posed the question as he pushed his empty plate away.

I put my fork down, picked up my napkin, wiped my mouth. Then I took a drink of iced tea, shifted in my chair, and bit my lip, all of which he watched. One hand cupped the sweating tea glass.

"Well . . . yes." My expression must have changed for Drew folded his hands together on the table as if he knew I needed some time to collect my thoughts.

"I . . . I need to find someone, find out where he is, what institution. I don't know where to begin. I thought you could be of help." I was hedging and couldn't stop myself. "You see, I knew this person a long time ago, and I heard he was later imprisoned, and I need to find him." I gulped down some tea, looked at Drew over the glass.

He was watching me, carefully weighing what I said, thinking. He waited for me to say more. When I didn't, he leaned forward. "What can you tell me of this person? His name, relationship to you, where he last was, that sort of thing."

I noted his sudden professional demeanor, how he asked his question in a soft voice as if he were coaxing a reluctant witness, encouraging her to tell the truth, the whole truth, and nothing but the truth.

I sat up straight, looked him directly in the eye, and told him Julian's full name. "He was my—" Just for the slightest microsecond I paused. "He's the father of my son, Jude. And Jude now wants to contact his father."

"I see." He didn't blink.

I dug my nails into my hands, felt something at my neck. A section of my hair had fallen loose from the bun. I reached up, pulled out the few clips holding it up, and loosened my hair, let it fall down.

When and where did you last see him? What was he convicted of? Do you know when? No idea where? Nevada, maybe? Were you married to this individual? Have you ever heard from him? How about his family? Where might they be reached?

I provided what little info I could. "I was only eighteen when I got pregnant and I never told him. I had Jude all on my own—with the help of my family, actually. I decided I never wanted to see him again, hear of him. I never expected it might someday be important to Jude." I sighed deeply, feeling on the verge of tears.

"What makes you think he's still in prison? Twenty years . . . ho!" He shook his head. "Maybe he got out on parole or served his time."

I looked at him, surprised. "I don't know why I assumed he was still in prison. Maybe 'cause I heard he got sentenced for something serious. Yes, I remember now, a life sentence. Doesn't 'life' mean the rest of your life? But you know, there is someone I could call and ask. My old friend Jewell. She knows everybody's business." Even as I said that I dreaded calling Jewell. I knew that was why I first tried Drew.

"You call your friend, and I'll begin looking into it. If he's still in prison, I can locate him." He ordered coffee for us when the waiter came by. "How'd you come to be in Nevada?"

After we left the restaurant, we browsed shops in Old Town. By the time we parted company, he knew my entire background. It was such a relief to be completely open with someone, to not have to worry about when and how to tell him about the past, wondering how he'd react, whether he'd lose interest when he heard I had a son. Drew promised to call as soon as he had something to report.

We celebrated our high school graduation together, the first time since junior high the four of us, Julian, Herman, Jewell, and I, got together. In a class of three hundred, we were a handful of two handfuls of Indian students who made it through. Jewell and I had planned to go party at the Indian colony that night with older guys she knew. It was a big deal that they were older, nineteen, for God's sake, but at the last minute we changed our plans when Julian and Herman pulled up at the curb to ask us if we wanted to go with them to the lake for the class party. We hesitated, looked at each other.

Jewell gave them a hard time like she always did. "Why would we want to party with you jerks when we can party with some real men?"

"Real men!" Herman snorted, then erupted in sudden laughter. He looked at Julian behind the wheel. "She said 'real men.' " He shook his head, burst out laughing again. Jewell stiffened beside me.

Julian smiled, leaning over to look through the open window at us. "C'mon, Jewell. For old time's sake." When he said that, he looked right at me. I experienced such a funny feeling at that moment, suddenly remembering those long-ago times when the two of us were alone together. *Julian, Julian.* His name had been a song in my head through the years. I had turned the volume down low, but still it was there, and I knew it. I said nothing to let him know I hadn't forgiven him for dating Tiffany, the blond cheerleader. And Brandi. Heather. Francine. Girls who never saw me, never once spoke to me.

"Whadda ya say, Cissy?" Herman teased, calling me by my nickname. By his slurred words, I knew they had been drinking.

"Devon won't like it," I said, bringing up Devon's name to throw in Julian's face. Jewell stared hard at me. She was the only one who knew I had already broken up with him. Julian stared out the front windshield then back at me, then out the window again.

"What Devon don't know won't hurt him," Herman shot back. "Time's a'wasting. You coming or not?"

Jewell looked at me and shrugged. "Okay with me, if it's okay with you."

I shrugged back. "What the heck?"

"If it's a bomb, we'll look up the party at the colony," she whispered as we climbed in the backseat.

I don't remember much of the graduation party except Jewell got loaded to the max, all sentimental about old times. She got out of hand, went into a crying jag, and Julian and I had to take her home.

I dipped my brush into a smear of red paint and I gave form to the galloping horse I had penciled at the top rim of my seed bowl. A few brushstrokes and his mane, his tail, flew back. I had one more horse to paint in a spiral of seven horses that wound around the rim to the small opening, then the pot would be ready for firing. The phone rang. I put down my brush and pot to answer it.

"Jewell! Thanks for calling back. How are you?" I spoke into the phone, my tone upbeat, not betraying the swirl of emotion within me.

That's all I had to say for the next five minutes. Jewell went on in detail about where she was when I had first called a few days earlier, where and what she'd been doing for the past ten years, the last time we had talked. She now had three daughters, a preadolescent and two teens, all driving her nuts—were we ever like that, she wondered. Soon after high school, she had married Max, the Stewart student she dated in our senior year. He had turned out to be an enterprising soul, now running his own crew as a housing contractor, putting in bids for tribal projects. Jewell had gotten a bachelor's degree in education from the University of Arizona and was running an Indian ed program, making sure, by golly, that the public schools did right by federal funds earmarked for Indian students, not like they had ripped us off when we were in school. In between her personal update, she asked quick questions. You married yet? Still doing pottery? Traveling?

She spoke to someone in the room with her. "Honey, I'm on the *phone*. Go ask your dad." She spoke into the phone again. "Sorry. Kids! I envy you, Cecelia, still being single, no kids, no one telling you what to do, whining that they're hungry, tired, they need this, they need that. No one told me marriage was hard work. If they had. . . ." She trailed off. Despite her words, her tone was smug. She didn't mean what she said. Jewell had always thrived on people needing her. In high school, I was one of those people.

"Jewell. I'm trying to contact Julian. Do you know anything about him? Where he is?"

"Julian! Funny you should ask about him. I was thinking of him 'cause—I'll tell you later. He's still in prison as far as I know. Been there, let's see, almost twenty years—can you believe that long? I can't. I don't even know what he was convicted of. Assault with a deadly weapon? Maybe it was felonious assault—the same thing?—some kind of bogus charge, anyway. It's all crap. I never did believe any of it." Her tone became indignant. Her mouth was right over the phone and I could hear her breathing. "If anyone knew him, we did. He was probably framed, screwed over with some made-up charge, the way they did to all those AIM guys. He was in tight with AIM in its heyday." She snorted. "Lot of good it did him. Where is AIM now when he needs them? We were probably the only true friends he's ever had. Last I heard of him—remember, I was away at school in Tucson when the whole thing happened—he was still in prison. Been no news since. Seems like they stuck him in prison, threw away the key. Guess they got him busting rocks or making license plates. God!" She breathed hard into the phone. "No one I talk to has heard from him, even of him, in years. Have you?"

"No." My voice was hoarse in my ears, defensive.

"Oh, right! Otherwise you wouldn't be asking." I could hear the curiosity in her voice. I braced myself. In high school, Jewell had hawk eyes that could make uncanny assessments with a sweep of her eyes, a sharp mind that recorded every minute detail to be retrieved later on a moment's notice. She could put two and two together, subtract the distractions, and detect the deepest secret. She would wedge into any crack she'd find and pry until she'd break you down, learn everything you knew and more. I hid myself from her all the years since high school, keeping the distance between us, mumbling my excuses for her persistent suggestions for a reunion.

"What a waste of talent." She was still searching for information, probably hoping I'd add something. My tongue cleaved to the roof of my mouth.

"Actually, I always thought Julian liked you more than he ever let on. He was always showing off for you." She laughed and I joined her weakly.

"If any one of us was going to end up in prison, I never would have picked him. Any one of the rest of us bums, but him, no."

"Listen, Jewell, I've got to tell you something." I took a big breath and blurted out the pertinent details about Julian and me. It seemed that once I opened my mouth my story was getting easier and easier to tell. For once, Jewell went quiet. When I finished, when it was out that I had borne Julian's son, Jude, now in his twenties, there was a brief silence on the other end of the phone.

Then, "My God, Celia! Why didn't you ever tell me? I don't know what to say. Congratulations? I'm sorry? And you said Julian doesn't know, either? *I* should have known! This is too much!" She spoke to one of her kids again, "Go away! I'm busy." Then she called out, "Max! Help me out here!" Back into the phone, she said, "Okay, Cecelia. I want the whole story. How did you and Julian, you know, get together? Why didn't you ever tell him?"

It was like old times when we hashed over boy problems. At various points, Jewell was appropriately sympathetic, indignant, outraged, then helpful. "I see why you need to find Julian. I can't imagine how he'll feel to learn he has a son. I'm going to have to meet this kid myself, Cecelia! I'll ask around about Julian, let you know what I find out. I'm thinking that you should also let his parents know. They'll freak to find out they have a grandson, poor things. I heard they took it hard when Julian got tossed in the slammer. Julian's mom was always so nice to us. She made the best gravied stew and fry bread, ever. Ummm! Hey, they'd know how to reach him. They moved away, I don't know where, but I'll try to find out about that, too. I can't believe we don't know beans about where Julian is."

"Wouldn't Herman know anything? You ever see him?"

She cleared her throat. "Herman was killed about a month ago. His younger sister, Kerrie, the one we called Brat, called to tell me."

"Oh no." My voice was tiny, like it came from someone else far away. "What happened?"

"He was shot outside a bar. From what I heard, it involves a love triangle. You know Herman. Always had a girlfriend. And one or two more on the side. That guy! A regular Romeo." She gave a little laugh. "He was married for a while but guess it didn't work out. Anyway, he started seeing this one woman, Darla Stevens, really pretty Indian woman from Elko. She was divorced from her old man, but he was a jealous son of a gun. Apparently, he picked a fight with Herman outside the bar, and he shot him in the chest. Killed him instantly."

We were both quiet for a moment. "I'm sorry to hear that. It's so hard to believe. Really, he was too young. Not that any of us are spring chickens anymore, but you know what I mean."

"Yeah." Jewell was silent for a minute.

"Remember . . . ?" I began hesitantly. "Remember how Herman used to drive Mrs. Cox crazy with his phony fainting spells on the playground?"

Jewell laughed. "Yeah! He used to fall down on the cement court, all limp whenever his side was losing at basketball."

The first time Herman faked a collapse, we immediately ran for the teachers. We gathered around to watch, excited that he might have died right before our eyes and scared at the same time that he might have. The P.E. teacher knelt beside him, raising his head, gently slapping his cheeks. Another teacher stood over him to provide him shade with her shadow and instructed us to keep our distance. "Give him room to breathe."

Someone called for Mrs. Cox, the school principal, who came charging across the playground, her ugly black ankle-length coat flapping like buzzard wings around her. She pushed through us, offering assurance that everything was all right, just step back, she'd take care of things. When her first aid ministrations failed to revive him, she stood up, and in a shaky voice that feigned calmness, she called to her secretary, "Beverly, call an ambulance!"

At her words, Herman sat up, acting disoriented. The side of his face had dirt and gravel stuck to it, his hair all matted. In a weak, pitiful voice, he asked, "Where am I?"

He pulled that stunt repeatedly and got away with it each and every time! The next time he did it, Mrs. Cox tapped her black clunkers next to his head and shrieked, "Herman! Herman, you get up right now! Right this minute, young man!" And when he failed to respond when she poked him with the sharp point of her shoes or even when someone threw the basketball and hit him in the stomach, she'd yell for Beverly to call for an ambulance.

Picturing Mrs. Cox with her cat-eye glasses askew, her frizzy hair sticking out all over, utterly losing her cool, I laughed so hard I could hardly speak. After Herman did that a couple more times, the rest of us would just keep on playing around him, stepping over him, sometimes on him but not on purpose. Sprawled out in the middle of the court, he'd lie there until Mrs. Cox personally came. Even if the bell rang, he wouldn't get up for nothing, not until Mrs. Cox came.

Jewell and I laughed at the memory until our laughter subsided to little gasps, and we settled into a calm silence. Remembering Herman in that way made me feel better for a minute.

When Jewell spoke again, it was in a different voice, subdued, regretful. "He was a lot of fun. Him and Julian. Too bad the way things turned out for them."

"Isn't it?"

That night just as I was drifting off to sleep, I heard the faraway wail of an ambulance. I recalled waking up earlier in the summer out of my dream of horses to that same sound, whispering Julian's name. I opened my eyes to the dark. Was it Herman's death I dreamed about? Herman and Julian had been best friends, practically inseparable. *Please, God, let it be Herman and not Julian.* I was instantly struck with guilt and began reasoning that Herman was already dead, nothing I could do to change that, so it wasn't like I was wishing something bad for him. Maybe Herman just wanted to say bye, get the wheels in motion to bring us all together. He never did like conflict. Herman was that kind of friend, faithful to the end.

Practically My Whole Life

JUDE—AUGUST 1996

I sat on the back porch, slouched into the old patio chair, flipping through the newspaper as a distraction, skimming news print, reading here, there. Cecelia and Drew were in the kitchen, fixing dinner. I needed to get away from the faker. Drew didn't fool me. He was no Indian. The moment I met him, I saw right through his act, his scam. He was looking to save the day, find my dad so he could prove he was a good guy, and get me to look up to him. He wanted to legitimize himself by getting an Indian woman and wrap up the deal before my dad complicated the scene. I just hope Cecelia wasn't that stupid. His voice drifted through the open window. I rattled the paper, scanned the headlines to occupy my mind.

A whole series of articles focused on the heat wave: "Heat Wave Continues Unabated; Elderly, Infants and Homeless Adversely Affected." Drought conditions prevailed, water conservation measures were in effect for city residents, campfires were banned. Rain evaporated before it hit ground. Forest fires raged throughout the West, destroying thousands of acres of national park lands, forcing park closures. Four firefighters narrowly escaped death when a wind-whipped fire jumped the fire line, trapping them in a ring of flames. They hit the ground, covering themselves with their asbestos shields. One was quoted as saying, "In a moment like that, suddenly you know what's really important in life."

Damn, it is hot, I thought. Some iced water would be good, but I wasn't about to go back inside. I folded back the paper. It seemed the heat was making people testy. The planned reintroduction of gray wolves in west-

ern states was meeting with vehement opposition by ranchers. Cranky
U.S. senators up for reelection in the fall were cross-examining FBI officials about the 1992 FBI raid of a suspected white militia group at Ruby
Ridge. Former FBI agents were singing like canaries, confessing past sins
of how they had infiltrated select political groups as far back as the '60s,
directed smear campaigns to discredit leaders, harassed and arrested them
on trumped up charges, mishandled and manufactured evidence in FBI
labs, and down and out lied in sworn testimony against group members
during trials.

I looked up from the page. The whole story of government conspiracy
was worthy of becoming an Oliver Stone movie starring Tom Cruise as the
conscience-stricken FBI agent trying to do the right thing in a paranoid,
corrupt agency. But how come the white separatist involved in the shoot-
out at Ruby Ridge got over three million dollars for the death of his wife
and son and a congressional investigation, and Leonard Peltier just got
thrown into the slammer after the shoot-out at Oglala?

Huh.

Next page. Record crowds of men seeking to reclaim their roles as
leaders in the home were flocking to men's movement rallies. Columnists
praised this guardedly, wondering if this was a male backlash in response
to feminism. In another story, super-predators, young criminals with no
sense of remorse or fear, were predicted to be unleashed soon on society.

I wondered if all these different news articles weren't related in some
way. Maybe someone could write a rap song based on the stories, make a
music video with forest fires raging in the background, heroic firefighters
digging trenches, seeking to confine flames leaping up ponderosa pines
rising 200 feet in the air, gray wolves leaping through hoops of flame while
ranchers in white cowboy hats, federal marshals, and young skinheads
with Nazi insignias tattooed on their thickened biceps picked them off as
they leaped through. Female backup singers, a blond, a Latina, and a black,
would sing "Hot, hot, hot!" as the sweat glistened on their near-naked
bodies. As the music swells to a crescendo at video's end, the committed
dads in the men's movement, wearing sports caps, Bermuda shorts, and
Denver Broncos T-shirts, rush in with fire hoses to douse everyone. The

camera pulls back and the word HELL is superimposed on the scene as the people twist and gyrate in the water falling like rain, steam filling the scene as the camera fades out.

"Jude, it's time to eat," Cecelia announced from the door.

"Hey, Jude, come try this," Drew called from the kitchen in that annoying "let's be buddies" voice he used on me.

I pulled back from the video playing in my head and vaguely waved my hand at her. She stayed at the door.

"Are you coming in?"

"Later."

I was once a boy who needed to love, and be loved by, his father. Now I'm a man who desperately wished for that love. I wanted a dad to show me how to be a man. To play ball with me, take me fishing and hunting, show me how to change the motor oil, cuff me on the head, put a hand on my shoulder. I needed a model to measure myself against, someone to tell me where the path goes and what to do when it disappeared or came to a dead end.

My whole life, I have always longed to know my dad. I wasn't the only kid growing up without a father, but I was the only one who didn't know his father's name. Who he was, what he did, where he was at. What his favorite team was. Why he wasn't with Cecelia. Did he ever think about me, wonder where I was, what I looked like? Maybe he didn't give a flip. Maybe he had b.o. potent enough to gag a bum. Maybe he was a boozer getting bottled all the time, so he could barely hold down a job. Then again, he could have a family he treated good. Whatever the hell he was, he wasn't around for me, the bastard child. At least he knew who he was. I didn't.

I heard Drew laughing inside. He irritated the hell out of me. It seemed like he was always calling on the phone, or Cecelia was going somewhere with him, or worse yet, he was over here. He sure was taking his sweet-ass time about locating my dad. If I answered the phone when he called, I'd bark, "Did you find anything yet?"

I picked up the newspaper again, shook it out, read a few more articles until my eyes grew heavy. I leaned back in the chair, covered my face with the newspaper, and fell asleep.

I dreamed about my dad. He was standing, motioning me to come. I could see his body from the chest down but not his face, which was in shadow. He was huge, dressed in a bright orange jumpsuit like the kind detainees from the county jail wear as they pick up trash along the freeway. For some reason I grew afraid, stopped in my tracks, and turned at a noise I heard. A little boy about ten years old approached, then hesitated a few feet away. He stared at me with dark eyes. A chill went up my spine. "Who are you? What do you want?" I demanded, fear evident in my shaky voice. He continued to stare, mute. He stepped closer. Though he was just a kid, I raised my hand as if to strike out defensively. The boy's face darkened in anger. He stepped back, tossing what I thought was a rolled white sock at me. It fell at my feet. I picked it up, surprised that it was a softball. I looked up, but the kid was gone.

"Jude. Jude! Are you hungry?"

I took the paper off my face and focused my eyes on Cecelia standing over me.

"Come on in and eat." She looked closely at my face. "Are you okay?"

I looked at her hands, which were empty. I sat up, shook my head, let out my breath in a whoosh. Perhaps she took it to mean exasperation because she quickly added, "Drew's gone."

"Yeah, I'm hungry."

I got up and followed her inside.

To get away and clear my head, I spent part of my time down at Isleta, hanging out with my cousins and uncles. I sat with *Meh-meh* Two Bucks and Auntie Reena's old man, Buckley, in Reena's kitchen one morning. She had served us coffee, sweet bread, and canned peaches, urging us to eat. Knowing I was available, Buckley had called me to help him in the field.

"Two Bucks" was *Meh-meh*'s nickname earned for the rodeo escapades of his youth. "Yeh," he told me over his cup of coffee, "I'm one of a kind. Two Bucks. Too much for one woman but not enough for two." He threw back his head and let out a deep laugh. Then he started coughing. *Meh-meh* was getting old. He was still a big man, but his brown skin hung on him, and he moved slow. He was no longer farming the fields, no irrigating, mowing alfalfa, baling or hauling hay. Just tending a small garden of corn, tomatoes, chile, and melons in his backyard.

He pointed at my baggy pants with a finger thickened and gnarled as the exposed root of an old cottonwood tree. "Those pants are big enough for two men. Sure you don't got some extra tools in there?" He hit my arm with the back of his hand.

Buckley winked at me.

Back in his day, Two Bucks used to strike terror in the hearts of all us kids 'cause he never let us get away with any mischief. Cecelia says it was the same when she was a kid. But he had a tender spot. Once when I got bit by a red ant and was crying good and hard, he first doctored me with mud that took away the sting, then led me out to the ant pile. "Show me which one bit you. I'm going to kill it," he said.

"I don't know which one. They all look the same."

"Well, when you see the one that did it, you let me know. I'm not going to let any ant get away with biting you." He took away the hurt with that.

"*Too quai,*" let's go, Buckley said when our cups were empty. The family spoke to me in bits and pieces of the Tiwa language.

I nodded and picked up my work gloves from the table. We headed out to haul a load of bales.

"Come back for lunch," Auntie Reena called.

Out in the field, beads of sweat dripped down my face as I lifted another bale into the trailer bed. I took off my T-shirt drenched with sweat. It felt good. Work hard, eat well. I'd sleep soundly tonight.

It was hard not to get bitter and resentful, jealous of other kids with dads, even kids with part-time dads, loser dads. I started telling people my dad was dead 'cause that was easier than the truth. It got me sympathy. My dad died in the Vietnam War, I decided, jumping on top of a grenade to save his buddies. His death kinda drove my mom crazy, I explained, and we couldn't mention his name. My mom really couldn't raise me, and my grandma was sick, so that's why I stayed with my aunt in Phoenix. After a while, I just said I didn't want to talk about it, and no one pushed me on it.

But I lived with a lie and a desperate longing for the kind of family I watched on TV shows, imperfect but forgiving.

I didn't do very well in school. While the teacher talked at the front of the room, I'd fill my notebook with detailed drawings. I stumbled through the grades, passive, overlooked because I was passive, which created conflicting feelings in me, both relief at not being hassled and anger at not being challenged. I just drifted along, graduated with no plans. If no one cared, why should I? I started doing drugs, marijuana and cocaine, dropped some "ladies," as my Hopi friend Dwight called them. I didn't even know what they were, only that the world began to glow and I floated on air.

Dwight was my friend since high school. We were tight. Friends were the only ones I trusted. Adults always wanted something more from you, like you weren't good enough just the way you were.

To earn a living, I drove delivery trucks, unloaded stock, took inventory at a lumberyard. I also worked maintenance for a short while at the Indian hospital, good bucks there, but too boring. I bussed tables at a family restaurant, busted my ass for a small-time moving company, assembled electronic parts for a big-name business. All jobs going nowhere. Whatever, as long as I had pocket money for the ladies.

Dwight had a motorcycle we used to fly around on. We would go out to the nearby Salt River and Gila River Pima reservations, visit friends there, ride the dirt roads. One summer evening I remember, we were on our way home. It was around ten o'clock, the air just barely cooling off. For some reason, the engine stalled on us, and we were forced to walk the bike. We didn't mind, what with the ladies keeping us company. The desert night was pitch-black, the lights of Phoenix in the distance. We hadn't gone very far when Dwight suddenly stopped without warning so that I walked right into him.

"What the—" Before I could ask why he halted, I saw the reason. A dark figure was approaching.

"It's Butch!" Dwight was amazed and excited.

"Who's Butch?"

"My cousin. What's he doing here?"

"Ask him." I felt cool air moving over us.

Dwight handed the bike over to me, and he moved toward Butch. It's not clear in my mind what happened next. The night was dark, my ears were buzzing from the effects of the drug. I don't remember that Dwight said anything, then I heard a scuffling noise, and I strained my eyes in the dark. It looked like Dwight was dancing with Butch. I pushed the bike forward, and Dwight yelled over his shoulder, "Get the bike going!"

I heard the fear in his voice, and I automatically responded, running past them with the bike. I stopped, swung my leg over the seat, balanced the bike, turned the key. The engine responded, and I opened the throttle. I heard Dwight running up from behind. As soon as I felt him on, I gave it gas and we leaped forward, the back wheel briefly spinning in sand before we flew down the road. I didn't stop until we reached my place.

My hands hurt from gripping the bike handles so hard. I worked my fingers, checking out Dwight. The side of his face was bruised, and he was covered with dust.

"What happened back there?"

"That Butch is freakin' crazy. He got me down on the ground and was trying to choke me."

"Why? What was he doing walking down the road?"

"He wants to take me with him."

I was watching the light from the lamppost. It was splitting into pieces, falling like rain to the sidewalk. I turned slowly to Dwight.

"Take you where?"

"He's dead."

"You mean we saw a ghost?"

He nodded. I don't remember how we got into my place, something about climbing in a window, but once inside, Dwight told me that Butch had died the summer before. We both were so frightened we stayed up all night with the lights on. That incident scared us straight for a short time.

We saw Butch again one night the following winter after the basketball game at the Salt River tribal gymnasium. Dwight hadn't told me, but he had seen him again the previous month when he went home to Hopi. A similar struggle had taken place, but Dwight managed to get away and run all the way back to his grandmother's.

"Shouldn't you do something about this?" I asked him.

"I did. I was told to stay sober."

"Have you?"

"Till tonight."

"Oh man. That's it. We're going home."

That was the last time I saw him. I avoided him after that, not wanting to lead him back into booze and drugs, not wanting to risk seeing Butch again. Dwight's sister, Alma, and her husband came to tell me of his death. April Fool's Day. He drove his motorcycle off a mesa. She didn't believe that. Neither did I.

I swore off all drugs and booze then, but even without them, I re-mained a zombie, empty inside except for a deep anger that fed on my pain and confusion. Sober, I couldn't escape myself. I didn't like who I was—another Indian screwup going nowhere fast. It hurt so bad.

I had to do something. In the fall, I tried school and found a little piece of myself. A start, but it wasn't enough.

By spring, I decided I needed to locate my father and confront him with my presence. Whoever he was, whatever he was doing, however he re-acted, it was all right with me. I could handle it. Over the years in lots of different ways, I had asked Cecelia who my dad was, but she had never answered. Even as a kid, I picked up the message that she didn't want to. So out of respect for her, I quit asking directly and poked around the family, but nobody knew anything, not even the kids, who always find out the secrets adults try to hide.

If I ever was to know, like it or not, I had to outright ask Cecelia. I mulled that over for months before I acted. I know I blew her away with my question when I called her in June from my place in Phoenix, but I didn't expect that her answer would do the same to me:

"You won't get mad?" I was trying to work up to the topic before she slammed shut the door on it.

"About what?"

"I've been thinking for a couple of weeks now, well, actually since Father's Day, and even before that, really." It was more like my whole life. "Well, I was wondering about my dad? Where he is? If—"

"Jude. You know, I've told you before that was impossible."

She was maneuvering to close and lock the door, and I stuck my foot in quickly. "You don't have to get involved if you don't want to. I can ask my mo—" I caught myself there. I called Aunt Virgie "Mom" 'cause she was a mom to me as well as being my auntie. I finished with, "Aunt Virgie for help." Hell, I wasn't even asking for much.

"That's not the problem." Okay. I bit my lip, remembering I had told myself, "Whatever it takes." I settled into patient mode, ready to solve any problem, totally unprepared for what came next. You think you know your own mother, but when you find out you don't know shit about her, your whole world can turn upside down. What kind of woman doesn't know the father of her child?

"*I'm sorry. I was so young. I just don't know who.*" What the hell kind of answer was that? The kind that played over and over in your head, making you sick and angry at the same time, that's what. And after offering me nothing, not even a glimmer of hope, she wanted me to visit her, to give up a job that was beginning to define me. Like that would help. She didn't know what it took for me to work up the courage to ask about my father. At that point, I didn't want any part of her, not her stinking money, not any of her precious time.

When I hung up the phone, I was shaking. I sank down into the dingy plaid cushions of the couch I found at the flea market, staring at the blank TV screen, seeing nothing, no past, no future. The aching emptiness of earlier years swelled in me. Then I was sobbing, crying for myself and the family I never had. But my anger grew bigger than any sorrow I felt, and I was cursing through my tears, choking out the F-word over and over. All I had was fucking sperm for a dad. Breathing hard, I picked up the remote, flicked on the TV, then picked up the controller for the video game player, and pressed down hard on the On button. I played mind-numbing game after game till a friend from the community college showed up, and we went out and got wasted, another familiar form of mind numbing. I hated myself even more for that slip.

If it wasn't for Auntie Marli, I probably wouldn't have come to see Cecelia at all. She called Aunt Virgie one evening early in July when I was visiting her, then asked to talk to me. I thought it was just going to be the usual "Hey, Jude, how's it going" conversation. I could tell right away it was something different by her somber tone.

"Jude, I'm going to ask you to do something. I haven't ever asked you to do anything, so you know this has to involve something serious. I'm asking you to come see your mom."

"I don't—"

She cut me short. "Hold on. Listen to what I'm *not* asking, first. I'm not asking you to quit your job. I'm not asking you to stay a long time. All I'm asking is that you come for at least a week."

"Why? Why do you want me to come? Cecelia already asked me, and I told her no way. I got this job through the community college that pays real money, and I get training, too. I don't think they'd let me have any time off."

"Yes, that's what she told me, and I can understand why you wouldn't want to walk away from an opportunity like that. But what I'm asking you to do is important, too. Your mom needs to talk to you about. . . ." I could tell she was searching for words. ". . . the two of you. And it could affect your future. I mean, this is about family. Jude, you're in a family, and when family needs family, family should be there."

I had no idea what she was talking about. "Huh? What are you saying? Spell it out for me 'cause I'm not very good at guessing."

"Oh, Jude!" She was exasperated. "You're going to have to take my word for it that this is something important you need to do. Let me put it this way. Your mom needs you here. Never mind why. Would you please come?"

Suddenly I thought maybe my mom was dying like Grandma Judy had, and maybe Cecelia couldn't bring herself to tell me. Death could come as easily for any of us as it did for Dwight. I tightened my grip on the receiver.

"Is something wrong? Is my mom okay? She's not sick, is she?" I held my breath, bracing for the worst.

"She's okay, health-wise. Nothing's wrong, nothing bad like illness. No, no, no. Nothing like that. I don't want to worry you. That's not what's behind this. Will you come?"

The tension left me. I let out my breath. "I guess." My answer was begrudging.

She didn't say anything.

Really, it wasn't such a big deal. I cleared my throat noisily, shifted the phone to the other ear. "Yes, I'll come."

At Marli's invitation, I went to spend the day with her and check out the UNM campus. After her morning class, we sat in her office. Her eyes were bloodshot. Looked like she had been up half the night. She asked me to take a look at a disk that her computer couldn't access.

"It won't open 'cause your disk is ruined," I told her. "See." I pointed out the metal tab on the back, which had been bent at one end. "Don't carry your disks around loose. Buy a case to keep them in."

"Can't you straighten out the metal?" she asked, hopefully.

I laughed. "Nope."

She sighed heavily. "You were my last hope, Jude. I've reconstructed about half of my paper, but the ideas aren't coming out the same. As students say, it sucks. I don't know. Maybe I've just built up the original in my mind."

I don't know why she hadn't saved on the hard drive. "Disks are unreliable," I informed her. She looked blankly at me. "The more important the document, the wiser it is to save duplicate files on the hard drive and on at least two disks."

I handed her back the disk. She threw it in the trash can.

"That's what Earring Boy at the computer center told me. I've been running myself ragged trying to make the deadline. I don't think I'm going to make it."

I had to ask. "Why didn't you save on the hard drive?"

She sighed again. "I was working on my article both here at the office and at home, and I just worked off a disk. The article kept changing as I worked, and the disk just made sense. I don't know what I was thinking."

"Don't you have a rough draft lying around somewhere?" I indicated the piles of paper on her desk.

"Nah, I've already looked. I threw out rough drafts in a fit of cleaning. I had finished the paper, after all. Everything would be okay, but my paper was stolen."

I widened my eyes and opened my mouth. She related in great detail how Arnie, her ex, took off in her car and stole her camera and CDs, as well as her paper.

"Are you sure?"

"He denies it, but he did it," she stated flatly. She ran down a long list of his flaws, topping it off with "He's such a loser."

"You want me to rough him up a little bit, tell him to give the paper back?"

"Thanks, but no. Come on, let's go have lunch. Tell me about what you're studying. You sure know a lot more about computers than I do."

Over lunch I told her about my bad experience in school and my nowhere life, about Dwight and the turnaround in my studies once a tutor told me I was a visual learner and gave me tips on note taking and studying.

"Amazing. Makes me wonder how I learn. Through the school of hard knocks, I think," she said, staring thoughtfully into space. Waving her fork in the air, she said, "You know, I'm through playing the role of the victim. From now on, I'm a woman of action, not reaction. One way or another, I'll finish my paper. And it'll be better than the first one."

"Go for it."

"Likewise." We clinked our water glasses together.

The phone rang. I turned my head from the television screen. I could predict who it would be. What's-his-face, the lawyer. I flicked off the set, picked up the phone. "Yeah? Yeah, she's here. What have you found out, champ?"

It seemed I didn't have much time to savor the name of my dad before Drew butted in. Seven days to be exact. I drove up from Phoenix, barely got settled, went to the Indian Artisans Show with Cecelia at the end of the week, and then she told me the following Monday. I was on a natural high for those seven days after her gift of a name. I smiled with pleasure at the memory. Cecelia. She blew me away again. I mean, I about fell off the kitchen chair when she told me she did know who my father was and that she'd tell me. Yes! I could have leaped off my chair, jumped in the air, and twirled around the room like a little kid. So thirsty for knowledge of my dad, I drank in every word as she explained the situation between her and Julian, the reasons she did what she did with her life and mine. With a tinge of guilt, I realized I never had given any thought that my mother might be as wounded as me. I couldn't look directly at her, my heart was too full.

"My father's name is Julian?" She nodded, smiling faintly. My heart was beating like a drum in my ears. "I always wanted to know." Always. I took a deep breath and looked her in the eyes. "Thanks for telling me."

Her eyes were glistening, then her shoulders folded and she began to sob. With a great effort at control, I saw her take a big breath, wipe her eyes, hold herself upright. "There's more, Jude." Her voice wavered. "Your father is in prison."

She leaned across the table, placed her hand atop mine, letting me absorb that. "As far as I know, he's more of a political prisoner than a criminal. He got a life sentence is what I heard, but we'll find out where he is, what all the facts are. I'm sorry I have to tell you these two things at the same time."

I lifted my head. "We'll find him wherever he is. Whatever it takes."

We got up from the table and I bear-hugged my mother. Then I felt my own heart twist, then my mouth, and I was crying for the sense of family I now had.

"I recently met someone who works with Native prisoners. I can ask him to help locate your dad. We should be able to find out some information soon."

That's how Drew figured in. Only thing, his finding Julian wasn't coming soon enough for me.

I handed the phone to Cecelia. "What's-his-name still hasn't found anything."

I left the room as she was saying hello, automatically headed to the back porch, my place of solitude. I settled down in the chair. The cushion was molding to my body contours.

Julian. The name connected me to him. I liked to sit and think about the man, put some flesh and bones on him.

"You resemble him," Cecelia had said. That helped place me, but not to visualize him. He'd be forty-two now, be way changed from when he was my age. I did find out he was involved with the American Indian Movement, and that intrigued me. Militant Indians kicking butt. Standing up for their treaty rights and mother earth. All right. But my thoughts dead-ended. AIM wasn't more to me than slogans. Would I ever believe in a cause I'd sacrifice my life for? Cecelia didn't know the exact charge for which Julian was imprisoned, but she thought it got him a life sentence. Did he kill someone or was he involved in an event that resulted in someone's death? Was he involved in a kidnapping? That seemed like an AIM warrior thing, grabbing a liquor store owner, an FBI agent, or a mining rep and holding him hostage to make a point. It made a lot of difference to me that his imprisonment was political. In my mind, that put my dad in a whole different category than if he was robbing convenience stores or doing psycho murders. Suddenly remembering the testimony of the FBI agents reported in the newspaper, a thought came to me. *What if he didn't commit the crime at all? He's been doing time for twenty years—practically my whole life!* Cecelia told me not to jump to any conclusions, just wait to see what Drew found. I saw in her eyes, she was anxious herself. I suddenly felt protective of her.

It was such a relief to know my mother wasn't a whore. I could say it now. It's too hard to imagine what she went through all these twenty-some years. She must have been hurt badly, which leads me to wonder about my parents, and then I stop myself. After finally finding out about my dad, I don't want to be forced to take sides. Cecelia was right. Don't jump to any conclusions. Hope for, and believe the best.

At a family dinner, *Meh-meh* Two Bucks was giving Marli a hard time. He had asked her what classes she was teaching at the university. She told him the title of her Native studies courses, "Cultural Values and Survival" and "Native American Life and Thought." Hearing them, he said, "Maybe I should enroll in one of your courses, so I can learn how to be Indian."

"We don't teach anyone how to be Indian. That's impossible," she said in an exasperated voice.

She was saved by Auntie Reena's call for dinner. After she fixed her plate, she sat down across from Cecelia and me.

"I've got something to tell you guys. I am so embarrassed," Marli said.

"What?" Cecelia asked, reaching for a slice of oven bread.

"Yo." My mouth was full.

"I have the original copy of my article."

"Did Arnie give it back to you?" Cecelia asked, amazed.

Marli took a sip of her drink. Her cheeks became flushed. "No. A student did. It seems I accidentally mixed in my paper with the graded ones I returned to the class. She returned it this morning and said, 'Oh, I've been meaning to bring this in. Like, you know, I thought this might be kinda important.' Just a little bit."

"No!"

"Oh, man!" I laughed.

"I am just so embarrassed." She gave a short laugh. Then she stopped with her plastic cup midair, a startled expression on her face. "My God, this shenanigan is worthy of Clyde!"

"Who's Clyde?" I asked.

The artists on either side of Cecelia's booth at the next intertribal art show I attended proved to be entertaining. To the left of us was a stone sculptor who brought only one piece to sell, a buffalo about three feet high. He was a funny guy, giving out jokes as good as he got them.

"This the only thing you brought? You better sell it!" customers told him.

"This is the only thing I brought. You better buy it. It's the last buffalo and a bargain at three thousand dollars!"

Everybody laughed, but nobody bought.

On the other side of us was a silversmith. The way the wife acted, you'd think she made all the pieces. She kept interrupting him every time he spoke with an interested buyer.

"Tell her how long it took you to make that piece, Dennis." When he didn't respond in the few seconds she allowed, she told the woman who had lifted her sunglasses to look closely at the pin she held in her palm, "He spent hours just cutting that piece. It's one of a kind."

"Yes, I can see that."

"It can be worn as a brooch or on a necklace." She leaned over and motioned the woman to turn the piece over. "See? This piece I have on is like that."

"Is that right? I believe I'll take this. Do you have any others? I still need to get something for my neighbor. She's watching our dogs for us."

"Show her the others, Dennis. That one is twenty-five dollars. I'm sorry we don't take checks, just cash or credit cards." She pulled out the cashbox and was ready for a transaction. She gushed on, "I just love my piece. Everyone always remarks on it. I'll put a couple of Dennis's cards in with your purchase. If you're interested in more, you can contact us at the address."

Sheez. And my mom wonders why I have no interest in getting married. I've never had a serious girlfriend, never have done much dating. I'm in no hurry.

I nodded my head in their direction. "How can you stand it?"

Cecelia looked at me like she didn't know what I was talking about.

"That one," I nodded again at the wife who was still going on.

"Oh. I tune it out."

"Some of the artists here are more strange than their art. There's a guy over there, white as flour. Some Navajo guys were teasing him, saying they had to wear their sunglasses when they looked at him to avoid the glare! He was wearing a fringed leather vest and a black hat with a beaded hat band. He had on a turquoise bracelet with these incredibly huge chunks of stones. If he hit you on the head with it, you'd be out for days. Another woman with hair dyed pure black looks like an old, moldy hippie in a long skirt. She's got these weird braids." I laughed in remembrance. "I thought this was supposed to be an Indian art show."

"They're all supposed to be Indian."

"Reminds me of Drew." I threw that one in. She didn't say anything. Lately, she hasn't been responding to my comments about Drew. When he called yesterday, I told her she had a call from Mr. Big Toe.

"Big Toe? Who's that?"

"Your friend, Drew. You know, he's Indian in his big toe."

I changed the subject. Our space faced west, and the afternoon sun was halfway in our booth. "This is hard work."

"Yes, it is."

"You like it?"

"Yes, I do."

"You do good work, Mom."

"Thanks."

After the show as I sat unwinding on the back porch, I let my thoughts go. In the darkness behind my closed lids, I floated down a river, gazing up to the night sky, the moon, bright, a large ball in the sky. The little boy in my dream handed me the softball. I felt it in my hands, round, solid.

"Thanks," I told him.

The Real Thing

The evening air was still warm as Drew and I approached the KiMo Theater where the Native prison art show, "From the OTHER Side," was on exhibit. An interesting site for the show, I thought. The KiMo in downtown Albuquerque was an old movie theater built in the Pueblo Deco architectural style of the 1920s, a short-lived style based on lavish embellishments of Southwest Indian motifs. Named a historical building and saved from demolition in the remake of Albuquerque's downtown image, the KiMo was renovated to its original grandeur and now served as a performing arts center. The exterior of the building was eye-catching with its colorful Pueblo-design panels above the second- and third-floor windows, blue-painted windowpanes, tiled box office, and Indian designs adorning the front.

Back when it first opened its doors in 1927, the governor of Isleta Pueblo, Pablo Abeita, won the contest for the naming of the theater, I told Drew. KiMo was supposed to be a Tiwa word, *Kim-mu*, meaning lion, but the name was mispronounced as "Ke-mo."

"Is that right?" he marveled as he held the door open for me. We stepped into the cool interior of the theater. The ceiling looked to be made of vigas, but I knew they were really plaster beams, textured and painted to resemble vigas. On the walls were Carl von Hassler murals of Pueblo villages with blue mountains and cloud-filled skies. I looked up at the painted skulls of long-horned steers mounted on the columns supporting the "vigas," then took in the wrought-iron railing lining the balcony, and rain cloud and thunderbird designs painted on light fixtures and beams.

Drew glanced around. "It's a bit cool in here. Would you like me to get your wrap from the car?"

"I'll be fine," I assured him.

"It's no problem. It would only take a minute—"

"No, I'm fine." I touched his arm to stop him from going back out the door. I appreciated his concern after we had earlier sat under an air conditioner vent in the restaurant, but I didn't want him to leave. For once, I wasn't arriving alone, wondering if anyone I knew would be there yet.

There was an edge of excitement and anticipation in the air, in the quiet buzz of people's voices, their purposeful movement in one direction, the click of their footsteps across polished floors that led to the screened-off exhibit hall where the artwork was on display. I loved attending the opening of a new art exhibit and all the fanfare that accompanied it. Some of the artists who were included in the show, though they weren't prisoners, worked with AIM, Native prisoners, or environmental or political causes and would be introduced at 8:00 P.M. Drew had said the city mayor and the Navajo Nation president would also be in attendance.

A young Indian woman in a beret, probably a university student, smiled as she handed us flyers for the benefit concert. I signed the guest book, and looked around the lobby for exhibiting artists or dignitaries as I waited for Drew to sign. Indian men carried a large drum into the hall. A few people, waiting for friends, perhaps, watched us, even as they pretended not to. A couple of women gave Drew a second glance, then as they noticed me, looked past me. For their benefit, I leaned in close to watch him write his address. He smiled up at me, put the pen down, and we followed a couple across the room.

A large sign posted at the hall's entrance warned that the exhibit included content that some viewers might find offensive; parental discretion was advised for children under eighteen. I paused. People moved past without even stopping to read the sign. I reread the warning, swallowed, and turned to Drew, but he had already entered the room, where a modest

crowd milled in front of various works. Paintings, drawings, and photographs were hung on the walls of a large, plain room with ceiling-to-floor
windows spilling in light from Central Avenue. More paintings hung on
freestanding screens. Multimedia work was set up on pedestals in the
center of the room. On the far wall near the windows, a U.S. flag, images
painted on it, hung upside down.

I stopped before the first exhibit I encountered, a series of glossy black-
and-white photographs of police arrest scenes. One photo captured a
policeman with upraised billy club bending over an Indian man in soiled,
rumpled clothing lying on his back on the ground. In an effort to protect
himself, the man shielded his head and face with his hands and arms, and
drew in his knees. The officer's legs were bent, locked into position, to give
power to his blows. In the background, another officer was running toward the scene, his hand touching his billy club hanging at his side. Paper
wrappers, brown bags crumpled around bottles, cigarette butts, and other
trash littered the area. It had to be Gallup, I surmised, by the pawn shop
and bar signs visible.

A second photograph took me by surprise, caused me to inhale sharply.
A Navajo woman wearing a long velvet skirt sat in the open door of a squad
car, her blouse fully open, her large, sagging breasts exposed, her nipples
large and dark. Her head hung down to her chest; stringy, unwashed hair
obscured her face. She was utterly defenseless. Unable to look at the photo
further, I glanced at the artist credit and noted that the photographer won a
journalism award for exposing police brutality in—I was right—Gallup.
With a sense of dread, I scanned the other arrest scenes. The blacks of the
photos were rich and sinister—the squad car, the pistol and holster, the
shadows; the whites, in contrast, looked dingy. I didn't have the stomach
to study them individually.

I headed toward Drew staring up at a painting. Someone called his
name and he turned to greet an acquaintance. He held his arm out toward
me, indicating he wanted his friend to meet me. He introduced me to Tom,
a lawyer he worked with. Tom turned pale eyes on me, studying me as
Drew told him I was a potter-sculptor and unnecessarily described my
work in detail. "And her storytellers emanate such dignity, an aura of their

own," he was saying. Tom's eyes dropped to Drew's hand placed casually on my shoulder, moved back to my face, and then to Drew, whose eyes were shining as he talked. Conscious of the intimacy Drew's hand on my shoulder implied, I gathered my hair over that shoulder. The movement caused Drew to lift his hand, and I shifted my stance slightly away from him.

When Drew finished, Tom gave me a slight nod and politely asked, "Is that right?" He squared his shoulders to face Drew. A look of annoyance momentarily crossed his face, and I realized he and Drew were engaged in some kind of ongoing competition, a one-upmanship. "Nice to meet you," I smiled curtly at Tom, holding out my hand, then turning to Drew, I said, "I'll look around."

I crossed the room to examine a multimedia display. It took me a few seconds to realize that the stark enclosure I was looking at was a prison cell in which Barbie dolls of various skin tones were situated. Naked, with blood-red paint streaked on their bodies, including their private areas, they were posed in various positions, lying down, sitting, standing in a corner, the hands and legs of some bound with string or handcuffs fashioned from string stiffened by glue. Their eyes and mouths were blacked out with Magic Marker. My hand rose to my throat, and I took a step back. The title of the piece, "Inmate Barbie," shocked me in its play on Mattel's packaging slogans. By the time I made it halfway through the exhibits, my heart was pounding. The expression of oppression and anger in some of the pieces overwhelmed me, not that all the pieces were provocative. Drew was still talking to Tom, only now two other men had joined them in a collegial circle. I could hear their deep voices, see them gesture with their hands, but only make out a word here and there. On one hand, I was relieved to be alone in my reactions to the exhibit; on the other hand, I felt vulnerable, standing alone before scenes of real and implied violence.

I turned back to a painting to see an Indian man staring at it intently. Sensing my presence, he turned and smiled. "This one is nice, isn't it?" he said. I had to agree. Entitled "Sunrise, Sunset," it was the sun-streaked sky viewed from a cell window. Standing there, we talked quietly about our reactions so far to the exhibit. He introduced himself as Pete, the head of a drum group who would be singing at the benefit performance. "All the money earned at the benefit will go to buy firewood for sweat ceremonies at different prisons," he told me. "You planning to go?" I nodded, and he told me a little of his sobriety struggle and how his involvement with a drum group helped keep him on the right path. As we moved along to other paintings, sharing space with other viewers, he introduced me to social workers he knew through his work with the Albuquerque Indian Center.

"This is Cecelia Bluespruce," he said to a huge Indian guy named Dallas and another older man with eyeglasses, named Joe. "I don't know what she does, but maybe she'll tell us if you two behave."

We laughed, and I told them I was a potter-sculptor. "Now, hey!" Dallas said. "A silent auction is part of the benefit performance show. Perhaps, you would like to donate something."

I agreed and we exchanged names and phone numbers. The three liked to joke a lot, and I felt my tension dissipating. I looked again for Drew and saw him still in conversation in the same place. At that moment, he turned and saw me. He gave a start and turned back to his group, made his excuses, and headed toward me.

"So sorry," he apologized. Pete, Dallas, and Joe looked at him curiously, then at me. They went silent, and as they figured out Drew and I were together, they backed off. "Call me and I'll come pick up whatever you'd like to donate," Dallas said. He nodded politely at Drew and moved off with Pete and Joe.

"They're nice guys," I told Drew.

He nodded. "What do you think so far?"

Disturbed by the art, I suffered nightmares. Painting after painting in heavy brushstrokes had depicted wolves. Wolves with yellow eyes. Red eyes. Matted fur. Hiding in brush, staring out from behind bars or security fences with coils of concertina wire at the top. Other multimedia work included smears of human excrement and blood, and desecration of the U.S. flag. A few paintings were pastoral scenes, eagles and hawks soaring among clouds, the night sky, the painting I viewed with Pete. Review of the show in the arts section of the newspaper emphasized the objections to the desecration of the U.S. flag by veterans and the pornographic content of some work by a Satanist priest.

After a nightmare, I'd lie awake, wondering what Julian had experienced in prison, if he was anything like the boy I remembered. Of course not, I told myself. How could he be? And I'd grow frightened, questioning the wisdom of trying to locate him. But Julian's upbringing didn't fit the profile of the typical Native prisoner, Drew said. Being in prison for so long would make him a survivor, a leader. I appreciated his words and their calming effect. They gave me strength.

The benefit performance at the end of the week drew a motley crowd of young and old, professionals, activists, university students, Indian people from the reservations around the state and from the Albuquerque urban community, people who came for the silent auction or to support the effort, and those who came only for the entertainment. This time I went with my guard up, told myself this was not a date though Drew and I went out to dinner before the show, and Drew acted like he thought it was.

We heard speeches and testimonials by family members of inmates, former convicts, a religious rights activist, Indian people who had suffered police brutality or got caught in the cracks of the judicial system, and recovered alcoholics leading the sobriety movement. Pete was one such presenter, speaking movingly of his hard journey to recovery. He emphasized the link between substance abuse, violence, and crime that leads to incarceration. In between speeches, local Indian bands performed. The speakers must have been turned on full blast. I felt the music reverberating in my chest; some older people made their way up the aisle to the lobby.

During intermission while Drew was in the men's restroom, as I browsed the donated artwork, I ran into Pete and Dallas.

"Good talk, Pete!" I told him.

He waved off my remark. "I just speak from inside," he said, patting his chest over his heart. "Who you with?" he asked, curious.

"Drew Kamore. You know him? He works with the Southwest Native Prison Project."

"Seems like we should, huh?" he said to Dallas.

"Huh?" Dallas said, cupping his ear. "Dang, I can't hear anything. The amps are turned up too high in there."

"Is he your husband?" Pete asked.

"No!" I was taken aback by the question and surprised at my vehement response. "He's a friend. I'll introduce you when he gets back." We stood talking for a few minutes about the poor review the art show received, shaking our heads that the media always gravitated to the sensational, like the work of the Satanist, at the expense of other works that made important political statements.

"I had nightmares after the show," I confessed.

Dallas nodded. "I helped put it together. We should have considered audience reaction in exhibiting some of the pieces, but we didn't want to exclude or censor any artist. This is the first time we've done something like this. Next time, we'll set up guidelines before we solicit work. I heard the Satanist wants some of his bizarre rituals honored the same as the religious practices of other Native Americans."

"How does an Indian become a Satanist?" I asked, truly astounded at the notion.

Just then Drew returned. I introduced him to the others, including his tribal affiliation in my remarks. As I spoke, they looked him over, shook his hand, then glanced at one another.

"Nice bolo tie," Pete said. "I ought to get me one." He made a motion as if he were adjusting a bolo.

"So you're a lawyer? Do you know Buddy Small? He's a Cheyenne lawyer working on advocacy for Native prisoners." There was a challenge in Dallas's voice.

Drew looked down at the floor, shook his head. "No, I don't." Drew looked at me briefly and then away.

"Well, you should make a point of knowing him if you work in advocacy. What reservation did you say you're from?"

His face slightly flushed, Drew launched into a lengthy explanation of how he didn't grow up on his reservation, but his family originally was from the Northwest. His grandmother was enrolled and lost her land holdings when they were leased out to white farmers. With her thumb-print as signature, she granted permission and they later used that same thumbprint to sell the land. The BIA did that to most of the tribe and now the reservation was checkerboard. With what little land base they had left, the tribal council wanted to open a casino, and they were going to do it over the protests of tribal members.

"You know Henry Road Jackson? He's from that neck of the woods."

Drew shook his head. "Can't say I do."

"Anne Laws? Bill Palmanteer?"

"No," Drew said stiffly.

"Who do you know, besides your grandmother?" Pete and Dallas laughed, but cut it short when they saw me frowning.

"Well, hey, it's a pleasure to meet you, Drew. Come on down to the center and visit with us sometime." They shook his hand lightly and Dallas added, "You, too, Cecelia. Come on down for one of our gatherings. Bring some of that Isleta bread with you!"

The sound of guitars being tuned came from the auditorium, signaling the show was resuming. People began to return to their seats, though at least half of the crowd headed for the exit doors.

"Shall we go in?" I said to Drew, who stared after Dallas and Pete. He seemed relieved at my suggestion. As we went back in, he told me of all the Indian leaders he did know, when and where he'd met them. Why was he so defensive? His name-dropping seemed silly. I suddenly felt tired as I sank into the same seat I'd occupied earlier. A young couple a few rows ahead sat with their heads close together, leaning into each other. Out of nowhere, I remembered the one concert and the movies Julian and I went to, how my hand felt in his, how it felt to rest my head on his shoulder. A vague ache washed over me.

If it weren't for the fact that the top Indian bands, nationally known, had yet to play, I might have called it a night. As it was, I sat through the performance of a long-haired, shirtless Satanist who cut himself as he jumped wildly around on stage, screaming his lyrics. Many indignantly left partway through his act and didn't return for the remainder of the show.

"What do you think?" Drew asked as we drove home.

I couldn't put my finger on exactly what I thought, what I felt. The experience was strange, confusing, overwhelming, even humorous at times, though the humor was not always intended, like when groups of dubious talent played on too long despite the frantic gestures of the emcee to cut it short. "It was a good cause, but—"

"But what?"

I closed my eyes to think. I felt numb. All I saw was a whiteout. There were no familiar landmarks, nothing to guide me as I took one blind step forward.

I said the first thing that came to mind. "It could have been better coordinated."

"I thought it was a good mix of talent."

"Bloodletting and screaming is talent?"

"It's artistic expression. Freedom of expression is important. One individual's idea of art and how to express it should be respected."

"Well, yeah, but I felt violated in some way by that guy. I'm sure I wasn't alone in my feeling. Sometimes the group, and what's best for the group, is more important than the individual. At least that's what I was taught, what I believe."

"Community standards can lead to censorship. The status quo can stifle art." His voice had a slight edge as if he was annoyed at having to state the obvious.

"Are we talking about art or goofiness? Most Indian artists know the difference between artistic license and violation of tribal norms. If an artist has internalized community values, he or she will respect them and have no desire to violate them. If an artist chooses to do his own thing anyway, well, he should know he's taking a big risk and will have to face the flak." I sighed, thinking of the wild-haired Satanist. "But that's a problem in itself. The sense of tribal community and responsibility is diminishing."

"Why do you think that?"

"Oh, Drew! Lots of reasons. Loss of traditions. Urbanization. Intermarriage. Acculturation. I'm too tired to get into it now. My ears are ringing. Aren't yours?"

Marli, Rupert, Drew, and I sat at the picnic table in my backyard, eating grilled burgers and hot dogs. Jude ate his hamburger as he stood by the charcoal grill. He didn't want to sit at the table with us, with Drew, actually, and the fact wasn't lost on any of us, though on the surface we all accepted his excuse that he needed to tend to the steaks. Right from the start, Jude had disliked Drew.

"What's up with the white guy?" he asked me when we were alone in the kitchen.

"Jude! He's part Indian."

"Huh! Talks like a white guy and acts like one, too."

"Be nice. He's helping to find your father."

"Some help." His voice was bitter. "He can't find nothing. If you ask me, either he's incompetent or he doesn't want to find him. Or—" He looked at me accusingly.

I didn't know what to say. For some reason, Drew could not locate any inmate currently incarcerated or imprisoned within the past twenty years by Julian's name. He had even checked state institutions though I was pretty sure he had been sent to a federal prison. He double-checked the spelling of his name, *Julian James*, searched again, and still nothing. Without any further specifics, all we could do was wait on Jewell and see what she could find out.

Drew had called me daily for the past month. After the first few calls, he dropped the pretense that it was all business. I had been so excited at first, then we went to the inmate art exhibit and then the benefit concert, and my excitement dimmed, I thought, because of the emotional overload of the bizarre elements of the exhibit and performance and the tension of trying to locate Julian. I was waiting, I now realized, for the initial attraction to deepen.

Jude's blunt assessment of Drew made me uncomfortable. Drew did talk and act like a white guy. And it bothered me. But was it Drew himself who bothered me or Jude's hostility to him? All I knew was I had no words to defend Drew. And I needed them.

"Hey! Sounds like the phone is ringing," Marli said.

I ran in to answer it, but the handset wasn't on the base. I listened for where the ringing was coming from and searched frantically in the vicinity. After what surely had been ten rings I still couldn't locate the phone. Marli came in.

"Did you get it?"

"No. Help me find the phone." I pressed the page button repeatedly and Marli searched. Finally, she pulled it out from between couch cushions.

"Jude! He never puts the phone where it belongs." I was annoyed. "And he keeps turning off the answering machine. Pisses me off."

Marli looked at me sympathetically. "They'll call back."

"I hope so. Thought it might be Jewell."

"Guess that explains why I can't reach you sometimes. I was calling you the other night. I was so upset."

"Why? Wait. Let's go in the kitchen."

Marli leaned against the sink while I stood by the table where I could see the guys in the yard through the window. "Auntie Reena came to see me, and I was so shook up by what she told me. I just needed to talk to someone about it."

"What was it?" My hands on a chair, I leaned forward.

"Remember the Indian Artisans Show when she was supposed to show up and meet Rupert, then she never showed up, and we wondered what happened to her? Well, it turns out she was there long enough to find out who Rupert's dad is." Marli's lips were drawn tight.

"Who?" I held my breath, curious.

"Her ex-husband! The uncle from Laguna we never knew!"

I gasped. "No lie?"

She shook her head, sober-faced. "Then, get this, she went to Uncle Two Bucks to ask him if that meant Rupert and I were cousins!"

I felt my eyes grow. "What did he say?"

"You know Two Bucks. Bless his heart. He said, quote, That man was never your husband, much less an uncle to any of the kids. Don't worry about it, end quote."

I laughed. "Good answer. I wouldn't know her ex-husband if I met up with him face-to-face. What did he do? Cheat on Auntie?"

"You better believe it! She gave me an earful of what he did. Told me she was afraid Rupert might be the same."

"Rupert?" I looked at him through the window, hamburger in hand, talking to Drew, unaware he was under discussion. "No way. He's a homebody."

"That's what I told her."

"What is it with women in our family? We have a knack for picking them, don't we?"

"God! Tell me about it!"

Drew dropped by unexpectedly one evening. All week I had mentally rehearsed conversations with him, trying to find a way to back off from the relationship without jeopardizing the search for Julian. Drew had just driven in from Tsaile, Arizona, where he had attended a tribal government symposium at Diné College on the Navajo reservation, and he was still hot on the topic. I was wondering how I could work the conversation around to my rehearsed lines when Jude walked in the front door. He had been headed for the recliner to sit down, but as soon as he saw Drew, his eyes narrowed and he veered off for the kitchen. Unsmiling, he just barely lifted a hand in response to Drew's greeting and grunted at my question, "How was your day?"

Drew went right on talking about the need for tribes to exercise their sovereignty, but I quit listening. I wondered if he realized Jude had been rude, or if he even cared. Drew went on at length, so absorbed in his articulation about the problems of identity experienced by Indian kids adopted and raised in white homes and how tribes needed to assert juris-diction over their adoptions that he didn't notice my withdrawal.

So legalistic, all coming from the head, not the heart! At first, our discussions were stimulating and challenging with all the questions he asked, but lately it seemed I was a sounding board to fine-tune a politically correct position, or my name was used to validate his connections to community. Didn't he have any ideas or standing of his own? It made me wonder who he really was, what with his focus on his grandmother as if identity was not personally acquired, based on his own individual and cultural experiences, but could be experienced vicariously across generations, through books, by association.

Some artists opposed the rigid proof of tribal affiliation and verification of original, handcrafted work required by Indian art associations. I had observed such opposition typically came not from community people, but from those whose claim to Indian blood was murky or, many times, suspect, not just by lack of tribal enrollment but lack of community ties and grounding in Indian culture and values. Drew's monologue eventually meandered to this point.

He declared tribal blood quantum requirements to be colonialistic, a replacement of tribal naturalization processes. Tribes using imposed criteria to decide who was officially Indian and who wasn't, who was "holier than thou," as he put it, were just puppets in the government's hands. This self-serving point in its judgment of tribes as passive pawns wasn't being "holier than thou"?

I frowned. There were names, careers, and money to be made by claiming an Indian identity, not only in the arts market but in other realms. Marli told me of some university professor in Washington who recently resigned in disgrace as director of a Native American studies program when it was discovered his claim of Indian blood was fraudulent. People who didn't have a drop of Indian blood in them were setting themselves up as the Indian expert or role model, or pitching books about their identity angst or Native spiritual insights, taking the place and voice of Indian people. Without the Indian claim to fame, they had nothing to distinguish themselves in the cutthroat, competitive Anglo world.

"Oh, come on, Drew. That's crazy!" He was taken aback that I stopped him on this point, and he shifted on the sofa. Yes, it's true that the Native world has been drastically, irrevocably altered by colonialism, I told him. And yes, intermarriage, assimilation, and acculturation have also occurred, further complicating things. "But tribes have always defined themselves. Tribalism is all about being a member of a specific community, clan, or extended family with a recognized territory and traits. Tribes have to draw the line on membership somewhere. Otherwise, we'll join the melting pot," my voice raised here, "which is the real colonial agenda."

I held up my hand as he started to interrupt me. "Indian people are tired of being ripped off by fakers and wannabes. There's a world of difference between *being* Indian and *claiming* Indian ancestry, which many Americans can truthfully do. It's dangerous to think that a drop of Indian blood gives anyone special claims and rights to being Indian. You can't be Indian in the past tense. Being Indian is like being pregnant—" He crossed his arms at that. "You can't be a little bit pregnant, part pregnant, pregnant because your grandma once was. You either are or you aren't."

Eyes cold, in a superior tone, he said, "Your analogy is faulty."

"Too bad!" I angrily retorted.

He cleared his throat and somehow we made it past that point. Later, when he turned at the door to say goodnight, I saw in his eyes that our discussion had breeched something.

"Goodnight, Drew," I said evenly, holding his gaze, closing the door. I sat on the sofa for a long while after, sorting through my feelings, knowing that our relationship had gone flat. He didn't get it. The degree of Indian blood wasn't the point. The point was being true to yourself and true to others about who you were.

I thought about this the next morning as I added another coil to the wall of a pot I was working on, pinching the excess off, my hands coated with clay, such a soothing, pleasant sensation. I had been hoping for the real thing with Drew, a genuine relationship, which had eluded me all these years. For a little while, I had been able to pretend there had been something there, but all along I knew it had been only an illusion. Did Drew share that bitter disappointment, too? I dipped my fingers in a gourd of water now brown with clay. With one hand inside the pot, I smoothed the coils together, my thoughts moving to how I would finish the piece.

When Time and Chance Meet

Jewell finally got back to me, though she didn't have much to report. Julian's parents had moved to Phoenix from Stewart, then retired, last anyone had heard. She had already called directory assistance in Phoenix but found no listing for them.

Phoenix? How ironic. They had been near Jude for how long we didn't know.

"Everyone we knew at Stewart has moved away. But the Brat—uh, Kerrie—gave me the name of someone who may know where he was sent to, one of Julian's former activist cronies. She travels all over the place, but she returns home regularly. I asked her family to have her call me as soon as they hear from her. I told them it was urgent.

"Oh! And, Celia, before I forget. I checked on Browning like you asked. Both his sister and his mom, even Browning himself, said he never had—"

I stopped her before she could finish. "You know what, Jewell? Never mind. I don't really need to know that info after all. Thanks, anyway. I hope we hear something about Julian soon. Jude's pretty bummed. He wants us to hire a private investigator, but I think that could get expensive. I just don't understand why Julian couldn't be located in the prison system. Sometimes I get scared. It's like he got swallowed up in a black hole or something."

"Don't give up hope. Something will turn up." Jewell's voice was confident. Just like in high school, I hung on to her words.

I was in a clearing in the mountains somewhere, seemed to me like the Sierra Nevadas by the snowy mountaintops I could see in the distance and the cool breeze on my face. I was riding a pony, its thick, coarse mane in my face as I hunched over its back. The motion was like riding the wind—smooth and swift, with no thought, no ability to control direction. The pony was part of a herd of horses of unusual colors and qualities—mauve, calico, turquoise, jade, fiery red, an impossible sense of texture in their coats thick as mud, cold and shimmery as ice, still as air on a hot summer night. The ponies climbed foothills, then began ascending a mountain slope that grew increasingly steep. The herd moved in tighter; I could feel their warm breath and the heat of their bodies, smell animal sweat. As they climbed, the horses became deer, thick-coated, as strangely but beautifully colored as the horses had been. The ride was no longer smooth, my position precarious as the deer leaped over fallen trees and climbed slopes, almost vertical. I could see boulders, crevices carved into the mountainside by runoffs, and canyons of dense forage. Afraid I would fall, I melded my body against the deer.

Then, in the way it is with dreams, I became a deer, leaping and bounding, seeing almost all around me. The world took on a phosphorescent glow. I picked my way through undergrowth with ease, leaped from one outcrop to the next, stretched my neck gracefully. My agility was short-lived. I heard a sound like the sharp crack of a twig, then I began to fall, a gentle free fall as my feet sought ground. I watched other deer leap past me over a ridge, their hooves flashing above my head. Jingling filled the air, a blend of sounds, loud like the bells on a dancer's outfit and soft like turtle shell rattles. I expected dancers, deer dancers, to appear over the ridge. The wind blew softly. Just the boughs of evergreens swayed. I lay in soft leaves, waiting.

When I awoke, I had a strange sense of contentment. I had dreamed of horses again, but this time they weren't in the sky and the whole feel was different. The ponies, such a tumultuous mix of energy, had become deer, I myself had become a deer, was shot it seemed, had fallen, and then as others moved ahead of me, had bedded down to wait. The waiting was full of expectancy that I'd be given something in return for letting go, like deer taken by Pueblo hunters are thanked for giving themselves to others. Patience, solitude, peace. Which was it?

For several nights in a row after the dream of ponies and deer, I dreamed of flying with eagles who were really eagle dancers. I would tell others to fly if that's what they really wanted to do, just flap your arms, like this, I said, taking off. It seemed like I had always been flying; like breathing, you don't think about it, you just do it.

During this time, my energy was high. Auntie Reena's words came back to me: "Take your pain and make it into art. You'll know how." Almost on her own, a female figure with voluptuous, flowing lines, hold-ing a pottery bowl upside down under one arm, emerged out of a lump of clay. I shaped the body so the curves and contours of her breasts, hips, and buttocks were rounded and generous. I cropped the front section of her hair by her ears, Pueblo style, and gave her bangs in a straight line across her forehead. Later, I carved eyes like a deer, long hair coarse like a horse's mane, toenails on sensuous bare feet. I breathed on her still-wet form, covered her, and left her to slowly dry. Below the inverted bowl, I painted a trail of mica flecks along the side of her black manta, the traditional Pueblo dress, and atop her foot on that same side. I painted the night sky, clouds of stars on a black background, on the round base on which she stood. As a last thought, I painted seven tiny deer circling the inverted bowl. This last touch took me hours. Tirelessly, I formed other pieces, smoothed and sanded them, painted designs of feathers and clouds on pottery bowls, sculpted eagle and deer dancers, painted them in unusual colors, and kept my dreams to myself.

The shape of my storytellers changed, becoming more rounded. Their faces became more expressive. I formed sensuous lips, generous bosoms, made some pregnant, their swollen bellies painted or carved with spirals of star galaxies. The children set miniature boom boxes and television sets to the side as they sat at the women's feet. Those in front had expressions of rapt attention, mouths and eyes opened wide in wonder; those in back had a mischievous look in their eyes or made faces at one another. Drew would like these, I knew. He would feel their energy, recognize the change in style, raise his eyebrow and ask me a question. In some strange way, I missed our talks, but not enough to call him.

"Why the change of form?" I could hear him ask in that interrogative tone he used when he was trying to coax information from me. My hands stopped smoothing the pot I was working on, remained frozen in place.

"That's a good question," I said aloud to no one.

The phone was ringing. I debated answering it or letting the machine record a message. My hands were wet with clay and Jude was out, so I couldn't call to him to get the phone. It could be Drew. I hesitated. The last time we had talked soon after our fallout, we had a dispirited conversation about the lack of progress in uncovering any information about Julian. Still, he might have some news.

I picked up the phone. A woman's voice asked, "Is this Cecelia Bluespruce?"

"This is she," I answered automatically, irritated that I had responded to what was probably a phone solicitation.

"Oh, praise God! You don't know me, but my name is Peggy Braill. I've been calling several times now. I'm a nurse at Quince County Hospital. I'm calling on behalf of—"

Good grief, some charity group, I thought, about to cut her short. Then I heard her say, "Julian Morning Star, who's incarcerated in the nearby federal correctional center. I believe you are a special friend of his?"

My knees went weak. "Julian *Morning Star*?"

"Oh, that's right," she said. "You knew him by a different name. He changed his last name. Guess you didn't know that?"

No wonder! "How did you—?" *Know,* I was going to say before I ran out of breath.

"How did I find you? It wasn't easy!" She laughed.

Following the nurse's call, in which she revealed Julian's location and detailed his brutal attack, hospitalization, recovery, and return to the prison, I wandered from room to room in my house, marveling at the turn of events. I touched objects in rooms as if to verify their reality, briefly sat, then got up to wander to the next room, continuing to marvel. I was dying to tell someone the news. But rightfully, Jude should be the first to hear.

I sat in the living room, vaguely straightening magazines on the table, when I noticed my hands, coated with dried mud. I had forgotten what I had been doing. The pot I had been working on had sat uncovered for two hours. Too distracted to work, I dampened it, then covered it with a plastic bag, washed my hands, and went to sit and wait for Jude.

Graduation night Julian and I were parked up at the Cross, sitting on the car hood. It truly was like old times, he and I alone together. Up there above the campus, buzzed with alcohol, we relived the past, maybe getting a little sappy because of the beer, but we had grown up close, and soon we'd be parting paths. I had already tried everything I knew to get Julian's attention; nothing had worked, and I had plain given up, was content for conversation for old times' sake.

He asked me if I had ever heard the story of the guy buried up here. I got a chill, said no, and he told me a ridiculous story of an escaped con in hiding who killed someone walking on the road late one night, then buried him right here under the Cross. "On the anniversary of his death, every year the dead guy walks around up here."

"Yeah, right! When was he killed?"

"Long time ago, around this time of year."

"I don't believe you. You're making it up." I was talking big into the night. It was pitch-black all around us; the sagebrush on the banks around the dirt clearing where we were parked suddenly assumed threatening shapes. The streetlights down on the campus were little orbs, far away. Farther away, the lights of the Nevada state prison blared a cold fluorescent square of light.

"For real! He snuck up on the guy walking down the road, grabbed him from behind—" Suddenly, Julian grabbed me by the neck from behind. I screamed.

"Okay! Okay! Geez, you don't have to scream like that. Someone will call the cops on us."

I could have slapped his face. He scared me silly so that I spilled beer on my clothes. It was just his cheap old trick again of getting close without seeming to. I moved away, leaned back against the windshield, and wrapped my arms around myself, can in one hand. He sat by himself on the end of the hood for a while, finished his beer, and then sheepishly said, "I'm sorry. I didn't mean to scare you . . . that much."

"Well, okay." We both knew I would forgive him like I always did for his dumb mistakes. He slipped off the hood, stood to toss his empty can high into the air. Then he jumped up on the hood beside me and leaned back.

Looking at the stars can make you drunk. You don't need alcohol, though I still sipped at mine so I got a double dose of intoxication. Looking at stars can also make you fall in love. It's like looking into a baby's eyes, so awesome, so scary, so personal. All of a sudden, my love, my longing for Julian that had laid dormant for so long welled up, and I felt like I could cry.

Julian was talking, reminiscing, pulling up scenes from days gone by. I followed along and let him take me back with him. We shared some good belly laughs, remembering Herman sprawled out on the playground, giving Mrs. Cox grief, the huge water fight we had inside Jewell's house, how Melvin had started rumors of his own death, sending Jewell and Misha, his ex-girlfriends, into excessive public displays of mourning until the rumor was uncovered and they became incensed at his trickery. Indians are real good at tricks, we agreed.

But maybe the worst ones are the ones we pull on ourselves.

It seems like the stars were always the silent witnesses to the whispered promises Julian and I made to each other our last summer together. That night of graduation was the first. Looking up at the stars, at the vast spaces between them where time bends, whorls, becomes relative, our souls wandered together up there and entwined. We shared space, time, an unconscious awareness of one another. I understood that when he kissed me for the first time and I saw stars in his eyes; Julian, less intuitive, didn't.

"Cissy, I think I love you."

"I know," I whispered back. "I've always loved you, too."

If anything, I am grateful for the memories of the summer and how my love for him unfolded. But I made my mistake, too. I didn't want to share him with anyone. I realize in retrospect that if Herman and Jewell had known about us, neither one of them would have let anyone come between us, that's how fierce their loyalty was.

I think I know which night Jude was conceived. Not the first time we made love, but the night we saw all the shooting stars, our last time together. In our own special place we knew from childhood, we bared ourselves under the sky. The moon was a sliver, curved, arching, gleaming like my body. My hopes as high and distant as the stars, my love so strong! Even now, its strength has endured. Rolling, laughing, biting, clutching, Julian and I joined, exploded like supernovas, stars being born, stars dying, the beginning and the end in one. My womb was waiting, its own universe. Jude was, is, will be.

One of the first things Peggy had asked me was, "Is information about Julian an intrusion in your life?" Very honestly and spontaneously, I replied, "I haven't had a life since Julian."

I told everyone the most pertinent details that Peggy shared with me, but I kept private some things, tucking them into my heart.

"When Julian first came in, he was in bad shape, connected to the monitor and respirator, his body crisscrossed with tubes and wires, his throat a swollen mass, face blotchy, skin ashy. His vital signs were stable, but he remained unresponsive. Just the shell of his body was present. The man himself had retreated somewhere deep inside. I would call to him, 'Julian! Come on, guy, wake up.'" She mimicked her call to him.

"Yep, that's what I did for several nights. I deal with patients on the most basic level so that getting close to a patient, forming a bond, can happen quickly, effortlessly. One small thing I did for Julian right away was to undo his braid. Sleeping on a braid so thick would give anyone a crick in the neck! His loosened hair softened his face and made him look comfortably asleep, I thought. I stood beside the bed and prayed silently for him, and as I prayed, I saw him with the eyes of my heart, curled up inside himself in a fetal position, protecting himself. This feeling of compassion just flooded me." She sort of choked up on her words here. Then she cleared her throat and went on.

"Taking care of Julian was easy. He has a strength of will that takes people through anything. Some patients actually nurture their ailments, milking them for all the sympathy and attention they can get. Not Julian.

"His face never did quite lose a hard and guarded look, but there were times I walked in during the first week and caught him with a dreamy expression that made me wonder what he had been thinking. With a blink of his eye, the mask would come down, all trace of softness gone. He'd put his head back, real cocky-like, and watch from under lidded eyes. He seemed uncomfortable with touch, so I'd explain everything I was doing, chat him up, try to be encouraging. I constantly asked him how he was doing because he didn't indicate discomfort in any way. I suspect he didn't feel entitled to a thing.

"Like a night owl, Julian began to stay awake the duration of my night shift. He sat in low light, his bed raised to an upright position, staring and thinking. Thinking and staring. My goodness, he was thinking so hard, he'd stare at the corner as if he saw something there. I gathered from him, by the faces he made, that he thought the nurses on the day shift were hags, that he'd rather sleep through their shifts. Unable to speak a word, he indicated this to me by laying his head on his hands pressed together. For a while there, I was locked out, he was locked in, on edge. In giving him pen and paper to communicate, I acted out of pure practicality, but it turned out to be the best thing I did for him. The tension coiled inside him was released, and the brooding stopped. Wish I could say it was my nursing!" She laughed, then continued. "He began to pour all his time and energy into writing. He furrowed his brow in concentration, pursed his lips, put a single focus on the page before him; his body was present, but his mind was traveling across time. He wrote so candidly about his prison experience and his past.

"After the first set of his writing that he gave to me, I couldn't help noticing the softening around his eyes."

What had he written about, I had to wonder, that touched this nurse and moved her to find me?

Once Julian regained his voice, she said, he talked of me incessantly, of his regret at losing something precious in his life. Seeing a picture of me in a magazine had been a lifeline for him, a reason for him to try for parole, to hope.

Try as I may, I cannot imagine the man who spoke that, the man sent to prison for a crime he says he didn't commit.

When I told Peggy that Jude was Julian's son, and he wanted to meet his dad, she choked up. "He has a son? Oh, Lord Almighty!" Her outpouring of joy touched me. My eyes grew damp. The woman knew so many things about me, she was like an old family friend. She gave me her phone number and insisted that when we arrived to visit Julian, we must call her.

"Oh, I'm not so different," Peggy protested when I thanked her profusely for her call. "Every nurse does something special for a patient at some time in their career, something up and beyond the call of duty. One nurse I know bought Christmas gifts for a six-year-old patient and his siblings when the family couldn't afford them. Another organized a blood drive for a patient with a rare blood type, and one other taught an elderly patient to read and opened the world for him. At my age, I'm no idealist out to save the world, eliminate suffering, or fight for nuclear containment." She laughed as if the idea was ridiculous, adding, "I just do what little I can."

Then she prayed for me and Jude and Julian. For forgiveness, restoration, healing of emotions, wholeness. For a safe trip, for words to speak to one another when we met in person, for no further hindrance to our reunion. Never have I heard a prayer like that. I was used to formal, ritualized prayers, nothing so personal and specific. I found myself weeping, washing away apprehension, bitterness, hurt, feeling I could start life anew.

"My dad—when I meet him, I'll know who I am. I'll become a whole person for the first time," Jude told me with tears in his eyes. Then he asked a question I knew must have been on his mind.

"Do you think he belongs in prison, that he's guilty?"

I had already thought about it during the hours I sat and waited for him to come home. My answer came from my heart. "No, Jude, I don't."

Jude and I have become a whole family in the days since Peggy's call. We laugh easily, take nothing for granted. He often touches my arm as he talks, drapes his arm around my shoulder as we walk. I listen to him and am surprised at how sensitive my son is.

I must have written a hundred drafts of a letter to Julian, trying to explain the recent days of searching for him, the years past of trying to forget him. The words fell on the page in endless combinations each time. Words, words, words. Finally, I reduced them to their essence. *Do you want to see me? Do you want to meet your son, Jude? He wants to meet his dad.* The reply was swift. *Please come. Please forgive me.* Jude received his own separate letter, which he didn't share with me. He folded it to carry in his wallet.

I never asked him to, but Drew began reviewing Julian's case, assigning research to legal externs from the law school. He offered no optimistic projections. I asked for none, just thanked him for being a friend.

Drew called one afternoon to ask if he could stop by later in the day to share a report on Julian. Though we had talked over the phone a number of times in recent days, meeting in person was awkward. We sat at the table, a lawyer and his client.

"I saw Julian."

My eyes flew to his face. He looked at me, then at his hands folded together atop the table.

I could barely breathe. "When?"

"Yesterday. I met with prison activists who have been working with him, and they took me out to see him."

"How is he doing?"

He looked at me, then past my shoulder out the window. "He's fine. His health is fine, that is, and not really knowing him, I can't say how he's doing, but he seems strong. Intelligent. Wary. He asked very good questions." He paused briefly. "He has long hair, a braid down to his waist."

An odd detail, I thought, looking at Drew's mini-ponytail, then away quickly before he noticed.

I waited for him to go on, but he said nothing further.

"What questions did he ask?"

"For one, what's my interest in his case."

"What did you say?"

"I told him, initially, I was investigating on your behalf, but that in looking into the record further, I would be happy to assist him. When I told him that, he folded his arms, leaned back in his chair, and lowered his eyelids on me. 'What's it to you? What do you get out of it? You gonna be the hero and save the day?' He's very direct, fired the questions at me, but before I could answer, he shook his head, held up his hands, and said, 'I've been in here a hell of a long time, and I'm suspicious, you know? I'm not going to put my hopes on no lawyer, but you're coming from Cecelia, and I'm not going to turn you away.'

"Then he got quiet, and in a different voice altogether, he asked about you. What you look like, what did you think about him being a con, were you involved with someone." Drew cleared his throat, still looking out the window.

"I didn't tell him much. I told him those were things for you to share." Drew nodded at me. He waited for me to say something. When I didn't, he went on. "He understood. He asked about Jude. He's in awe of him, Cecelia, in awe of having a grown son." This time I looked out the window. "We talked some more about his situation. The prison administration has taken a hard stand on his case, refusing to investigate the attack on him. He told me that all along he's been targeted for harassment, labeled a dangerous threat to prison security because he stands up for his rights, that the goal is to neutralize him."

My heart began to pound.

"I gave him my assessment. The most important thing now is to push the administration to move quickly on transferring him. Julian's not safe. He knows that."

Feeling somewhat awkward, but needing to know, I asked, "How does he look?"

Drew cleared his throat and shifted in the chair. "He looks good for a man in prison, for someone recently out of the hospital, though he told me he dropped a lot of weight. He's obviously no one to mess with—that comes across. I say that because of his eyes. They're watchful, calculating. Within a few minutes, you know he's got you pegged. Can't say I impressed him. I'm just another lawyer. But when he talks about you or Jude, that hardness leaves his eyes." Drew looked down at his hands, cleared his throat, then looked up again. His eyes found mine. "I know cons all play the role of the innocent, but I believe Julian is sincere. There's something about him that comes through as straight-shooting. He seems to demand that of himself and others. In his words: 'Don't give me no bullshit and I won't bullshit you, either.' We spent the remainder of our time talking about religious rights of Native prisoners and the stress and boredom he faces. I don't know that I'm answering your question. I'd say he looks like a man hungry for freedom." Drew spoke of Julian in a neutral tone, even with a trace of admiration, but I noticed he clenched and unclenched his hands as he spoke.

I reached across the table and patted his hands, let my hand rest there a moment till he looked at me. "Thanks for telling me, Drew. And for going out there."

We had to wait for security clearance before we could see Julian, which was just as well since the last local art show of the summer, the biggie, the Santa Fe Indian Market, was coming up. As Jude and I drove to Santa Fe on Friday afternoon, huge, blinding white thunderheads moved in, cooling off the hundred-plus-degree temperature. Santa Fe, situated below the Sangre de Cristo Mountains at a higher elevation than Albuquerque, was always about five degrees cooler. The usual flood of tourists in town for Indian Market filled up every motel and hotel in the city; traffic was congested on the narrow downtown streets, and parking space was almost impossible to find.

By 6:00 A.M. Saturday morning, the downtown streets were closed to traffic for the weekend, and Market organizers in bright orange vests redirected traffic flow. We exhibitors were allowed to park in front of our booths to unload wares from our vehicles, and then we had to search for parking. My booth was situated on the east side of the plaza. Double rows of booths lined the streets on the four sides of the city plaza and extended up and down Palace Avenue and San Francisco Street and down other side streets. Even before the show officially opened at 7:00 A.M., before we were fully set up, people began to buy, and they didn't stop once they started. Pieces in my new style of work were the first to go. Perhaps the blue ribbon awarded for my sculpture of the woman with the inverted pottery bowl, "When the Stars Were Born," was a contributing factor. By mid-afternoon, I had sold everything I brought and could go home.

Jude and I took our time packing up the supplies, and then we spent the rest of the afternoon browsing some of the other hundreds of booths. While Jude wandered off on his own, I was able to visit with friends who were still selling. It was a good year for Indian Market, we agreed. The economy was booming, people were happy. Are you going to the Kansas show, they asked, and were surprised when I said no. They were even more surprised when I told them Jude and I were going to meet his dad.

Jude was thrilled at seeing celebrities, Arnold Schwarzenegger and Maria Shriver with their kids, among the crowd. "I saw Indian students all bunched up on the sidewalk. I wondered why they were so excited. Then I saw them gathered around Arnold Schwarzenegger. They were asking him to autograph their programs, and I joined the group," he said.

"Did you get his autograph?" I asked.

"Nah. But I did talk to him. It was cool," he nodded, pleased.

"One year, Robert Redford was in town making a movie and some woman recognized him in an ice cream store, standing in line behind her. She was trying to be cool about it, so she didn't say anything to him, just purchased her cone and left the store. A few minutes later, she came back and indignantly told the clerk he had neglected to give her cone to her. 'He gave you your cone, ma'am,' Redford said to her. 'It's where you put it—in your purse!' "

Jude laughed.

"Did you do anything like that in front of Arnie and Maria?"

"Nah. I'm too cool. Hey, guess who else I saw?" He paused a moment. "Your friend, Drew." He said "friend" with a certain inflection.

He watched me closely to see my reaction. "Oh, yeah?" I answered casually.

He patted my back as if in sympathy. "Sorry to be the one to tell you this, Mom, but he was with someone else. A blond. She was—how shall I say?—built. Can't say she was ugly. She had her arm on his."

"Well, good for him," I answered.

Jude's eyes were twinkling. "Guess I should tell you she was old. And she wasn't really blond, more like silver-haired, and there weren't one, but two old ladies."

His mom and auntie? "I want you to be sure to tell your Auntie Marli what you saw. Tell her, two old ladies who looked like they could be his mother and aunt. Come on, let's go home. It's starting to sprinkle."

Before the Santa Fe Indian Market, I had set aside my largest storyteller with a multitude of children enfolded in the woman's arms, gathered on her back under a shawl, sitting at her feet, peeping out mischievously from behind her, babies in cradle boards propped nearby. If I had sold it at Indian Market to a collector, maybe a movie star come to the "City Different" to soak up some cultural ambiance like Schwarzenegger, I could have possibly received a good asking price. Instead, I took it for Peggy, who had befriended us all.

Auntie Reena and Marli came with us at their insistence for support. Even Jewell planned a later visit to Julian, as did the Brat. Drew said the letters and visits would be noted in his file and look good for the record.

We left Isleta just before dawn. The morning star was still visible to the west. After the initial excitement of starting out, we all settled down, Jude complaining of the choice of radio station.

"Let's listen to the Navajo radio station," Marli suggested.

The sounds of the Navajo Nation took us down I-40 past Laguna and Acoma Pueblos, through Gallup and the Navajo reservation spread across two states, and past the hideous billboard signs advertising the chance to sleep in an Indian tepee and other bright yellow signs screaming for travelers to stop at a roadside business and see "real Indians" and buy "authentic" pottery and jewelry, the kind of claim that had made legislation necessary to protect Indian artists and unwary tourists. By the time the Navajo station faded, the sun was high in the sky, my heart braced for what lay ahead.

Under a clear blue sky, Jude and I walked up to the gray, intimidating institution located on a "government reservation," surrounded first by concrete walls and then two runs of chain-link fences, all three topped with double strands of concertina wire. Guard towers overlooked the grounds; tiny figures, obviously armed, were clearly visible against the skyline. We approached the admissions building, passed through a steel-plated security door and an electronic scanner, and endured the strip-searching eyes of guards, as well as a pat-down. Shaken, suddenly feeling less than a person, my only thought as I took a deep breath to calm myself was, There's freedom in forgiveness.

The Race Is Not to the Swift

JUDE — SEPTEMBER 1996

We have passed through the gates and scanners, made it past the guards. Our footsteps sound loud and flat on the waxed linoleum floor. The whole place has the feel of a social services office, full of despair and tiredness. The lighting is stark and bright; reflecting the fluorescent lights, the floor gleams like moonlight on a lake.

I pat my shirt pocket to make sure the poem my dad sent me, which I usually keep in my wallet, is still there.

Looking ahead, I see my dad, an Indian male. My heart beats faster till I feel I can hardly breathe. He's sitting, tense, hands on his knees, head turned away from us. His hair is long, braided down his back. As we approach, his head turns. His eyes move quickly across my face, take note of details, miss nothing. Our eyes meet and hold steady. We connect. He shifts his gaze to Cecelia. His eyes shine with love. Now he's standing. Tears slip down his cheeks. He wipes them on his sleeves and holds his arms out to us.

Epilogue

JANUARY 1997

Honeymoon

(For Cecelia Bluespruce and Jude Morning Star)

The night is a woman wrapping

                    her

                         arms

                you   tenderly

                    around

Holding you till your heart is quiet, your breathing steady.
Donning white buckskin, she rises quietly,
        walking barefoot across the sky, never once looking back.
She's never the same,
        you love her, you hate her for it,
The way she teases, moving in
        and out of clouds and trees.
The soft breeze carries her laughter, her mocking words:
        You will never own me.
Tired of the game, she grows indifferent, turns her back.
        Just when you give up on her, she shimmers, beckons to you,
            makes your heart glad.
Sometimes she is full with life in her belly,
        you ache for the beauty of her form.

Then she is gone, taking a part of you with her.
You wake and wonder at the emptiness within you,

<pre>
                    a
                    perfect
                    r
          e   o
        l   u
          o   n
              h   d
</pre>

Julian Morning Star
No. 10105-702
Federal Internment Camp
Maximum Security
© 1997, *Renegades in Exile*

About the Author

E velina Zuni Lucero is Isleta/San Juan Pueblo and lives in Isleta Pueblo. She received the 1999 First Book Award for Fiction from the Native Writers' Circle of the Americas for her novel *Night Sky, Morning Star*. She holds a B.A. degree in communications from Stanford University and an M.A. in English from the University of New Mexico. Lucero is on the creative writing faculty at the Institute of American Indian Arts in Santa Fe, New Mexico.